Advance Praise for *Subduction*

"Kristen Millares Young's *Subduction* is the powerful debut novel from a writer that comes to us fully formed. This book is as unforgettable as it is timely, a story that keeps us riveted from beginning to end, written with abundant grace and lyric intensity. Beautiful, smart, and urgent. Read this book now."
—ROBERT LOPEZ, author of *Good People* and *All Back Full*

"In this commanding novel, Kristen Millares Young captures the brutality of an anthropological gaze upon a Makah community. Her complex, exquisitely shaped characters embody the calamity of intrusion and the beauty of resilience."
—ELISSA WASHUTA, author of *My Body is a Book of Rules*

"Kristen Millares Young's *Subduction* is a taut, atmospheric tale that gave me what I hope for in a novel: characters that I can care about with stakes that really matter. This is an enormously impressive debut. I'll eagerly await more from this writer."
—STEVE YARBROUGH, PEN/Faulkner Award Finalist

"'Love is a kind of home,' Kristen Millares Young writes in *Subduction*. But in the world of this beautifully written novel, home is also a place of secrets, murder, and loss. A tale of taking and giving, resistance and surrender, *Subduction* raises troubling, provocative questions about our struggle to belong."
—SAMUEL LIGON, author of *Miller Cane, Wonderland*

"*Subduction* will give you a sense of life lived in the most remote corner of the lower 48, the Makah reservation in Washington State. The ever-changing Pacific Ocean, the emerald forests, the geoduck clams, and the scruffy sea-scoured dwellings are merely the foundation of Kristen Millares Young's suspenseful, atmospheric first novel. The characters leap off the page and into your heart. I wanted to swallow the story whole, and I was happy to know it would take time to savor it. An auspicious debut!"
—PATRICIA HENLEY, National Book Award Finalist

"Set in the Pacific Northwest, *Subduction* is a lyrical forest of storytelling rooted in indigenous voices and invaded by those who would steal the tongues and hearts of the ones they love while bartering and betraying the idea of belonging to a land, a birthright, and a family. When you read Kristen Millares Young's words, you understand how it is we can steal, can betray, can love."
—SHAWN WONG, author of *Homebase* and *American Knees*

"*Subduction* introduces a welcome new voice in Kristen Millares Young, here telling a taut, fraught story of two people who meet and engage in circumstances that surprise. Both have lived but are seeking to live yet more fully, even as they're beset by their pasts. Whether the way to such realization is with the other is a core part of this vividly written story. Set on Makah Nation land, part of Washington's Olympic Peninsula, *Subduction* is a searching exploration of historic legacies in the present day. The result: a book of reckoning, full-heartedly told."
—RICK SIMONSON, Elliott Bay Book Company

SUBDUCTION

a novel

Kristen Millares Young

Red Hen Press | *Pasadena, CA*

Book design by Sandra Moore

Library of Congress Cataloging-in-Publication Data

Names: Millares Young, Kristen, 1981- author.
Title: Subduction : a novel / Kristen Millares Young.
Description: First edition. | Pasadena, CA : Red Hen Press, [2020]
Identifiers: LCCN 2019041298 (print) | LCCN 2019041299 (ebook) |
ISBN 9781597098922 (paperback) | ISBN 9781597098946 (ebook)
Classification: LCC PS3613.I532276 S83 2020 (print) | LCC PS3613.
I532276 (ebook) | DDC 813/.6—dc23
LC record available at https://lccn.loc.gov/2019041298

The National Endowment for the Arts, the Los Angeles County Arts Commission, the Ahmanson Foundation, the Dwight Stuart Youth Fund, the Max Factor Family Foundation, the Pasadena Tournament of Roses Foundation, the Pasadena Arts & Culture Commission and the City of Pasadena Cultural Affairs Division, the City of Los Angeles Department of Cultural Affairs, the Audrey & Sydney Irmas Charitable Foundation, the Kinder Morgan Foundation, the Meta & George Rosenberg Foundation, the Allergan Foundation, the Riordan Foundation, Amazon Literary Partnership, and the Mara W. Breech Foundation partially support Red Hen Press.

First Edition
Published by Red Hen Press
www.redhen.org

For Brian

In the one hand,
you are holding the mirror.

On the other hand,
you are the mask.

Put on the mask and look in the mirror.

—*Wilson Duff*

For nothing is fixed, forever and forever and forever, it is not fixed; the earth is always shifting, the light is always changing, the sea does not cease to grind down rock. Generations do not cease to be born, and we are responsible to them because we are the only witnesses they have.

The sea rises, the light fails, lovers cling to each other, and children cling to us. The moment we cease to hold each other, the moment we break faith with one another, the sea engulfs us and the light goes out.

—*James Baldwin*

SUBDUCTION

Chapter One

THE SHORE PULLED away. Froth churned from its feet to hers. The engines hummed through her bones.

From the aft deck, Claudia looked back toward the city they made home. She searched the skyline for places they had been happy—the top of the Space Needle, a waterfront park, the Ferris wheel—until her westward passage split the horizon into expanses of gray demarcated into sea and sky by hue alone.

Puget Sound opened in fathoms below the ferry.

Claudia left town without saying her goodbyes. Seattle was a small world. Movers must have swarmed her house to clear out Andrew's belongings in the space of one morning. The neighbors would have seen.

What had they seen? She couldn't bring herself to ask whether her sister had been on site to supervise, and Claudia hid her phone in case someone felt like sending unsolicited glimpses of Maria deciding what to take, practicing wifeliness. Slipping Andrew a kiss for courage as the first box was packed. Claudia pictured Maria's thick curls, her narrow shoulders, her rounded hips. Birthing hips.

The broadcaster's voice echoed through the loudspeakers, cautioning passengers about unknown items and suspicious activity.

It was cowardly of Andrew not to deliver the news in

person. Worse still, Maria. Did they think she would handle it poorly? That she was dangerous?

Listening to the roar of the props, Claudia saw what her fate might have been—her body lying in the bathtub, blue and bloated. Afloat. Her stomach twisted. It was more than she could take—or forgive. They knew what they were doing, she thought. Yet they think I deserve it.

Gulls swept the boat's wake. She was surprised by how close they came, how she could see feathers tracing their sinuous curves. How they were suddenly beautiful—not the splattering scavengers they had been, but flight itself.

Right now, everyone I know is stuck at a desk, and then there's me, Claudia thought, on my way back into the field. As a child in Mexico, she wanted to go somewhere—anywhere—away. She had always studied people. She never envisioned herself as an anthropologist, preferring something more dashing, like explorer. But here she was, en route to the Makah reservation at Neah Bay, an old whaling village on the northwest tip of the lower 48. Indian Country.

Last year, she noticed Andrew timing her periods, his prick vanishing ten days after she first bled. Which was almost funny because lately, she found herself wanting to be careless, to chance it.

Folding up her body on her side of the bed, ovulating alone whenever she could manage it, she had made it through her thirties unscathed. That was when they were still trying.

And now, she thought, I'm old. I'd have a baby with Down's, if I could have one at all.

I just wanted something from myself. Still do. Something bigger for myself. Bigger than myself, bigger than all of this. I don't know how to get it without wanting it. Why couldn't he understand?

Besides, what kind of man fucks his wife's sister? Claudia tilted her head to consider the inverse. What kind of wife would allow her husband to become so close to her sister that he could fall for her, fall inside of her, fill her up?

Only a conniving bitch would wrap her legs around her brother-in-law. Maria's legs were curvy. Great gams, Andrew once said. In horror of excess flesh, Claudia carved herself to gristle. Maria's thighs bloomed. Claudia imagined they would shake in sweaty reverberation during sex, a shuddering and prayerful response to the call of loin striking flank, so unlike the flat slap of muscle her own lovemaking had become.

Last month, when her fingers crept between buttons to his curly nest, his hand rose to still her wayward progress. She left her arm on top of him, trying to act natural, like this was cuddling. They pretended to sleep.

It took ten minutes to amass the strength to roll onto her back and concede. It was terrible to be uneasy in her own bed. She hadn't felt that way since college. But this time, it was her husband, and having had his love and lost it made her physically ill, a malaise so invasive it was as though she were at altitude, her body shutting down extremities, fingertips first.

She signed the papers to be done with it. He wanted out.

A giant gull hovered much higher than the others, dark against the sky, a trick of light diffusing its outstretched wings into comets. Claudia followed as its silhouette moved forward, too quick for a bird, her steps taking her into the warm fluorescence of the cafeteria, where people sat chatting over beer and chicken strips. She hurried westward, peering through fogged windows, passing rows of vinyl booths and plastic chairs before she rushed onto the foredeck and into the full force of the ferry's crossing.

Claudia clutched her billowing jacket and studied the cirrus clouds, searching their soft underbellies, muscles locked against the cold. She could not find the gull.

Her gaze dropped to an oblong head bobbing in a trough, nodding and dipping, a sleek presence that seemed sentient. The Sound foamed and fell back on itself amidst a charcoal tangle of currents. Squinting, she rose on tiptoe to check the next swell and sighted a line trailing behind it. Bull kelp.

The Olympic Mountains loomed. Her mind was awash in pearl and jade. The ferry neared Bainbridge Island, the first leg of a 160 mile journey that would take her west, along peninsulas carved by retreating glaciers and bridges built by enterprising men, until finally, she reached land's end and its people—*qʷidiččaʔaˑtx̌*—who had claimed their place among gulls and rock for millennia. She was merely passing through this world. Or above one, in any case, riding the back of an inland sea where fish were fighting and fucking and occasionally being carried off by nets, their minds naked with terror.

A merciless place, acidified by the dank exhales of engines. Though sea creatures shepherd their young in good faith, their only end is death, as it is here and everywhere on earth. Those that remain will end in mud, picked over by crabs.

Years ago, she drove around the Olympic Peninsula with Andrew, searching for adventure on summer weekends. Now the mantle of winter softened its range of crags. If she looked hard enough, Claudia could see ripples in the snowfields, the glaciers getting close and large.

She saw herself with Andrew, climbing a narrow saddle between creaking icefalls. Remembered the weakness and dread she felt while they reached the peak, bound by rope, carabiners clinking as they kicked steps into white crust. Wind screamed over ridges. Her rigging howled and whistled.

Andrew leaned into the gale, angling into its clutches. Her body aped his steadfast decision to keep going, but her spirit scurried down mountain, where trees bowed under snow crisscrossed with the tunnels of animals. They, too, had changed colors to avoid predation.

And now, to whom was she tied?

Claudia gripped the green railing, still wet from the last rain. A crow flew by, holding one small claw with the other. This too shall pass, she told herself, unconvinced.

She looked toward the water, and there it was again—the black head. A seal. It pivoted toward her. She heard its breaths in slight puffs that pushed aside the engine drone until a hush drowned all other sound and stilled her thoughts. A strange watchfulness intensified.

The sea opened and closed around the seal, swallowing its head. The ferry grew louder, the voices of other people tuning in on deck like an oldtime radio.

Shivering, she hugged herself.

The wooded shores of Bainbridge Island took shape along the sharpening coastline. Kelp twisted along dark beaches whose upper reaches sprouted mansions. Their banks of windows glittered, cold and steely as the early photos of homesteaders with severely parted hair and thin mouths.

It had all once been forest, right down to the water, the largest stumps serving as dance floors, fiddlers sawing sweet melodies as wood was shipped to whoever could pay, the roving bands of loggers more devastating than termites, than locusts, than anything that had come before.

Executives and their fleece-trimmed families lived there now, the latest in an oncoming wave of people.

It was close to Christmas. Claudia always had Andrew spend the holidays at Mt. Baker with her family. "You like my sister," she replied when he broached the idea of other plans. "And you know what Thomas expects." Andrew cozied up to her father's aura of wealth. Thomas was mostly stocks and properties now, not all in on timber as he once was. "The good old days," as he liked to say, "when no one gave a shit about owls."

It was better to be with Makahs for the holidays. She wanted to sit with other people's families, let their happiness buoy her, but she didn't know if she could take it, being near children.

Most Makahs would want to be with their kids, cooking and wrapping presents and bullshitting in front of the TV, not talking to an anthropologist about animal spirits and songs. She could knock on Maggie's door, though it seemed rude to show up, unannounced, at the home of a woman who lived alone. Or maybe she didn't want to put in the time, no different than the outsiders who first arrived wanting the goods quick and easy as they could be had.

Even the good ones were suspect. Like James Swan, who lived among the Makah Tribe in the mid 1800s. Who was an amateur ethnologist, customs inspector and Indian agent. Who taught schoolchildren and was respected enough that a Makah family took his name. Who considered his life a failure because he never struck it rich, and what else was being a pioneer about. Who transcribed their stories of cannibalism and grave robbing, of cooking marrow from baby arm bones to make grease and power, of strapping other families' dead to their backs when they swam creeks to purify themselves, anything to be a better whaler. Who ransacked the graves of Makah chiefs for skulls he sent east to the Smithsonian, a violation of respect and sanctity so great the institute was later compelled to return them.

These flawed forebears cleared the path for those who came much later. By the 1970s, hikers had stumbled across a handful of longhouses buried in the wild beach at Ozette, an old Makah village south of Neah Bay. It was the find of a lifetime, cured in salt water, hidden from prying eyes and hands. A professor and archaeologist named Doc Daugherty worked with Makahs to excavate, catalogue and display thousands upon thousands of artifacts. There were bows and hooks and shanks, bowls and whetstones, looms and paddles and nets, posts and beams and planks, shafts and shell blades for arrows and harpoons, and weapons of iron set adrift from the Orient in a time when junks still plied the seas. Cedar bark baskets survived, wetly, their weave holding the hair of their makers.

It had been hundreds of years since a landslide swallowed the longhouses during an earthquake big enough to send a tsunami to Japan. Nowadays, a whale saddle studded with otter teeth was a big hit during classroom visits to the Makah museum. A nettle fiber net housed there helped swing the Supreme Court in favor of Native fishing rights, proving the existence of that technology before first contact with white people, who came to take everything they could see, everything they could carry, everything for themselves, or for sale.

Daugherty was different. He was decent. The Makah

tribe held onto its stuff. Claudia was coasting in a dead predecessor's wake. She knew that. There were still some great men. She just hadn't met one.

And then there were Andrew's meds, the pills she found guilty for their faltering sex life, insisting that drugs were unnecessary.

"Unless I have to deal with you," he said during what turned out to be their last argument.

She didn't know when she began speaking to him the way she spoke to herself, with all the judgment and cruelty of someone not expecting to be overheard. She always meant to walk out when a fight got nasty, but she never learned how. What came next felt inescapable, unalterable.

"You don't know how to live in your own head," she spat, stung. "I have nothing to do with it."

He left the pills in an otherwise empty bathroom cabinet, ransacked like the rest of the house. In his stead, the orange plastic vial signaled, "Why bother? Who needs this life, the only one we learned to build in our years together?"

No answer to those questions, only a long hot bath and a bottle of wine and one more bad decision.

She thought an overdose would flash memories and the smell of sulfur, a fireworks finale. Instead, it was like nodding off on a redeye, getting colder and colder in the darkness between distant glimmers until they, too, disappeared.

The broadcaster's voice was smug. "Please return to your vehicles. We are about to arrive at our destination." Claudia pressed through the double doors into the feverish heat of the cabin, where people filed in to begin flowing down the stairwells.

Barnacled pillars towered on either side. The ferry coasted into the approaching dock in neutral, poised for the final reverse thrust. Inside the cars, everyone waited to turn on their engines, listening for the first eager sputter, that lone cough becoming two hundred streams of idling vapors before the ropes were tossed.

A fitful rain splattered the asphalt. Cold and wet and wind silenced the workers, who grimaced and pointed and made circling motions with their hands.

Eagles and vultures wheeled through the gloaming over razed forests and colossal silvered stumps that sprouted frail versions of themselves. Semis bearing logs no wider than a forearm rattled past, pulling her SUV from its center of gravity with whooshes that left her stiff and staring.

A truck came upon her, fast. It was dusk. The highway's shoulder disappeared along hairpin curves that wound from cliff top to strait. She braked on the steep grades and turned up the music to drown his horn, tipping her rearview to avoid his brights until she could yank herself into a pullout. With a final honk and the finger, he was on his way.

Con calma. Trembling, she cruised the final curves into Neah Bay through nightfall—the forest dark around her, headlands black and jagged against the strait—and soothed herself with her mother's admonishment against hurrying, given as she arranged from her hospital bed for Claudia to be sent north into the custody of the father she'd never met. *Todo se hace con calma*.

She used to bring Claudia beachcombing after every storm, hitting up the hotel frontage at dawn, before resort guests left their breakfast buffets to scavenge Baja's coastline. Among the nets and kelp and trash they'd find shark's teeth and sand dollars and, once, a big green glass globe that came all the way from Japan. At the end of a long day, holding

Claudia's cold hands when she was tired and little and crying, her mother told her to close her eyes and imagine being
a big green float. You're in the sea. You go up and down, but
you're always near the surface. That's your job, to stay close
to the light.

Rolling down her windows to wake herself with a cold
rush of briny air, Claudia slowed as she drove into town,
peering into the night, wondering if she would see someone
she knew. It had been months since she was out here. Light
poles cut jaundiced circles into gray pavement. Nobody.
Neah Bay was quiet but for the barks of sea lions and the
slap of boats rocking at berth.

Her headlights cast twin moons onto fog that crept
from the strait and surrounded her. Phosphorescence flickered from a few windows of the trailers lining Front Street.
A car passed her in the mist, its lights blurring into soft suns.
She could not see the driver.

She threaded the curves between the church and the
clinic. Leaving the low clouds behind, she entered a corri-
dor of lichen-mottled alders, their naked branches joining
hands overhead. She watched the shadows along the shoulders of the road.

A white flurry filled her windshield. "Holy shit!" She
slammed the brakes.

An owl, whisper close, smelling of rot.

She shifted into park and sat back, tires squealing in
her ears. Her heart pummeled her chest. She hyperventi-
lated, lightheaded. The crown of her skull seemed to shift
and move. She cringed and covered her head with one hand.
Cowering in her seat, she glanced out the window and
checked her mirrors. Nothing.

Claudia pressed both palms into her eye sockets, cradling her forehead. "You're just tired," she repeated. Her senses attuned to Wa atch River's splashes and murmurs. She dropped her hands, ready.

A large brown mink stood facing her. Eye level. Its neck was long, ears pointed, tail curled over its back. Claudia raised her hand as though to honk. It rose higher on hind legs, front paws dangling, and sniffed the air in all four directions, lifting its sharp muzzle, nostrils flaring. Her arm faltered and lowered onto her lap. She glared, willing the mink to move. It didn't move. It didn't blink. Pressure mounted between her temples. Her left eye twitched, uncontrollable.

With a slow finger, she pressed the buttons to roll up her windows, sealing herself in. The mink pricked its ears at the mechanical whine and got on all fours.

She punched the horn. "Get out of my way!"

The mink reared up and laughed. Horribly, impossibly, and yet there it was, human laughter ringing in her ears.

She startled at the sound of tapping. A man in jeans and an old work jacket stood outside her door, limned in light.

Wiping her mouth, she smiled at him, uncertain. Her engine was still running. She straightened and turned to see the silhouettes of children wrestling in the back seat of his car. His beams kindled the drizzle into a shower of small comets. She cracked the window, massaging her neck.

"You okay?"

"I'm sorry."

The man studied her face. "You should be careful on these roads. You could hurt somebody."

"I haven't been feeling well."

He nodded. "Where you headin'?"

"Hobuck Cabins."

"Know how to get there?"

"Yes."

"I'll follow you, just in case. It's on our way."

"Okay. Thank you."

"Get some sleep."

"I will."

"You do that." He got in his car and slammed the door.

Blushing, she shifted into drive. He thinks I'm drunk, she thought. Or on drugs. I wish I were. It would explain a few things. Did I dream that mink? What about the owl? Was I hallucinating? Jesus. She hoped not. She didn't know what was worse—freaking out about random animals or being found stupefied in the middle of the reservation's main road.

Still, she knew the animals were not random. Not here, on this land, among these people. Unease spread across her like oil. You're less than a mile from the cabins, she thought. Drive.

Small wisps of mist curled into shapes at the periphery of her vision. She refused to look at them, dismissing what she saw, what she had just seen. Her hands slipped on the wheel. She tightened her grip and turned left at the bridge, debating whether to introduce herself. Their lights were stark on the grassy riverbanks. Patches of fog scurried across the black river, too swift. She would hear about this episode as soon as she started her interviews in the community, maybe even before then. Everyone was sure to hear about it.

Few dunes had escaped four wheeling, the grasses yielding to scabrous patches of sand. Beyond them, the sea was shrouded. She used her blinker early to let him know he could move on. He stayed behind her, resolute.

Claudia pulled off at the sign for the office and parked at an unmanned booth with a dim vestibule. She left her lights on and the engine running, just in case. He pulled up next to her.

Ay Dios, she thought. I hope this doesn't get weirder. She called "Goodbye!" and approached the booth. An envelope was pinned to the wall under the awning, her name in neat letters. Her body relaxed. She was expected somewhere. No, "expected" isn't quite it, she thought, swatting off iterations of the word like "expectation," "expecting" and "expectancy." No, not at all. It was better than that, nicer. Someone thought of her. Though she paid for that attention, it warmed her. She waggled the envelope in his direction. Maybe he would go home and forget about it.

He raised a hand from the wheel, fingerpads forming a fleshy shark's fin, and drove off, his girls swiveling in their seats to stare, their faces reflecting her headlights with the pale disregard of distant planets.

Chapter Two

PETER COASTED DOWNHILL. The "Welcome to the Makah Nation" sign receded to a speck in his rearview. He stepped on the gas, ready to get this over with. And just like that, a cop swung into position behind him. Neah Bay PD.

Dread coiled in his gut. His eyes flitted to the speedometer. 35 in a 25. The officer spoke into his radio and settled back in his seat. Peter slowed and waited for the flashing lights. None came.

He peered out the passenger window. The wrinkled gray water of Neah Bay rippled north from the Coast Guard dock and around Waadah Island, unfurling toward a container ship suspended in a line of fog that pierced the strait. Damp driftwood beaches divided the bay from town. The reservation's main drag was lined by low buildings and trailers, some proud and tidy, others boarded up, defiant. There were still no stoplights. Dogs made dirt nests wherever they saw fit to bed down.

He was almost home.

Peter pulled over by a semicircle of young men on Front Beach, heads bent toward a common purpose. He lit a cigarette and watched the cop pass him to cut left into a big parking lot. The cruiser spun a circle to face Front Street.

Dozens of bald eagles spotted the mudflats, dipping their heads and slumping their shoulders, spreading water on their wings and shaking themselves clean, fluffing their leg plumage to step from one pool to another. Peter thought of his father, who in a rare fit of whimsy once said eagles pulled up their petticoats to bathe.

That he tried not to think of his dad, but did, proved his constant lack of self-control, an admission that he was less than a man. The only good hours were those he lost underwater, mind on the glare, sucking stale air and pissing his suit. Welding made sense. He could measure a day's progress without searching his soul. Nothing but light and metal. That's what he saw when he sat poolside with other trainees doing flutter kicks with fins on, abs burning—a tiny bright arc turning into piers and harbors, a long line of pilings carrying everything above.

He checked the cop, casual as he could. Still there. Sweat beaded the lines of his forehead.

If he spun around and stepped on it, he could probably stay ahead long enough to make it back off the rez, where a tribal cop was unlikely to bother. They could always call in the feds, or Clallam County. A state trooper, even. He doubted they cared about long-dead Indians.

Eagles shrieked from the highest branches of a cedar towering above the beach. Their whistling unsettled him. Two girls with green braids walked by, heads bowed over phones.

Raucous laughter drew his head to the right. Between the men's shifting, shuffling legs, Peter saw a crow hopping with a can in its clutches, thrusting its beak inside and tumbling before going aloft with a quick flap of wings.

Low hills slid toward the strait. Skinny trees grew in silent crowds over the clearcuts of his youth. The town clustered on the flatland along the water. Recognition clutched at him. This is your place. He batted it away. I don't belong here.

Peter listened to the sway and clank of the marina—that was new—and tried not to look for their old troller. It was easy enough. The fleet had tripled in size. Who made good? Probably the same names that dominated back in the day.

For as long as there was memory, Neah Bay had been a collection of families soaked in drama and the preservation of status, each head of family claiming chiefs for ancestors— never mind the slave blood that coursed in the night— mapping triumphs in public, charting in private the fall of a cousin, a sister. It was only a question of when tragedy would hit, he thought. Not how. There are only so many ways to wreck a life.

Maybe he underestimated his own. The big boats at berth told him that, and so did the new gym's digital sign. The Red Devils had a tourney coming up. He hadn't played basketball since high school. Had his mom kept his jersey?

One of the women who tried to claim him, Tammy— even her name was suburban, and that's where her folks lived, on the outskirts of Bellevue, though she tried to hide it—was always going on about racist mascots. He hated when she got involved with shit like that; it let him know he was part of her street cred with the guilty liberals she called compatriots. She had a master's degree and waited tables, for Christ's sake. Being on the ass end of capitalism didn't make her revolutionary, even if she liked to paint.

He tossed the filter and pulled onto Front Street. The cop eased out behind him, stayed close as they passed a VFW trailer. Didn't flip his lights until they approached a big building with long ramps.

Here we go. Peter was furious he'd stashed his gun in the

toolbox. This place never forgets. The officer strode up with a notebook, fingering his holster, speculative. Peter tried the breathing exercises he found online to fight anxiety. He hid his unease as best he could. No one likes a nervous man.

"Peter."

He kept his silence with both hands on the wheel, so there could be no excuses later.

"I seen you comin' down the hill. You back?"

"Depends. Maybe."

"You been gone a long time."

"Am I getting a ticket?"

"Don't recognize me?" The cop pulled off his aviators. His face was wide, like someone had stepped on it, pushing his cheeks into jowls that bulged. Still, there was something in his eyes, a brightness that moved beneath, bringing intimations of boyhood.

Peter squinted. "Randall."

Randall's hand crowded Peter's face. They shook, compressing each other's fingers until Randall grinned and called it off. "Three kids, a wife. You?"

"Flying solo. On my way to see my mother."

"About time. You should come over, meet the kids."

"Who's the lucky lady?"

"You and Maggie don't talk, eh?"

Peter was no longer panicked, but he was getting irritated. Why exactly had he been pulled over?

Randall smiled, sure of himself. "Roberta."

Roberta read Peter's lifeline when they were kids. "You're gonna die before you get old." She traced his palm with a chipped red nail. She smiled, hair spilling silken on the inside of his wrist, showing her dimples. "You're gonna have lots of lovers, though. Lucky guy."

"Lucky? To die young?"

"Yeah." She pressed his hand between hers. "You know, go out when you're still good looking, the ladies chasing you right into the grave."

"You think I'm good looking?" He flipped his hand around to take her by the wrists, fingers meeting and overlapping, body screaming to bring her close. He never forgot what she said, or what they did. It never felt inevitable to love someone again.

The ache echoed through his chest. Roberta was the one who tracked him down with the diagnosis—dementia—his mother squirreled away with so many other secrets. Roberta hadn't said anything about being married. To be fair, he didn't ask, hustling off the phone to nurse the old hurt alone. She must not have told Randall about the call. That was encouraging.

Her husband was a big cock in a small town, but he had his gun at the ready. It was good to keep that in mind.

"Congratulations."

"You can go along. I just wanted to say hi."

"Put on a little show, you mean."

A handful of elders gathered on the building's ramps.

"I seen you coming down the hill."

"Yep, that's what you said."

A man in a Seahawks baseball cap, eagle feather dangling from its crown, shuffled down the ramp. Peter steered his truck past him, stomach curdling with spent fear. An old woman covered with blankets sat in a folding chair across the street. Slow as a heron stalking the shallows, she turned to watch the action.

"I'm not ready for this." His dashboard rattled in response, like always.

Speeding past dead ends choked with blackberries and trucks on blocks, Peter wove around basketball hoops and sedans with flat tires. But Diaht Hill had come up in the world. Every third or fourth house had a new SUV pulled up front. There were neat woodpiles and clipped lawns. He slowed by the old carvings, here a thunderbird with mother of pearl eyes, there a mossy headed whale.

His family's patch of land was a postcard of a place he'd never been, at first. Just a tired doublewide. But soon he saw himself flying on a bike with the training wheels snapped off, heard big boots scraping the pavement behind him, his front wheel wobbling and tipping him into the gutter, bloody but toughing it out as his dad scooped him up and carried him to the couch.

He bade his memories be quiet as he stepped onto the street. And then his mother was standing there, smaller, distilled.

Peter took her birdlike shoulders into his arms, guarding his smile. Cataracts ghosted the blacks of her eyes. He touched the gray cloud of her head and hugged her. Knowledge of his own mortality emanated from the bones shifting, frail as popsicle sticks, beneath the loose skin of her back.

Through the tickle of her hair, the trailer's tufted brown carpet came into focus. He braced himself, blinking against the vision that came to him unbidden. Blood and oil spreading on plaid linoleum, pooling around his dad, spread eagle and unmoving.

"Thick as a tree." His mother patted his chest. "I made coffee."

She pulled him in, shooing a herd of cats from the porch and shutting the door against the smiles and stares of neighbors.

It was dark inside and smelled of wood smoke, coffee, cat piss and a dank funk he could not place. He fought the urge to breathe through his shirt.

"Jesus, Mom."

She edged past yellowed stacks of the *Peninsula Daily News* and milk crates filled with old phonebooks. A narrow path snaked toward the bedrooms through mounds of debris tall enough to block the windows. His disquiet deepened.

He followed her, lifting his arms, trying not to touch anything. The piles brushed against his calves, his knees, his thighs, his hips.

She pushed open the door to his childhood bedroom. His jersey hung on the wall. The floor was clear but for cobwebs waving in the corners and balls of dust that spun in the wake of their arrival. Had she known he would come? Or just held out all these years?

His daybed squealed in complaint when he sat on its swayed back; he remembered his teenaged vigilance, oiling the bedsprings through a narrow red straw to mask dull nights of jacking off.

"How about that coffee?"

Peter stepped sideways through aisles wide enough for a woman. A wood stove warmed the room; this place was a firetrap. He gathered strips of cedar bark and bear grass from the coffee table, making his way down to a layer of graph paper covered with basketry patterns. Her notebook lay open to a series of dots forming the long curve of a whale and the arc of its tail. Behind, six figures leaned forward in a long canoe. All paddled but the man in front, harpoon at the ready.

Moving so slow it hurt to watch, she slid the tray onto

the table and sank into the chair that was his dad's favorite, despite its pattern of covered wagons. Cups and spoons clattered, coffee staining the creased packets of powdered creamer. Peter did not react, not wanting to embarrass her. He flicked a pack until one end was fat and tore it open, drowning the lumps, patch by patch.

"It's good you're here."

He tossed the spoon on the tray. A cold film covered his palms. He rubbed them dry on his knees, overwhelmed by the desire to wash his hands. Two tabbies appeared, meowing and rubbing his shins. He stamped his feet.

They sat, sipping. The rain was tender at first, then violent. The trailer shook with its force.

His mother held her mug like an offering. Her swollen wrists distended sideways; the acute angle of attachment and disproportionate size of her joints made her hands seem welded onto the wrong body.

He jiggled his leg. "What's with the stuff?"

"I've been saving it."

"What for?"

"There are things you will need to know."

Peter studied the path along the floor, trying not to take the measure of his absence by the height of the piles. He went away inside himself to fill his face with forced cheer. "Let's go through it. While I'm here."

"How long will that be?"

"I don't know."

She pressed on the cap of an orange vial. Her whole body shook. Failing twice, she extracted a round pill with a jagged nail.

"What's that?"

"Methadone."

"Wow."

"My rheumatoid arthritis."

"You could make good money with those on the street." His joke came out like an invitation.

"The clinic counts our pills."

Peter flinched, looking around for something to say.

"You make me wish I still smoked, son. And you're late."

What did she mean by "late"? She always claimed to know things. A lot of Indians claimed to expect shit that happened. "I saw a crow flying backwards, and then they called to tell me my cousin died, but I already knew." If she knew so much, why hadn't she done something?

She was it, the only one who knew what they'd done after he came upon her in the kitchen, her face purpled, forehead smeared with blood and oil, his dad's head in her hands, broken.

He'd never told anyone about that night, which lived in him nonetheless as waking dreams. He would break his promise to guard their silence. He needed to talk to his mother before dementia took the memories he most wanted from her, the only things he needed from her, because he sure as fuck would not load this crap into his truck when he left. And he would leave. She would not snare him with need. He was older now.

"Peter." She repeated his name.

He jerked as though he'd been kicked. It wasn't usually this bad. Being here was making him worse.

"Sorry. You were saying?"

"I was asking if you're with someone."

"I'm not here to make brown babies, Mom."

"Geez, you're touchy, eh?" She pushed her mug from the edge of the table. "Why don't you unpack? I'll make lunch."

"What are we having?"

"Canned smoked salmon and French fries—your favorite." She touched his knee. "Help this old woman up?"

Putting his boots toe to toe with her slippers, he slid his hands along her forearms until his thumbs came to rest at the crooks of her elbows and rocked back, waiting for her thigh muscles to catch as she straightened, her smile showing a strong line of teeth grown crooked.

The top of her head reached his clavicle. "Put the cups in the sink."

They zigzagged to the kitchen. "Mom, you can barely get around in here."

"I manage."

"The cats pissed on your newspapers."

"Finally put to good use."

He snorted. "We'll get rid of some stuff, okay?"

The scanner squawked and burbled, gushing forth a domestic disturbance at 200 Line. Peter lowered the volume, fighting the old feel of a fist on his face. She heated oil in a cast iron pan. Stooping to pull a bag from the bottom drawer of the fridge, she untied the handles—potato peelings—and considered the garbage can in the corner. He did everything but whistle and stick his hands in his pockets. Blushing, she plunged a hand into the garbage and retrieved a saggy plastic bag, giving it a good shake to free wet coffee grounds from its folds.

From the kitchen, Peter studied the maze of mementos. The crates were trussed into a globe that tapered and curled up into a fan. A whale. He turned his back on it and scraped a chair from the breakfast table, sick with regret. Her madness pressed at him from all sides. He forced himself to get used to watching her stagger. "The oil is smoking."

She scowled and snatched the pan off the burner. Oil sloshed onto the red-hot coils. Flames licked the cast iron's inside edge, broadening into a circle of blue fire she stared into with a strange inquisitive smile, like that of a shy child.

"Don't move!" Peter stepped in to lift the pan high and level, keeping the blaze away from the piles as he hurried to the front door and kicked it open, ripping the screen from its frame. Cold air blew the flames toward his face. Cursing, his arms hot and quivering, he lobbed the stream of fire into the grass. It leapt and fizzled.

"Burning down the house already?" On the porch next door, Dave tucked an empty bottle into a cardboard six-pack holder at his feet and withdrew another with the same gesture. "Thirsty?"

"No."

"Sweet tea . . ."

"Next time."

"Welcome home! Remember me?"

"Yep." Dave, too, was whorled with years, his body bent in odd places, the strange stoop and slope of age.

"Maggie don't have to have her place all tore up like that. We tried."

"I'd better go."

"Married? Kids?"

"Nope."

"I'll draw you a map of the best poon in town."

"I'd like to see that."

"What have you been up to?"

"I'm a commercial diver. Underwater welder."

His mother shouted from inside. "Quit meddling!"

"Just talkin', Maggie." Dave jammed the bottle's neck

through the crook of his knee and twisted the cap. "Ahhh. There she goes."

She beckoned Peter. "I'll clean up and try again."

Peter carried the pan back to the kitchen. "Hasn't changed much."

"Stopped boozing."

"Huh. When?"

"Right after you left. About time, I guess. Chases tail less than he used to. So that's something. I got tired of his advances. Ha! More like retreats."

Peter tugged until he heard the doorknob click, wincing as his boots crushed kitty litter spilling from a tray wedged between the toilet and the wall. Rummaging through the drawers, his hand brushed against a folded Buck knife. His father's.

He saw his dad whittling a stick for s'mores, smelled logs smoldering in rain, laughed again about genuine Indian smoked marshmallows. Heard the splatter of rain on their matching slickers, gusts blowing their hoods back and sending them stumbling across the *Magdalene*'s deck. Saw his dad cut two plugs from a still gaping salmon, its hooked jaw working, soundless, as he popped one in his mouth, grinning and chewing and offering the other, shouting above the wind, "Sushi! Japs love this shit! They'll pay top dollar. Not like timber. Remember that." Saw a pile of nets seeping blood around still feet. His dad went out right around this age, but at least he left something, had people who would remember him. Peter's midlife hovered over him like an avenging angel, ready to exact its tribute in quiet desperation, and here he was, back at home, trying to deal with the only person who still gave a shit about him.

He needed something to calm down. He opened the medicine cabinet with a sense of reverence. Shelves and shelves of vials. Turning on the faucet to cover the rattle of pills, he rotated a few.

May cause nausea. May cause dizziness, drowsiness or brief hallucinations. Do not operate heavy machinery for 12 hours after taking. Call your doctor immediately if a rash appears. Cease taking immediately and call 9-1-1 if you begin vomiting.

Peter shut the cabinet. It didn't matter where he went or what he took. Their shadow was always on him. His mother hadn't asked why he came home, and he hadn't given her a reason after decades of refusing to step foot on this reservation.

They were so goddamned alike. Biding their time.

Chapter Three

CLAUDIA STROLLED THE dry goods aisle, forcing herself to find the cheapest brand of coffee. A white-haired lady in a warm up jacket rolled by in an electric wheelchair with a wreath tied to its back, clipping a middle aged man, his wide face broadened by the center part of his long hair.

"Beep, beep, beep." He backed up.

"Beep beep!" She toggled the switch on her armrest to charge at him.

They disappeared into the frozen foods aisle, laughing. Claudia wanted to follow, gladdened, but she never allowed herself near breakfast waffles and ice cream.

This Christmas was the latest in a long line of holidays she filled with work, goaded by her father's derision of vacation. Even as he grew old, her father treated visiting family as though they weren't there, locking himself in the study to make calls, coming down to dinner when the day was heavy upon him. She, too, was proud of her ability to insulate her focus against the presence of loved ones, saying "no" to people who cared about her and "yes" to those who didn't. Perhaps she was sick, but she liked it that way. She would make it in this country.

Last Christmas, their father had prevailed upon dinner with lengthy discourses about world politics and the economy. Claudia relied on Maria to bring cheer, stockpiling energy for later, when she could think.

"Thanks for showing Andrew around today." She raised her wine in salute. Two glasses, max, she'd vowed, but here she was at three. It wasn't yet time for dessert. She had to work later. Maybe tomorrow.

Stop drinking, she thought, and took another sip.

"Please don't thank me. It was fun!" Maria leafed through her salad. "You should get out more. It would be good for you." Her sunglasses had left a pale stripe on either side of her wide eyes. "I make so much art after I've been in nature. I love cross country skiing. It's so mellow. You can take in the scenery, you know?"

Maria still spoke like a Mexican, which meant she said "love" like "lowve."

"I had a great time." Andrew smiled at Maria and reached for Claudia's hand. "We should go up there tomorrow, Claudia."

"Oh, sweetheart." She gave him a rueful squeeze. "My proposal is due."

Thomas chuckled. "I thought you'd written the keynote by now." With a stiff cough and the wet clatter of ice, her father regarded his crystal tumbler with displaced contempt. She knew the reason. In his cosmology, she was too clumsy to make it on her own. She eroded his dynasty. Before him was the errant branch of a family that roared westward, chewing up trees and men and sky, and never retreated. A wasted generation, which future historians would skip.

Claudia let go of Andrew's hand and took another sip. "It's complicated."

Andrew sawed his steak with unnecessary vigor. "No

problem." Blood oozed into his mashed potatoes. "I'll go up to the hill, get a few turns in."

"Great." Claudia speared a green bean. "I'll finish by dinnertime. We'll have a nice evening together."

The next afternoon, when she came down to the kitchen for a snack, she heard Maria speaking Spanish with the maids in the other kitchen, refusing as always to comply with their father's edict to "maintain the proper distance." Claudia couldn't make out the words from the lilt of female voices. A rumble of laughter. She knit her brow and checked her watch. Had Andrew come back? Still on deadline, she went upstairs and closed the door.

At her prodding, when she began her PhD, he launched a boutique architecture firm. Life was busy for them both. She taught classes and worked on her dissertation, analyzing gendered notions of love in Mexican border songs, thrilled to see her name in journals. *Ethnomusicology*, *American Anthropologist*, *Ethnography*. He saved copies for display on their coffee table.

But when he began delegating to employees, she was just getting started on her true task. Tenure. She was in the very infancy of her career. Between committees and conferences, she sought solitude whenever possible, excluding herself from vacations and weekends only to be tormented by procrastination, the sound of her keyboard a fickle companion, dipping into and out of a smoking habit that made her a liar a thousand times.

She kept at it, her writing disrupted by distant bellows as Thomas argued points on a call. They worshipped success together. Mostly, the halls held nothing but shadows and silence, blessed silence, and the words flowed. Work felt holy.

And so it would seem she had missed the glances unfurling between Andrew and Maria.

Claudia wheeled over to the produce aisle, trying not to ruin her makeup with tears. Right. Something for breakfast. Onward.

A young couple—pimples and hoodies, flip flops peeking below wet jeans—herded a small child past Claudia. The boy spun in circles between them, arms outstretched. The father's sweatshirt was printed with AMERICA: LOVE IT OR GIVE IT BACK. The mother put down her basket—milk, apples, Cheerios, cans of alphabet soup—and stooped to pick up the boy.

Claudia scanned the bananas—too green, too ripe, well, this splotchy bunch could do—and eavesdropped on a conversation in the deli corner.

"Oh, that must be nice for you." A girl wiped down the metal counter in front of an old woman and fiddled with rows of fried chicken wings. "How long is he staying?"

"He just got here. You two should meet."

That voice, like beach stones tumbling under surf. Claudia peered around a shelving unit stacked with shrink-wrapped bell peppers. A grizzled halo, pants ending two inches above the socks. It must be. Pull youself together and get to work, Claudia thought. Now's your chance.

"Maggie?"

Maggie turned and waved, albeit vaguely. Claudia put the bananas in the child seat and pushed her cart over.

"It's Claudia! Good to see you again!"

"You, too."

She remembers me! Claudia stepped from behind her cart, making it official—we are going to chat. But why was

Maggie staring like that? She seemed perturbed, anxious, her eyes clouding and refocusing.

Claudia was recalculating her approach when Maggie looked up at a man coming out of the cleaning supplies aisle, a bucket of bleach dangling from his hand, forearm tensed against the weight. Dressed in jeans and a hooded jacket with pushed up sleeves, he moved rangily, like he spent his life outdoors. He slowed—in spite of himself, it seemed—approaching with a once over that was not as subtle as Claudia would have liked. His hair was long enough to tuck behind his ears. His eyes turned down at the corners. A mouth so full it was womanish. His skin stretched over the angles of his face, hollowing at the cheeks, shining along his wide brow. She couldn't place him.

But now, she'd been caught. His eyes were big and black and looking more and more amused. She was naked, exposed. Her ears popped with a muffled ringing almost like silence.

"Hi." He offered his free hand. "Peter."

Claudia took his palm, her wrist torqued so their fingers could slip around each other. His skin was warm; hers, chilled.

"Claudia." She turned to Maggie. "How have you been?"

"Fine."

Claudia tried to emit genuine feeling, to offer Maggie the sweet comfort of shared memory—our friendship is real—but her cheerful expression was deflating. Maggie was acting like she hardly knew her. Claudia spent hours, days, weeks talking to this woman, recording her thoughts and reviewing cultural tidbits culled from prior data gathering interviews that masqueraded as conversations. Unprompted, Maggie shared secrets, the kind that weighed on whoever held them in keeping. Perhaps she was ashamed now, because here was the son, and Claudia knew things.

"Staying long?" Peter put the bleach down.

"A couple of months. I just arrived. I'm stocking up."

Wait, she thought. I don't mean you. I'm not stocking up on you.

Mindless chatter was where she stumbled the most. She revealed what she didn't want to reveal, her mask no mask at all but a bullhorn for social awkwardness, solitude, self-doubt. Everything she tried to keep at bay came tumbling out of her mouth as superfluous commentary.

Relax, she told herself. Focus. We're having an interaction. I'm lucky Natives take their time talking.

"You over at Hobuck?"

Impossible to hide where she was staying in such a small community. "It's so beautiful on the beach."

He seemed delighted. "What are you doing way out here?"

"Your mother's been helping me with my research. Stories and music."

"Whaddya know about that."

"Not as much as I should! That's why I'm here. To learn. Maggie, are you still volunteering at the museum?"

"Oh, here and there. Not too much these days."

"I brought a transcript of our last chat."

Maggie's eyes were blank.

"We talked about how your husband was a singer, like his mother?"

"Oh, sure, sure." Maggie drifted toward the deli. Her sneakers made small squeaks.

"I learned a lot. Should I bring it to the museum?"

Peter watched her work his mother, his smile hardening.

He spoke before Maggie could reply. "Why don't you come by the house? I'm interested in family history."

"Oh, you live there now, too?"

And again. She'd embarrassed him. A grown man living with his mother. But here, housing was tight. Families lived together. It had been that way since the longhouses.

Peter was smiling, thank God. "Just moved back." He picked up the bucket. "We're on Diaht Hill, third pull out. My black truck will be parked out front. Come by Monday morning." He guided Maggie toward the cashier before Claudia could thank him.

Lingering in produce, waiting for them to clear the checkout line, Claudia tossed a head of garlic into her cart and ducked past the meat section, grabbing a chicken for show. The deli girl was staring. She did not look amused. We weren't flirting, Claudia wanted to say. This is work for me. She'd forgotten the gutsick social paranoia of small town life, where every relationship mattered, or at least made itself felt.

The coffee maker gurgled at her. She turned in haste, clocking the counter with the right half of her pelvis, and doubled over. Her cabin was not expansive enough for real pacing, but she tried, a small star of pain exploding in her hip as she limped down the hallway, emitting a reedy stream of air from pursed lips.

There was the small matter of what she'd seen. The owl. A harbinger of bad news. Ill spirit of a drowned soul. *Siyowen*.

And that mink. Kwa-Ti. A trickster. A Transformer.

His laugh had started high, a hyena-like hoot that thickened into something more human, with bass in it, like listening to a man talk with your ear on his chest. The piercing clarity of her delusion haunted her, plucking anxieties from her subconscious with the lucid cruelty of God. It was a vision. Some One was trying to tell her something. Kwa-Ti was a shapeshifter, greedy and boastful. Bound to deceive, he pretended to serve those around him, suffering the consequences only to come back for more, scaling up by orders of magnitude, always. A warning.

No. It was a hallucination, she decided. All kinds of people see things that aren't there. Yes, but those people talk to themselves. It was a dream. I passed out at the wheel, she affirmed, desperate not to stand among the crazed. I was exhausted. It could happen to anyone. In the days since, she slept and slept and still was tired, as though she hadn't slept at all. Waking was like drowning at the bottom of a well.

Claudia brought a mug and her bathrobe sash to the breakfast table, where she set up her laptop and printer. In the oven, the butterflied chicken was tightening, its ruddy muscles pulling away from each other without their fatty veil. She sat, passing the sash beneath her seat and over her lap, tying herself to the chair with a grim smile, and opened the first document, copying the entire transcript into a blank file she saved in a new folder, entitled *Drafts*.

> M: *Sam's mother was a real singer. I seen her perform at pot-*
> *latches when I was a girl. The men drummed in a circle,*
> *and she leaned in over their shoulders, her voice all high,*
> *cuttin' through. Nobody could sing like her.*
> C: *What did she sing?*
> M: *Oh, you know, family songs.*
> C: *Do you know them?*
> M: *The songs belonged to her husband. He passed one on to*
> *Sam.*

C: Could you sing it for me?
M: I can't remember too good.

Her cursor paused. Grammatical errors should remain, though it filled her with shame, somehow, to leave them there, knowing that Maggie and Peter could read through the diction to the distance between the woman who was asking the questions and the woman who was answering them. They won't notice, she thought, skeptical. Maggie shifted in her seat when she said it, aware of her error. Or maybe she used the mistake and her confusion as decoys, a bird's broken wing trick to lure the weasel from her nest.

For all intents and purposes, Claudia's presence was predicated on one thing. Maggie would give her what she wanted, would tell her things about spirit animals and songs that she wasn't supposed to reveal to anyone outside her family. Maggie knew it, too, of that she was sure. The lonely, the young and the old possess emotional acuity, an astute sense of positioning born from need. Last summer, Maggie was killing time, keeping her erstwhile companion close because she needed company. Claudia's reappearance had to be palatable to this reconfigured family, its prodigal son returned.

For all intents and purposes—Claudia used that phrase incorrectly in an article submitted to her grad school's journal. The reviewer returned the paper, unaccepted, her error—*for all intensive purposes*—circled in red, marked **ESL?** She stared at those letters for a long time before the dimpled pages told her she was crying. She was glaring at the screen now, to no avail.

M: I can't remember too good.

It would remain in the text, a gauntlet thrown.

> C: *Did you teach your son the songs?*
> M: *I tried, but he wasn't interested. And then he was gone.*

Would Peter challenge his mother on that point? Could he make her sing?

> C: *Who went to the dances?*
> M: *Everybody. I could pull out a Neah Bay telephone book and show you. I keep them, just in case. Directories, we used to call them. I've got stacks in my house. People keep passing on. I can't bear to throw their names away.*
> C: *What else do you keep?*
> M: *Oh, everything. I'm about to run out of house!*
> C: *What kinds of things do you keep?*
> M: *Anything that helps me remember. I'm a saver. Like Peter's jerseys. He started on the basketball team, took the Red Devils to state his junior year.*
> C: *Do you have anything . . . cultural?*
> M: *What do you mean?*
> C: *Materials that pertain to your culture, things that make you Makah.*
> M: *Well, jerseys fit the bill, I guess. I'm not sure what you mean.*
> C: *I'm not explaining myself well. Do you hang onto old stuff?*
> M: *Sure do.*
> C: *Maybe I could come over one day, help you go through it.*
> M: *I wouldn't want you to go to the trouble.*

Muffled thumps and flutters pulled her from the transcript. She looked at the kitchen window, and there she was, her pallid face framed in darkness, mouth speckled with the frantic bodies of moths. They hurled themselves at the light of her laptop, their futile bumps and hovers like fingertips drumming a tabletop. She was out here alone. Lashing herself to the chair was unwise. She tugged the bow; the silk sash slipped its knot, slithering to the floor.

She could not conceal her greedy nature without deleting the whole damned document. Would Maggie remember what she said? Regardless, Claudia could not advance beyond this first draft of their history, aghast at her own depravity. She was hustling a hoarder.

> C: It would be no trouble at all!
> M: Peter will help me, when he gets back.

Claudia left her breach of basic decency intact. It was a hook. An anchor. Peter would need an assistant. And who better than she?

> C: When will that be?
> M: He'll be home soon. Any day now. I feel it.

Claudia stood and stretched, slipping on quilted oven mitts to pull out the chicken. Hot fat swished, sizzling as she scavenged juices with a spoon, trickling her meager haul over the desiccated drumsticks. Placing the mitts on a burner, she kept the oven open to warm her hands. Like a bum in front of a trashcan, she thought, examining her ragged nails. She would buy polish. Maybe she and Maggie could do their nails together. Some Makah women were into makeup and that sort of thing.

She wiggled a drumstick. The joint moved easily. She picked up the knife.

She thought Chicanas cornered the market on penciled eyebrows, but it turned out lots of brown girls had a way with brows. There was a certain kind of Native woman, just like there was a certain kind of Latina, who saw her own face as a blank canvas, or, more accurately, a map of flaws, a tenuous topography to be torn down and rebuilt in private with tweezers and a pencil. Many girls began their lives believing they'd be artists, but most only learned to draw over themselves.

She slid the blade around the chicken's thigh, working it away from the body with small, sliding taps of the knife's tip.

She made a career of such merciless scrutiny, which led her to this jagged point on the Pacific, the same sea she swam as a child. Peeling strings of meat from bone, Claudia worked late into the night, deleting phrases that betrayed her. Excising the errata was as fierce and satisfying as standing before the bathroom mirror, squeezing blackheads from her nose. Please get over your disgust, she told herself. Like you haven't done that, like you're not going to do it again.

Chapter Four

CAUGHT BETWEEN HIS daybed and the wall, his arm was chilled. A downpour rattled the trailer. His trapped hand clutched the bedpost, asleep. Touch sent painful tingles through the warm, alien skin. He left it and watched rain dapple the glass.

The dream, again. That night teemed through his mind like he had never stopped bailing his dad's blood with a sawed-off milk jug, crying and shaking and sloshing clean water on the gunwales while his mom watched from the troller.

"Gimme some light!"

"Looks good," she hollered. "Let's go!"

The skiff dipped and spun with the restless ocean. Staggering, he stripped and flung his clothes overboard and his boots into the troller. Winding line around his wrist, he leapt in.

The cold bit hard. He thrashed and scrubbed at his stained hands, his mind tugged down a long spiral to the sea floor, his father's big frame falling through the deep like a feather, blown off course by sharks that would bump and nose and return, grimacing.

His arm snapped up, tangled in line she hauled in, one fistful at a time.

"Want me to take over?" Hacking out the words, his

throat and lungs raw with salt, he clung to a cleat, covering his nakedness.

"I know the way."

The skiff orbited the buoys. Two ravens circled, croaking. They flapped toward the wooded coastline emerging green and misty in the early light. To the north, dark jade mountains. Vancouver Island. Just south, Shi Shi Beach buckled into sea stacks towering above the froth. She motored past Tatoosh Island into the mouth of the strait, scanning the horizon through smears of cloud.

Waves wept from rocky shores. He checked over his shoulder. The land was gone. Sobs echoed, endless and rising beneath the boat, reverberating through his body, whirling him awake. Again.

"Shit." He rolled out of bed, wiping his wet face, trying to shake off the dream that loomed like a hangover too many mornings.

The air in her room was humid with the warmth of slumber. A murky wail erupted from her chest, chased by splutters. Her hands raised above her head, snarled in sheets printed with basketballs and hoops. His childhood sheets, worn to holes. He took her arm. The fleece sparked and shocked him. "Ow. Mom!"

"Huh?" She pushed her face between her dimpled elbows. "What's the matter?"

"You were crying. In your sleep."

"Sorry." She eased out a hand. It quavered against the folds of her neck.

"Don't be." His voice was groggy. "I'm going now."

"You're going to leave me." Shadows moved across her face. She plucked at the sheets, fitful.

She had no right to guilt him, no right to be weak just

when he was ready to reckon with the ache he held so close it had grown into his skin. This old woman came along and stole his mother, leaving someone too frail to fight. Peter went back the way he came, sidestepping through her crap, and pressed his spine against the doorframe.

"You were dreaming." The price of his silence was flight. Always had been. "It's four in the morning."

"Time to get up." She raised one knee, then the other.

"Go back to bed." He reached for the doorknob.

"I'm old, son." She massaged her thighs with the heels of her hands. "Sleep doesn't come when I call."

"Well, good morning then, and good night."

Bleach water sluiced down the drain. Peter scoured the bathtub, mulling over whether his mother was demented, forgetful or a mastermind. Maybe she got bad on purpose to bring him back. Being here felt wrong. This was not how it was supposed to go. He rinsed the brush, yellow gloves slippery. Bit by bit, his mind rested on what was in front of him until every surface was clean but his own.

Refreshed, or at least showered, Peter paused by his mother's room and tapped the plywood with his knuckles. Hearing nothing, he banged harder. No response. He girded himself to see her sprawled on the floor and hip checked the door. Nothing. Her bed was made. The rest of the room was knee deep. Where was she?

Bread cooled on the kitchen counter. He snuck a piece.

"Mom?" He swallowed the last bits, cleared his throat and called again, louder this time. "Mom!"

A crow cawed. It began to rain.

Could she be with Dave? Peter hurried next door. No one answered his knock. Inside, the TV blared celebrity news—boob jobs, cleanse diets and DUIs. Peter gave another three blows.

"I said, come in!"

A teenage boy cradled the remote in the middle of a couch covered in burn holes and car magazines, the television so loud that Peter had to shout.

"I'm Peter, Maggie's son. Your next door neighbor!"

The boy made no move to get up. "I'm Beans. Dave's my Grampa."

"Is he around? I'm looking for my mom."

"The waitress at Warm House called. Maggie headed up 200 Line again."

"When were you going to tell me?"

"Grampa's got it handled." Beans changed the channel.

"I would have gone!"

"He's got nothing else to do."

"I'd like to know if my mom is wandering."

"She goes straight for 200 Line every time."

"Why?" His mom told him about a big development—housing and services—being built clear across town in hills where folks used to bathe and pray, out of the way of the big wave that would come when the ground shook, which was just a matter of time.

The kid stared at a starlet's court-mandated monitoring anklet.

"I said, why 200 Line?" Peter moved closer, noticing for the first time that Beans was stoned to the bejesus. The set's blue flicker illuminated the patchy beard on his baby cheeks.

"I don't know, she says she can hear drumming and stuff."

"Why didn't you come tell me my mother is wandering around hearing things?" Peter stepped in front of the television with folded arms. Beans leaned to one side for an uninterrupted view. "Look, I'm here now. I want to be notified when stuff like this goes down. I'll be the one to get her. I'm going to leave my cell phone number on the counter. Give it to that waitress—what's her name?"

"She won't call you. She doesn't know you. No one does."

"She can get to know me."

"I'm sure she'll like that."

His mother tottered along, her back curving toward the earth, flanked by Dave and an EMT who had draped his jacket over her shoulders and held an umbrella over her head. They nodded at him as he pulled alongside.

Peter watched Dave brush his mother's head and shoulders with a cedar bough, shaking his rattle and singing in shifting, repeating tones. He stayed far enough away that the song was an idea of song. The melody slid toward him, passing through the downpour's insistent conversation with the pavement.

After Dave brought her back, Peter tried to stay out of the way. This mute woman was foreign to him. Her bones creaked when he led her to her chair. He wrote down the names of her medications and called the clinic, asking what they were for and who prescribed them and could he talk to that person, but the lady who answered the phone said Maggie didn't have paperwork on file naming a health care surrogate or giving him power of attorney. He started another list, detailing signatures he would need when his mother woke up to the world.

He cleared the hallway and living room, hoping to provoke a protest. None came. She watched him like a television, sitting in her armchair for days. He dismantled egg crates and threw phone books and newspapers into a trashcan fire he kept flickering in the front yard. The rest he shoved in garbage bags.

He hoped he wasn't being negligent by letting her snap out of it. What if she'd had a stroke? Or maybe she took the wrong combination of pills. That's probably what it was. I'm a bad son. She needs a doctor. Someone in Seattle should look her over. Would the tribe pay for it? Or did she belong in a nursing home? I didn't come here to send her away.

He waited, working his way down the hall, reading headlines from newspapers draped over each pile.

> TWO MAKAH APPEAL THEIR WHALING CON-
> VICTIONS
>
> TACOMA — Two Makah men convict-
> ed of two misdemeanor violations of the
> Marine Mammal Protection Act have ap-
> pealed their verdicts in U.S. District Court.

The yellow corner of the *Peninsula Daily News* tore in his hands.

> In the hearings, Arnold blocked Fiander's
> attempts to defend Noel on the basis of
> the Makah's 1855 Treaty of Neah Bay that
> guaranteed them the right to hunt whales,
> on tribal culture and on religious freedom.

He held up items—a crusty garden glove, a button blanket, stained potholders, strings of olive shells—and studied her face for an aftermath. He did this for days and into the nights, clearing a wide path, stacking bags along the wall, beating down dread, heartbeat swift and erratic, breath hurried. "We'll go through these bags later. What do you think, Mom?" Did she nod? Her eyes became alert, as though her mind bobbed along the surface of things, but her mouth remained below, thick with jostling silence. He stumbled, sweaty, through the trailer, trying to sever his mind's recurrent return to buoys lolling in the Pacific.

He burst onto the porch, drawing air like a dying fish, and nearly tripped over a bucket of geoduck clams tucked next to the door. He was hungry. His mother must be hungry, too. He hadn't taken care of anyone, not even himself, for years. It stunned him how ill-prepared he was to be needed.

Squatting, he lit a cigarette and studied the clams by the glow of his lighter. Covered by clear water, they probed the strange surrounding stillness with slick taupe siphons.

Rimmed with dirt and dead flies, the windows still opened. Fresh air flooded the trailer. The stink clung to his clothes and the carpet. He got down on all fours, sniffing. His dad always checked the registers. Peter pulled the couch to one side and smelled the grate. He almost passed out. Bingo.

Before he foraged for whatever died below the trailer, he thought twice and locked the screen door. He would hear her this time.

Dropping his head into the damp dirt, he cast his flashlight around the trailer's underbelly, pushing into the darkness, testing deep slumps in the fabric with a push, hoping to find what his dad called the "dead skunk bounce." He'd begged to hold the flashlight as his father prodded and cursed, ash falling onto his cheek, cracking jokes. "This underbelly has more saggy udders than a dairy farm. No, wait! Than a bar in Forks!" Peter laughed out loud, remembering.

"What's so funny under there?"

He froze, hearing old man wheezy grumbles. A faded, stained pant knee lowered into the grass, followed by tremulous hands. Dave's face appeared sideways. "How's it hanging, Peter?"

"Hey, Dave."

"You know your mom could apply for a new trailer." Dave settled in, hands folded on his knee.

"Really?" Peter flipped onto his elbows and pulled his bandana down.

"Yeah." Dave brightened. "I don't know why she won't, what with all the history in there."

Peter's silence was a vast sucking mudflat.

"Just making conversation, son."

"I'm busy."

"I can see that." Dave wobbled and smacked the trailer to steady himself.

"Wait!" Peter army crawled into the light. "I know I haven't been around. We had our reasons. But I'm here now. I don't want to find out my mom's wandered off secondhand."

"Beans told you I was bringing her back, didn't he? He's my grandson—my blood. That's not secondhand."

"I'm here to help."

"Might need more help than you can give." Gripping the vinyl for support, Dave bore down and plunked his foot into the grass, snorting a bit. "Push it away all you like. That stuff comes back."

"I'll handle my own business."

"We'll get you straightened out." Dave threw his words over his shoulder. "You can come watch me work. If you keep your mouth shut."

Peter cut a hole in the undercarriage, loosing a flurry of rodent flakes. Another. It was like a crypt down here.

"If you're going to lock me in my own home, better make sure there's not a hole in the front door," his mom shouted. "I might climb out."

"Look who's talkin'." He folded his mouth down, containing his happiness out of habit.

"Look who's talking back. Haven't changed a bit."

Surrounded by small piles of rotted squirrel, he grinned, the bandana hugging his cheeks.

His mother's fingers traced the ridged clamshell, tracking the geoduck's age in calcium Braille. Its tough neck slumped, exposed.

"I'm misplacing things, I know that." She slid a thin blade around the siphon, slipping the severed flesh into a bowl, and lifted the shell with both hands before letting it fall into the bucket with a hollow clatter. "Even words. Sometimes I can't find them for a long while." She smoothed hair from her forehead, lodging shards of shell in the strands, and searched out his eyes. "But you can't misplace love. Even if the self that's talking forgets, I am inside. I know you. I love you."

Her hands, small and balled up like a child's, barely encircled his waist when he hugged her, not thinking for once. His chin rested on her head; the mist of frizz that hung around her crown tickled his cheeks. In one breath, she smelled like a powdery old woman; in the next, she smelled like the sea.

"Look what I've done." She pulled back, cataracts glinting. "You're covered in clam!" She dabbed his shirt. The wrinkles around her mouth tensed.

"It's going to be alright."

"I know, son. I know. But then it won't be."

"I'll take care of you." There. The words escaped without his say so. The unsayable had been said.

"But who will take care of you?"

"Let me worry about that." His fingers curled around her arms. "Make the fritters. I'll get started on the windows."

The shells splayed open like wings. She held them over the bucket.

Roberta opened the door with a quick knock, the kind of knock that isn't meant to warn whoever lives inside. Peter was caught wearing boxers to a reunion he'd been daydreaming about for years. He tried to rearrange his expression from "What the fuck?" to "Welcome!" but the strange pulling of his cheeks told him his face landed on a grimace. He stood, solemn, as three kids blew past him to crowd around his mother, who let them stir the batter.

"You're quite a sight." Laughter had worn grooves into Roberta's cheeks, intensifying her angles. Her cheekbones had risen and rounded. They nudged up next to her eyes, opening a fan of wrinkles toward her temples.

"It's good to see you."

"No hug?" She held her hands out, right arm drooping with an enormous slouchy purse.

"Let me get some pants on."

Peter hustled down the hallway, glad he'd been able to resist his first and near fatal impulse to scream and cross his hands over his chest like a goddamned girl. He stepped twice into the wrong leg of his grimy jeans. He could hear Roberta call his mother "Auntie"—she started that when their mothers made them stop dating, and it pained him to hear it again. Those were her children. Were they all by Randall?

Roberta had her arm around his mother, who was smiling and saying, "Now just look at these kids. Can you believe it?"

"They're beautiful, Roberta. How old?"

"Sarah's five, Layla's seven, and John is twelve. Kids, this is your Uncle Peter."

Two high voices said hello.

His mind scrambled on Roberta's nearness. White wires threaded the shiny black curtain that hung around her shoulders. What she must think of him. Left his mother to rot. Roberta would have seen it happen in real time, the slow creep of trash like moss on a log.

The boy stared him down. She cleared her throat. "You've cleaned up."

"Not done yet."

"She wouldn't let anyone else do it, you know." She squeezed his mother's shoulders. "Waiting for him, eh?"

The oil in the pan hissed and spat.

"Still don't talk much." Roberta kicked his foot.

"Don't know what to say."

"You can't be eating. You're skinny."

"Is that Indian for in shape?" Peter flexed a bicep, like he did in high school, when she would clutch his arm with small fingers.

"Don't talk to my mom like that," John said.

"Relax, buddy, he's joking." She palmed her son's head. "We're old friends. Family."

"I've never seen him before."

"That means you should be extra nice to him, not the other way around. Our great-grandfathers were brothers."

His mother spooned golden clam fritters from the oil, soaking the paper towel and the plate beneath it. "Who wants one?"

John grabbed two and walked out. "I'll be at Dave's!"

Roberta blew on a fritter. "He's testy lately."

"I was a punk at that age. If you remember."

"For you, son?"

His mouth blistered. He tried not to make a big deal of it, but his cheeks puffed out like a blowfish. Roberta smiled into her hand.

"I've still got it, don't I?" Maggie tested a fritter with the back of her forefinger. "Too hot, Sarah. Wait a minute. You don't want to end up like him."

"I'm fine. Let me at another one. I'll show it what's what."

"The rest of this batch goes to the girls." Tiny hands made quick work of what was left. "Stay for dinner, Roberta?"

"Well, I thought I'd pop by and clean those clams, but you beat me to it. I have to make dinner for Randall."

"Invite him over!" His mother spooned more batter into the pan. The oil attacked from all sides, bubbling and frothing.

Peter was sick to his stomach. A cop, in this trailer. Chill out, he told himself. Roberta would have kept up her visits to her uncle. Dave was right next door. Randall had been coming here for years. He'd seen the piles, the stains. It was an old kitchen, an old story no one was thinking about but Peter—and maybe Dave, who acted like he felt bad, real bad, after Peter's dad went missing. They always threatened to net smelt after a night out. Dave said he thought Sam was joking. "You know, catching tail." After the accident, as his mom took to calling it when search parties found the skiff, Peter avoided hangdog eyes; some people were glad to fade away. Not Roberta. Peter took off before he weakened enough to tell her what happened. He was glad she couldn't see who he was inside. And then she got over him and married Randall, who was fair game because his mother was Yakama, far from the family tree.

"You brought the clams?"

"We dug 'em up this morning."

"Thank you." Peter always felt a slight sense of vertigo when he was about to do something he'd regret. He tried to keep himself from saying what he was about to say but couldn't, even as his pulse quickened and the nausea started. "Leaving them in still water kills them faster."

"Oh, yeah?" Roberta tucked her hair behind her ears. "Figures. My grampa used to wrap them in an old shirt. The girls wanted to make them feel at home."

"When they're in a closed environment like that, they asphyxiate."

Layla piped up. "What does that mean?"

"They suffocate."

She looked puzzled. He tried again. "Like drowning."

She grinned, sure she had him. "They can't drown! They live in water!"

"Um, it means they run out of oxygen. They use up what's in the water." I should listen when I have that feeling, he thought. Why don't I listen?

His mother snatched up the spatula, dragging the greasy paper towel with it. Fritter crumbs formed a constellation across the linoleum. He stared at the stained plaid, saw his shirtless dad sprawled in jeans, bleeding out. He blinked and blinked again, started counting, clinging to the numbers.

"Mom!" She was stooping below the counter. He pulled

her up and used the paper towel to wipe up the crispy bits, fighting his revulsion at the warm wetness against his palm, fighting the sound of sopping up swirls, fighting and wiping harder to hide the shake in his hands.

Someone tapped his shoulder. Roberta's childhood face stared at him from between Layla's braided pigtails. "I think you got it, Uncle Peter."

A semicircle of women stood above him. He stopped. "Got carried away." He smeared his palms on his jeans. "So. Fritters for dinner?"

The girls gathered close to their mother. She clasped a braid from each. "They're tired. It's been a long day. Maybe tomorrow."

Peter tried to think of what to say, mourning their forgotten hug. "We've got company coming. A lady from out of town."

"Anyone I know?"

"I doubt it."

After they packed up and left, he scuffled to his room and dove back into the musty palm of his bed. Sleep called to him, a siren swaying in the dark. Tomorrow, we'll work it out, he thought. That woman will turn up, get them talking about old times. Maybe he could take her out later, somewhere off the rez.

He hadn't looked in on his mom for hours. Padding down the hall, he flattened his ear against her door and held still. Was that her breathing?

"Stop snooping, you big snoop!"

"Sorry! Just checking."

"Good night! Keep going!"

Chapter Five

CLAUDIA GLANCED AT the transcript in the passenger seat, trying to quiet her anxiety at presenting this truncated testimonial to its source. She would not be the first outsider to lie to a Makah. Elizabeth Colson, a Radcliffe-educated anthropologist who examined the extent to which Makahs had assimilated American culture in the early part of the last century, was frank in her admission of deceit. She claimed to be gathering stories about the past, all the while studying tribal members in real time.

It was Heisenberg's uncertainty principle at work—the mere act of observation can change the observed. But Colson expressed no shame about misleading the very people she asked to reveal themselves. Perhaps sensing her duplicity—arriving, as she did, shortly after the attacks on Pearl Harbor—some Makahs called her "Spy Lady." Quarrels broke out among those who learned of what she'd been told. It was said that no one still living could know enough to speak for the record, and those who did were frauds and braggarts trying to advantage their own kin.

Claudia really should have wrapped up the research last summer, but in retrospect, the data she had gathered felt like fragments. Rubble. She needed to do a deep dive into one family. Makahs would talk about anything as long as she didn't ask too soon or too directly, but they felt safest sharing gossip, so that's where she started. Anyone who wanted to hear the good stuff had to listen to the rest first. It was shocking what they revealed if she sat on couches or took someone to the clinic, small favors not meant to be repaid except by the continued tolerance of her presence.

Peter's thick forearms popped into her mind, surprising her. She'd have to watch it around that one. The road began its ascent up Diaht Hill. Kept gardens and wild ones flashed past, lined with woodpiles, fronted by clean cars and their derelict cousins. A few bushes were strewn with ropes of lights and tinsel that wilted beneath new rain.

No one was outside, allowing her to ogle each trailer. Some of their occupants barely earned enough to get by. Others had millions riding on fishing equipment and licenses. Few reservations could claim such material wealth without the benefit of casinos, which too often generate more debt than cash, but geographic isolation helped the Makah Tribe, to some extent, as did a well-earned reputation for ferocity. The Spaniards first tried to take possession of Makah land in 1775. Driven away by constant skirmishes, they left little but the Ozette potato from Peru, whose knobby fingerlings sprouted throughout the reservation. Dark tales accompanied their departure—despoiled Makah women, dead men, an abandoned fort and a river said to be poisoned by glass bottles left by the failed conquerors. The story went that the bottles disgorged their contents when the rains came. Smallpox broke out. Or so Colson was told.

Sources gathered by the historian Joshua Reid show that white traders spread lies about diseased bottles that could be uncorked, if the natives didn't turn over more furs. In the multinational race to claim the lush northwest, the English, French, Spanish and Russians bickered with each other and traded blue beads, wool blankets and bad weapons to the natives until there was nothing left of the sea otter rookeries but thick pelts in China. Enterprising as any trader they met, Makah chiefs grew so wealthy they burned oil until the rafters were black, funding legendary potlatches and with them, a great flourishing of carving, singing and dancing.

Travelling aboard ships that stopped wherever they could profit, smallpox slaughtered without regard to rank, rending centuries of cultural knowledge and leaving a bewildered grief. People scrubbed the scabs with salt water and sand. Corpses everywhere. Babies nursed on dead mothers, and after, few knew who the motherless children were.

Peter's black truck, a Toyota Tacoma with fancy off-road tires, was parked in front of a trailer that looked tired, like the rest of them, a bleary door below a plywood porch. Something had burned a black moon into the lawn.

Makahs never showed up without gifts for their hosts. Claudia was tempted to turn around and come back when she had a present and maybe a plan. She slung her purse over her shoulder and got out, cradling the transcript and a digital recorder. The transcript acted as an oblique reminder that Maggie had long ago given permission to record their interviews, the way journalists imply interviews are on the record by asking subjects to spell their names. What if Peter refused? Claudia paused. The rain spat on her back. She would ask Peter for permission but hedge her bets. She switched on the recorder and dropped it into her purse just as he opened the screen door.

P: *You're earlier than I expected.*

C: *Hi, Peter! Sorry about that. Should I come back later?*

P: *No, no. That's fine. Come on in. Coffee?*

C: *That would be wonderful!*

P: *Cream or sugar?*

C: *No. Thank you.*

P: *Nice to see some restraint in a woman. Mom just stepped into the shower. She'll be out in a bit. Let's go to the kitchen.*

C: *Okay. Great.*

Steps, coughing, police scanner crackling . . .

P: *Have a seat.*

Chair scraping, coffee pouring.

P: *So. You've been speaking to my mother.*

C: *Yes, I met her several years ago.*

P: *Have you ever been here before?*

C: *You mean, in Neah Bay?*

P: *No, in this trailer. Our home.*

C: *Maggie and I conducted our interviews at the museum.*

P: *When was the last time you saw her?*

C: *Last summer.*

P: *Did you notice anything different about her?*

C: *Well, she's getting older. That's clear. It lends urgency to our work.*

P: *I mean, did you notice anything wrong with her?*

C: *No? I don't know how to respond.*

P: *How was her memory?*

C: *She . . . you know, she meandered a little, but I always thought her non sequiturs were charming, and they seemed culturally appropriate.*

P: *What?*

C: *Non sequiturs are when someone says something that doesn't logically follow from the prior statement.*

P: *I know what non sequiturs are. It's funny, though, that you found them, what was it, "culturally appropriate." Why's that?*

C: *I . . . well, I've noticed that Makahs have a habit of an-*

*swering the question they want to hear, rather than the
question I ask. That's all.*
P: *Like politicians.*
C: *Like anyone, I guess. Maybe they find my questions in-
appropriate. Maybe they think I need to know what
they're telling me before I know the answers to my actual questions. Maybe they'd rather talk about something else. I can't be certain. It's part of my job to be
somewhat intrusive, but I'm aware of how awkward it
is to be interviewed.*
P: *Give me an example.*
C: *Are you okay with me being here?*
P: *I'll tell you to leave if it comes to that. Give me an example.*
(5:00)

Claudia paused and replayed the recording, surprised by
her own sincerity, laughing at his completely inappropri-
ate "compliment." Nice to see some restraint in a woman!
Please. How did he think any men were still alive? Still, she
liked Peter; he intrigued her. For some reason, she was capa-
ble of being more honest in the field than she was with her
own family; in the end, she could leave the reservation and
would too, which everyone knew.

Many of her colleagues delegated the act of transcribing
fieldnotes, pressed for time or perhaps horrified by hearing
themselves fumble toward enlightenment. Excruciating as
that was, this was her favorite part. She dwelled on her mistakes—the interruptions, saying the wrong thing, slipping
sideways into unwise silence or worse, unsolicited explanations of purpose—when an insightful question or a direct
answer was warranted.

C: *Okay, an example. So, maybe I would ask someone what it
means that Makah dancers always enter the dance floor*

in a counterclockwise circle. And maybe they would wait a while and say, "Did you see my granddaughter at Makah Days? She was the best dancer, and she looked so pretty. She's going to be Makah Princess next year."

P: Well, that's easy. I can tell you why they're not answering. It's stuff you have no business knowing.

C: That could be it. They may also be afraid of contradicting what someone else told me. And, by the way, I'm not in it for business.

P: You'll sell your book, won't you?

C: Ha! Maybe. But I won't make any money.

P: Wouldn't you be selling our knowledge?

C: I contextualize what's been shared with me. Anyway, your participation is voluntary. And I make sure to thank my informants in the acknowledgments.

P: Your what?

C: Oh, informants? That's an old word for people who work with me. Participants, that's what I meant. That's the term we use now.

P: Informants. Sounds like spies.

C: I know, it's strange. Archaic, really. That's not how I think of you. I just . . . you know, you're not like most of them.

P: Who? Your spies?

C: No, most of the Makahs I've met.

P: You're saying I'm not Makah?

C: Maybe it's your years away, but you act a little different.

P: How so?

C: They're less, um, sharp, by which I mean, direct. Or . . . ah . . . argumentative? They're a bit more welcoming. Of me, I guess. More hospitable.

P: What, you don't like the coffee?

(10:00)

C: No, the coffee's good. Thank you. I didn't mean that.

P: You don't like being questioned.

C: No, that's fine, too. My research is collaborative in nature.

P: I'll tell you what I don't like.

C: Okay, tell me.

P: I don't like you telling me what's Makah and what's not.
C: I'm sorry.
P: No, you're backpedaling.
C: You're on fire this morning!
P: You're pretty hot yourself.
Laughter.

Claudia blushed. She should have shut him down. Peter was handsome, but there was something more, an edge that had been lacking in Andrew, who was so solicitous of her moods, right up until he wasn't.

Peter called her bullshit. She couldn't believe she had the nerve to tell him about his own people. In reminding him he'd been gone, she'd implied he wasn't as "Makah" as someone who had stayed. Historically, Makahs cultivated passivity as a social weapon. If someone insulted Peter, his lack of response would symbolize his relative strength.

In the world of bondage, that was called topping from below.

P: Truce?
C: Can I ask a few questions?
P: Sure.
C: What's in those garbage bags?
P: Oh, she wants to know what's in the bags.
C: I'm right here in front of you.
P: I'll answer that in a second. Did my mother tell you what's going on?
C: I don't know what you mean.
P: My mom has dementia. So maybe she forgot to tell you she's a hoarder.
C: Um . . . she said she was saving stuff.
P: Did she tell you why?
C: I think it made her feel better, like things weren't being lost.
P: Did she ever tell you why?

> C: *Well, I was going to show you this transcript when she*
>   *came out. She said she was waiting for you to come back.*
>   *I think she wanted you to see it. I think she may have*
>   *been saving it specifically for you, to tell the truth.*
> P: *Why would she tell you that? She barely knows you.*
> C: *I offered to help her.*
> (15:00)
> P: *Help her do what?*
> C: *Go through the stuff.*
> P: *Why?*
> C: *I like her. And she seemed . . . lonely.*
> M: *Who's lonely?*
> C: *Oh! Hi, Maggie!*
> P: *Mom, you remember Claudia.*
> M: *I said, who's lonely?*
> C: *Well, we all are, I guess. It's part of being alive.*
> P: *Tells us to be grateful for company.*

Her hands jumped off the keyboard. She had been so fix-ated on Maggie that she completely ignored this loveliness from Peter. He was telling her he wanted her to be there. His voice had thickened—with anger, she'd thought, but maybe it was emotion, or even desire. He diverted Maggie's attention from Claudia's stupid accusation—he'd stranded his mother—and commanded her to be nice to their guest.

Peter tricked Claudia by speaking from the heart. Most of the people she knew didn't do that. It was easier to be ironic. Less vulnerable, more defensible. What did he want from her? She reminded herself of an early life lesson. Men want one thing. It helped to remember that people are more alike than they are different, even if they don't seem that way. It took until adulthood for Claudia to realize that most social awkwardness manifested a shared intent to forge connections. Why else would anyone put up with the painful pauses and missed signals of new relationships?

By the time she swallowed that epiphany, she had already decided she didn't need anyone and would go it alone. That's why Andrew had been a goddamned miracle, now gone the way of miracles.

> M: *Did you save any coffee?*
> P: *Wouldn't be a good son if I didn't. There's a fresh pot on.*
> M: *I'll help myself.*
> P: *Already did most of the work for ya.*
> M: *He's feisty today!*
> C: *I was just noticing that.*
> *. . . pouring . . .*
> M: *Let's move this party to the living room.*
> *. . . crackling . . .*
> P: *Here, Mom. Take the chair. We'll sit on the couch.*
> M: *So, ahem, ah . . .*
> P: *Claudia.*
> M: *Yes, yes. Claudia. What brings you to our village?*
> C: *Thank you for asking! I'm here to continue the research we created together last summer.*
> M: *What was that?*
> C: *Here, this should refresh your memory . . .*

Fuck! What a terrible thing to say to a demented old woman.

> *. . . this is the transcript I was telling you about at Washburn's. It's a written record of an interview you gave me at the museum.*
> M: *. . .*
> C: *We can go over it together, if you like.*
> M: *Let's not fool with it now. Let's visit. Peter will look at it later.*
> C: *You talked about your mother's beautiful voice.*
> M: *She sure could sing.*

C: *I wish I could have heard her!*

M: *They didn't ask white people to dances, back then. It's all mixed up now.*

C: *Did they let Mexicans in?* [laughs]

(20:00)

M: *Those Mexicans are going to run us all over. They already took Indian jobs. My parents picked berries and hops. Nobody does that anymore. It's a disgrace. Might as well let the blacks in while we're at it.*

P: *Mom! You can't say stuff like that.*

M: *What? It's what everyone's thinking.*

C: *I was joking, of course.*

P: *Not so good at that, are you?*

C: *I don't belong in the field, apparently.*

P: *If you're going to be here, get used to it. This is how she is.*

C: *Is that an invitation?*

P: *What do you think, Mom?*

M: *About what?*

P: *Should we ask Claudia to come back another time?*

M: *Is she leaving? Good, I have some things to get done around here.*

P: *I mean, should we pick up where you left off last summer?*

M: *What?*

P: *I could use some help going through those bags.*

M: *I thought we were going to do that together.*

P: *We will! Claudia can help us.*

M: *I don't . . .*

P: *Why don't you say goodbye now? She's about to head out.*

Claudia stopped the recording. Peter hustled her from the couch before his mother could voice the "no" inscribed on her face. Peter would work as a go-around, but he would not betray his mother's wishes, once spoken. Claudia was drawn to him in spite of herself, in spite of everything. And now she needed him. Maggie had a diagnosis. His consent might be required to work with a senile woman.

A series of tasks awaited Claudia—conduct and transcribe interviews, provide them with copies, since co-ownership of data was a hard-won tribal right—wind up and repeat until a pattern swirled below the surface like cream poured in coffee. Transfixed, she would stare into the testimony, mapping the billows of information until a new theory emerged. She had a lot of work to do.

Her laptop's white screen darkened and went black, reflecting her face. She traced the crescents waning beside her mouth, putting all she said into parentheses.

Chapter Six

THE CLINIC'S WAITING room was clean, well lit and crawling with children. In one corner, three boys peeked out from a fort of chairs, hoping to be noticed so they could get a good case of the giggles. A tired young woman sat near them, entranced by her phone. Peter steered his mother to the opposite wall, depositing her in a chair before he approached a middle-aged lady peering into her monitor.

"Hi, I'm here about my mother, Maggie?"

"Peter! You're back! I heard that, but seeing is believing, right? And here you are!"

He was pretty sure he'd never met this woman. She was sure as hell acting like he had. "Hello." His reflection looked uncertain. He layered on some oomph. "How are you?!"

"You don't remember me. Well, I've changed—six kids took care of that—but you haven't! You look the same." Her glasses hung on a neon lanyard around her neck. Flesh pillowed around the creases left by her wire frames.

He searched the contours of her expectant face, excavating what it might have once been. And there, in the flash of chin amidst a jawline that joined face and neck without so much as a curve, in the forehead that rose smooth from her tweezed wisps of eyebrows, in the swoop of nose that crinkled up with her smile it dawned on him, holy shit, we used to date, we did it on your dad's couch, and I'm sorry I didn't recognize you. "Suzy!"

She waggled her fingers. "How's it going, Peter?"

"Good, good! And you—six kids. Congrats!"

"How about you?" She checked his left hand. "Did you find what you went lookin' for?" She said it sharp, an edge to her lips. She was his last girl before he took off. He didn't let her know when he left. She had a habit of interpreting his silences so everything he didn't say was either what she wanted to hear or the worst thing anyone could think.

"I need to check my mom in."

She gave him a clipboard. "Fill this out. We'll get her taken care of for ya."

His back was to her by the time she muttered, "As usual." He swore she said it, but she made a commotion, tapping papers into a stack and swiveling in her squeaky chair to file them away.

His mother played peekaboo with the kids. Next to her, a grizzled man worn lean by life was hacking into a magazine. His mother always told him not to touch the stuff in waiting rooms. Why do coughers sit close? Get away from my mom, Peter wanted to shout. Don't you see she's delicate? But now the man was playing peekaboo with the magazine, the boys growing frantic with joy at so much attention.

Not for the first time, Peter wished for a brother, someone to play and fight alongside him, someone who understood what was going on without a big talk. He had been a latebreaking baby, the kind everyone thinks is an accident because his mother was in her forties and liked to party. She said she'd been waiting for him, and who knows? Maybe she had. He settled in on her other side, sliding out the greasy ballpoint stuck sideways into the clipboard. Losing himself in the forms, hesitating above every box, uncertain, his mom too distracted to fill in the blanks of family history, he scanned the long list of diseases. Which would he inherit? He needed to ask the doctor some questions.

His mother shooed him into his seat when the nurse came.

"Mom, that was the point of today."

"Oh, I thought we were having a nice time together." She took the nurse's arm, exchanging glances with Suzy. "I'll tell you everything."

"Go ahead." As if she were asking for agreement. "I'll be here."

He presumed she would try to impress the doctor with how well she was doing, not disclosing the night terrors. Everyone knew about the wandering, given how often she passed the clinic on foot. Did they know how much she had socked away in the house? Wouldn't someone have called the authorities? Doubtful. There were so many firetraps on the rez, where small hills of junk served as stockpiles against an apocalypse or the more certain future of not having enough to buy another.

On the wheelchair ramp, Peter scrolled through his cell phone contacts, smoke singeing his eyes. Old folks arrived in cars driven by younger versions of themselves. From A to Z, not a single person he wanted to call.

When Peter lived in a Tacoma apartment block filled with immigrant families and other single men who preferred solitude to responsibility, he spent countless hours smoking on the porch, kicking his legs onto the railings, watching rain fall through the yellow lights of the parking lot, which held back a grove of madronas that was nothing but a dusty strip in summer that dripped the rest of the year.

He waited on that porch until fall, waited for something to happen that would make waiting meaningful, but it did not. In fact, the only memory he salvaged from the bleak slog of that year happened in August, when he should have been swimming but instead was still on the porch, smoking, watching tallboys multiply along the concrete walls and filling them with butts, playing a slow form of Tetris with empty packs and beers until he realized he had recreated his mom's favorite basketry pattern, row by row, something along the lines of . . . – – – . . . over and over, and decided to take out the recycling.

He took out the garbage while he was at it, edging down the stairs with three bags per hand because he hated multiple trips, which is why he never had enough groceries, his fists sweaty and clenched as he neared the dumpster and a line of bins.

Just because he was a bachelor didn't mean he was an asshole. He took care of things. He recycled. Indians are like that, he thought, we protect the land when others look away, and if it weren't for us, there would be no good streams left for salmon in this state. While he was musing and sorting, tossing cans until the bottles became a stale pile on the bottom of a bag he upended in one long clinking rush—never feeling like more of an alcoholic than when he took out the recycling—he heard it, the dry crack, and barely had time to look up before the tree was falling, the thickest branch of the nearest madrona coming down in pieces like a marble column, crashing into itself and onto the dumpster not two feet from where he stood, rooted, the emptied bag in his hand.

Later, he would learn that madronas are like sea stars. Sometimes they'll tear themselves apart to survive. Following the sun like a flower, their branches twist and turn. Any branch cut from the light destroys itself, clearing a path to the sun, littering the floor, nourishing what remained.

He left Tacoma when his contract down at the docks expired, ditching the stained couch he hauled up from the corner where the college kids left it to the rain, containing in its crevasses two lighters, a spatula and a pair of lace panties. He still had the lighters, which worked—a miracle— debated on the spatula but kept it because he didn't have one, and fished out the thong with a bag-wrapped hand like it was shit from the dog he never allowed himself to have.

He didn't set out to be this way, a man whose defining possession—if he had one, if possessions could define any man—was his truck, but it was where he felt at home. That is, it was the only place he breathed easy. He was in charge. Fiddling with the radio, rolling the windows up and down at will, wiping the oil stick with a paper towel just for show at gas stations because he knew there was enough, he was most secure when roaming. When he squeegeed bugs off the windshield, he liked to fight a crust thick enough to show he'd been somewhere.

When she still had enough confidence in their relationship to chastise him, his mother said it didn't matter how far he went, she was with him and so was his past. "You can leave the reservation, but it will never leave you."

No, that's not what she said. She only ever referred to Neah Bay as "the village." That's what this place was to her, a village, and it scared him how his memory scrambled her words, shading them with his own prejudices, which maybe were not even his own.

He never thought he'd come back to Neah Bay, let alone live with his mother, but here he was, his truck idle at the curb he once hopped with his bike, practicing tricks until he got his driver's license. In an ideal world, he would drive off once he'd cleaned out her hoard, an act he hoped would clear her mind so she could resume care of herself, never mind that she was cooking for them both. She likes to do it, he told himself. It keeps her busy, just like the sewing.

After they got back from the clinic, his mom asked for his mending, pointing at the jeans he was wearing. He obliged, stripping down to his boxers and socks, and went back into his duffel bag for the jacket whose pocket sagged from its hinges like an old neck. Sitting on the couch, conscious that his pecker could peek out of its peephole if he wasn't careful, he watched her swollen wrists wave over his tattered clothes, needle pulling thread the way boats draw a wake, fingers diving for scraps she used to patch the holes in his jeans. While she's distracted, he thought, talk to her. About Dad. About anything. Free yourself.

"Mom."

"Mm-hmm?"

Her face hung forward, the wrinkles gathering at the lowest point of gravity, her jutted jaw. Needles emerged from her lips like spokes on a wheel.

No, not now.

"Would you like some coffee?"

"Mm-hmm!"

Defeated, yet again. Maybe Claudia would get them talking. As an outsider, she could ask questions that hurt and didn't care if they did. He'd seen that in the transcripts she'd turned over, noticed her buzzard's circle over certain weaknesses in his mother's resolve to keep the conversation light, conversational. Claudia had a way of caressing a sore spot, worrying the wound until fresh words flowed. He didn't know how to be alone with these people. His people, though he hadn't even graduated as a Red Devil.

In Neah Bay, everything he did got reported back to command central, his mother, or, worse, the head of his family, which had been his father, kind of, before he died. Except he didn't have the standing or the money to defend his status, so news of some slight offense by his son would travel from teller to teller, crimes multiplying and distorting along the way like a giant game of telephone. Peter reflected on his family wherever he went, operating against the expectations of other people, whose accusations—you haven't received the teachings—ricocheted from mother to son.

If he had spoken then, he would have said she taught him to keep quiet, to dispose of unwanted things and not ask questions. She was right in front of him now, and he wanted to slap her into spitting out an apology. It would make him whole, he was sure of it. But there she was, needles in her mouth, having moved on to his jacket. His anger had no place to rest.

When Peter felt like this, first place he went was a bar. Before he came back home, he'd been having trouble breathing. At night, his chest contracted, condensing into a big ball of something about to explode. He skipped meals and smoked packs. He drank and he drank and he drank. He wasn't alone. Misery saw to that. On the last day of his last job, the day he got fired, he welded zinc anodes to a piling and shivered in his suit, gut rotting from the night before, passed by rays with long spines and circled twice by a muddy bluntnose shark.

Kelp waved like hair in the current. The piling fluttered

with brown curls. Tiptoeing along the sea floor, a giant Pacific octopus dragged its ruffled head along, disappearing into a shadowy reef. Up from that dark hole rose a form pale and fleshy, long and thick as a man, face wide, jaw swollen, mouth open, a corpse, it was a corpse coming at him, it was his dad swimming up to see him, what would he say to him, he dropped his stinger and electrodes to strangle, punch, defend himself, anything, but no, now the thing was upon him, beside him, past him, it was a wolf eel, one ugly motherfucker, but no ghost. And it was too late. He already crapped his suit, much to the delight of the control team, whose topside wisecracks led to a brawl in the boat, which didn't go over well with management, and that was that.

Sure, he chose to drink a lot. Life gets that way. But he had his shit together. He was facing the right direction. It was fine. Better than fine. Drinking was more fun. That gets lost once a man's ruined, like his dad. At one point, it was fun, before every night held a sick edge, that sense of doom forestalled by one more cigarette, one more shot, one more easy lay, one more time, just this once, stumble home, lights out, and then it was light out, and his head hurt like someone stepped on it, and getting coffee was a triumph of will.

Yeah, Peter knew that feeling. But that didn't mean he was an alcoholic. He needed to ease off, and he had. Besides, a bar was just a pricey place to pick up women, and he had one in mind, close by. No husband in sight, and Claudia didn't rock the body of someone who had kids. She looked like a woman who'd focused on herself all these years, not that he could blame her. He was the same way, but it's different with men. He could always change his mind.

His truck breathed welcome and comfort as soon as he opened its door, inhaling deep, glad to be out of the

house. You could just leave, he thought, leave her behind
and take off, but he said it to satisfy himself, to feel the
sick twist in his stomach as he buckled in and reached for
a cigarette. Turning on the engine, deciding yet again not
to go for good, made him feel like a man. He took care of
his responsibilities.

The constant cloud cover of Neah Bay deadened the
sky but brightened the colors below, the sun sneaking into
surfaces till they shone, saturated. Christmas lights sagged
across the porch of his neighbors down the way, the big col-
ored bulbs casting pastel versions of themselves on the disin-
tegrated siding. A pink plastic castle rose from the lush grass.
Next to it, flattening into the uncut lawn, was its cardboard
package, still bright with the image of a happy white girl
hugging the castle. The cardboard edges and plastic cran-
nies were fuzzed with emerald green. Around the castle
spread a moor of broken Styrofoam.

Just beyond, a strip of young hemlocks separated that
property from the next, a luxury here where housing devel-
opments were hard to get, where even families with money
had to wait their turn, cousins piling up in spare rooms until
a new piece of land cleared the council. But there, now that
he was cruising closer, there at the edge of this small copse
of woods, a tarp hung from ropes tied to the lower branches.
One of the ropes had snapped—or was it cut?—and hung
askew from one corner, revealing the rusted orange truck
behind it, a 1977 Ford F250 with striped side panels in yellow and blue and red. Its engine block held a spray of blackberry brambles, a blue collar bouquet that grew all over the
Olympic Peninsula, down into Oregon, up into B.C. and
east to the Cascades, dimming to dust in the high alpine
desert stretching leeward from the mountains. His father's

truck, right there, of course, because he had moved back to the nation that kept its past close as could be, closer, and why junk a car when you could push it to the edge of your lot.

Wherever he went, there they were, memories of his father, pulling Peter into his past until he was here, but not here, inhabiting the places they had been happy together, for time is a place, he was sure of it, and his soul was stretched thin across it, near to breaking, an aching that was his only memory of love. He remembered sitting on the truck's patterned blue upholstery, filling his dad's coffee thermos with beer, careful to tip the bottle so foam wouldn't spill, keeping his arms loose in their sockets so when his dad hit a rut both bottle and thermos would rise and fall, nice and easy like kelp in a wave.

His dad always bragged on him—"my main man, the only one I'll let ride with me any day of the week"—when they got to where they were going, unless it was up a logging road to go feather picking, and they were alone. When they stepped from the truck he would palm Peter's head like a basketball, and the feel of those fingers warm on his brow still lingered. Never take outsiders to your sacred spots, his dad told him. If tourists find where eagles leave blessings, that'll be the end of them. But maybe Claudia would like to go with him, because he needed a friend, a companion, and he thought she would like it, might soften and take his hand when they got to the top of the mountain.

But not today. Ice melted in the cooler next to him. He swung off Diaht Hill, turning right at the clinic for the flat stretch of road running by Wa atch River, and heard his last six-pack swoosh from one side to the other. It sounded like hope, or at least a good time. A cigarette shook in his mouth. He could not catch its tip with his lighter. Not as he

cleared the stand of mossy alders. Not as he passed the tsunami evacuation sign marking the turn up Bahokus Peak.
Not as he drove by the quarry with its spray-painted terraces.
Not as he turned left at the tribal headquarters, which he
still thought of as the Air Force base, though it was decom-
missioned in the eighties. He needed someone to empty his
mind into, and the urge of it compelled him forward. He
hurtled toward her, and it didn't matter if she was a jagged
shoal or a brokedown old rock with seabirds on it. He let
the wave take him, heart spread wide, waiting for the lacer-
ation of first contact.

Chapter Seven

THE PACIFIC FROTHED at the shore, its distant gray spreading into white foam and retreating, flattened by its own mass against the long curve of the horizon. The sea has neither mercy nor pity, Claudia thought, not recognizing her plagiarism for a full minute. Chekhov. Check off the boxes on your formal education and file it away; it does so little good out here in the world.

Snuggled into her sofa, she sipped her coffee and watched wind whip the ocean. Caffeine would kill her cravings. Claudia wallowed in her appetite's sharpness, a reminder of her body and its needs. She ate her last banana yesterday, but she hadn't made it back to the store, or even to Maggie's house, gripped by a powerful sense of foreboding she did not quite understand. They're just people, she told herself. They don't hate you. That's just how their faces are.

The door thundered under a hard double knock. She froze. Whoever it was knew she was here. She shouldn't show distrust so early into her stay.

Peter filled the doorframe. There was barely any sky around him. She smiled. So did he.

"In the neighborhood?"

"Thought I'd see how you were settling in." He shifted, big boots scuffling.

"I've been meaning to get out on the beach. Walk with me?"

"Yeah, sure. I've been cooped up."

"I'll get my things."

They had talked on the porch, but once they passed through the narrow wooden gate to the beach, they stopped talking and just walked, shuffling and squeaking through the peaks and valleys of dune grasses, which were sparse and the kind of green that Claudia last saw on olive trees. The beach grew firmer, crunchy with bands of shells and littered here and there with heaps of kelp.

Elsewhere on the reservation, the driftwood seemed from another time, the fallen trunks taller than people, their rounded root systems tipped toward the sky, carving dark suns into the horizon. But here, where bonfires were a ritual of witness that involved beer and cigarettes, where tourists pocketed anything pretty with the sly acquisitiveness of raccoons, the driftwood was sparse, and so were the good shells.

Claudia had thrown out so much before she left Seattle, shedding her shells and pebbles with the practiced satisfaction of a dog shaking off a bath. Some of her beach glass had been gathered here. Peter kicked a can and scowled at the container ships off the coast. For all she knew, her trash boarded a ship on its way back to Asia, destined for a distant beach community and its own flocks of garbage pickers.

Peter cleared his throat and paused as he came between her path and the shore. The pale sun backed behind the clouds, snuffing out the shadows of his face, his black hair absorbing all the light, as black as anything around it, blacker.

Stop staring, she told herself, and smiled, bright, but he

did not return it, and kept instead a steady gaze that said he had seen her hunger. She dropped her eyes to the tangled bull kelp at her feet, their slimy fronds twisted around a net at the wrack line, where breakers made their final sally before retreating, restless. A cloud of black flies floated around her ankles; her tennis shoes squished into a nest of smaller sea plants.

She stepped past the wreckage of the last high tide and onto the smooth, flat sand, and they kept on, not talking, their footprints erasing themselves with damp exhales from beneath, the closest she'd get to *leave no trace*, or walking on water.

The sea stood up and toppled over, dragging kelp and sand into itself before rising again and again, reaching for the shore. Its passage left a thick sheen on the crust of crushed shells, which rolled on their sides and sighed, sated.

Their shoulders brushed once, and again, as they walked, footsteps moving toward and away from each other in subtle waves that stretched long with the languid tempo of dune ridges.

Ruddy cliffs held back a cedar forest that spilled over, curving toward the sea atop a dark headland, tide pools bared to the sky. She kept her focus on that outcropping, trying not to watch Peter from the corners of her eyes as they drew nearer. His shadow at her periphery had taken over her full attention.

Grazing his hand, her entire body aligned to him like filings on a magnet. She looked without looking, hearing his weight change on the beach.

She was relieved when they came to the headland's surf-addled rock, where the lava had cooled into pockets, trapping untold numbers of bubbles. Where air had been, life crept in—a profusion of glossy mussels and rough bar-nacles, orange and purple sea stars, lime and crimson anem-ones, and emerald plants she could not name.

Claudia crouched before the first pool, its stillness a pane of glass onto a world that did and did not pertain to her. A velvety red anemone swayed, stirred by some unseen force.

She pushed a finger into its cold home, slow and careful. The anemone tuned to her, its rubbery receptors waving in her direction, beckoning. They clung to her as she slipped her nail into the folds of its body, trying to be gentle. It held her, and she lingered, feeling how dear it was, this aggressive embrace, and how it was this creature's weakness—and not the ferocity of its intent, nor the cunning of its perception—which made it dear. Her power inspired a rising tenderness. She tickled but poked no further, inclining her head so a sky mirror drew over the pool and she could regard herself being maternal.

Beside her shifting face she saw Peter. His eyes were on her. The air thickened into mist, blurring their reflection.

"Come again tomorrow," he said, and left her there.

Chapter Eight

A MUG SAILED past their heads, scattering ash. Claudia hid behind him, peering at his mother, who emerged from the hall, screaming, "I told you not to smoke in the house!"

"Mom! We've been over this. No throwing!"

"No smoking in the house! Don't change the subject!"

"Okay! We have a guest."

"Who?"

"Claudia."

"Never heard of her."

"Stop poking around under my bed, Mom. Privacy. It's a form of respect."

"What would you know about respect? This is my home! I told you not to smoke inside, Sam!"

"Mom, I am Peter. Sam was my father."

"You're worse than him!"

"Slow down, Mom. You're getting ahead of yourself."

"Ahead of you." Her shout faded to a mumble. The veins on her hands flexed and bulged as she picked at the flowers on her apron.

Claudia whispered, "I can come back later."

"No, it's fine." He kept between them, just in case. "Stay. Or go and don't come back. You choose."

She patted his shoulder. "I'll take that coffee."

He stooped to pick up the crumpled cigarette butts. He

had caved and smoked in his room last night, thinking on things, wishing for a beer he wouldn't let himself have. Drinking in this house didn't feel right. Growing up with parents who drank made Peter sensitive to patterns. Maybe being a loner did that, too. Forgiving his folks could be as simple as recognizing they were dealing with problems they couldn't share. Turns out the same held true for forgiving himself. Staying apart from the old hurt let it harden around his heart. He knew that now that he was back on the reservation, living with the mother he had tried to forget. Keeping a window open all night didn't work any better now than when he was a teenager. "How about it, Mom? Shall we start this morning again?"

"Smoke on the porch."

"Okay, I get it." He touched two fingers to his brow in a mock salute. "Shall we serve our guest some coffee?"

His mom tsked at Claudia. "Coffee sours an empty stomach."

"Oh, don't worry about me. I've eaten."

"You look like you need a decent meal." His mom moved toward the stove. "Skinny."

"Um, thank you?"

"That wasn't a compliment." He grabbed the mug. Cracked. "Sit down. We'll feed you."

"Great, thanks." Claudia looked around. "Where do you want me? Kitchen table or the couch?"

He felt the hint of a smirk forming on his face.

"I'll join your mother in the kitchen."

"Just what I was thinking."

His mom was most at ease around the stove, peeling strips of bacon from the slimy package and laying them in the cast iron pan. Grease splattered the stovetop. She didn't fidget when she had purpose.

The scanner crackled, spitting updates on a burglary at Wa atch Beach.

... unauthorized entry ...

She fished frilly bacon onto a paper towel and cracked an egg into its grease. The egg spread thin and whitened, bubbling.

... white male wearing a snow hat, black jacket and blue jeans ...

He decided against turning off the scanner. Kept her company.

"So ..."

"Claudia."

"Right, right. Claudia. What brings you here?"

... extensive property damage, glass everywhere ...

"I'm here to continue the research we did together last summer."

"About the old days?"

... neighbor says ... known trafficker from Sekiu ...

"Yes, but also about how songs figure into your lives now."

... destroyed the hard drive, took off with some masks ...

Finally, his mother spoke. "What kind of songs?"

"You know, the ones connected to those old stories, about how animals were people with animal skin robes on, like whales and minks and crows, or ... how people and animals shared some kind of spirit essence?"

His mom's movements slowed. "What about them?"

"I'm curious about what they mean and how they're understood."

"Uh huh." His mom was bustling again. "How am I supposed to help?"

He jumped in. "I think we can figure it out together."

. . . checking the bushes behind the house . . .

"Sounds tricky." His mom's tone was gruff. Claudia's face was all sweet expectation, but he didn't believe it for a second. Keep up your spirits, sweet tits. Old people are grumpy. He needed his mom to work with him here.

"It would be worth your while, Maggie."

"Seems like it's more for you." Now his mom was in form. She'd been so lippy when he was a kid. He loved that about her.

. . . transporting witness back to her house to complete a statement . . .

"No, just the opposite! This project is about you and your worldview. It could help preserve your knowledge for future generations."

"We have our own ways."

"I'd like to learn them."

"Then pipe down and listen. That's hard for your kind."

Claudia exhaled hard.

"Just kiddin'!" His mother laughed. "Son, why don't you get busy?"

"Doing what?" He pushed back in his chair.

"Fixing that coffee you promised!"

His mom made small orbits around the kitchen, laying out forks and knives and a jar of homemade jelly—salmonberry, from the looks of it.

"So, Claudia." He concentrated on pouring. The coffee rose, thick and oily, in her cup. "What's the plan?"

"Excuse me?"

"Your research. How do you want to go about doing this?"

"First, we should get comfortable. Anything you'd like to know?"

"It might be useful to have your phone number, so I could text you if we're out and about, doing something you'd enjoy, or if we need to delay a visit."

"My carrier doesn't provide coverage out here. You can have my email address, but the resort Wi-Fi has been spotty."

"So there's no good way to reach you."

"You know where to find me."

"You realize this entire tribe is online, right? I mean, like, from kids to elders, people post stories and photos and stuff."

His mom smiled at her plate. "I didn't know you were keeping track."

"I don't go in for social media, myself. Seems like a bunch of snooping and bragging to me, but Claudia . . . you're going to have a hard time staying in touch without a phone or the Internet."

"I'll take that into consideration, thank you."

"Parents?"

"Dead."

"Sorry to hear that. Siblings?"

"None."

"Husband?"

"Back in Seattle." She coughed.

"Do we get to meet him? Is he coming out for a visit?"

"His work keeps him busy."

"Huh."

"A provider. That's what women want, son."

Claudia raised her hand. "I have a question."

"Shoot."

"Maggie, when you and I spoke last summer, you gave me permission to record our conversations, which was really helpful because it freed me up to concentrate on what you were saying rather than worrying about writing it down or remembering it right. I have a terrible memory."

"You seem pretty sharp to me."

"I can't depend on it. The words . . . they move with time. On a certain day, I remember it one way. Another day, another way. Or I make something up. With a recording, I can go back and check. I want to get it right."

"Listen harder. Or ask me to tell the story again."

"I admire that, I really do. But written records can be useful for everyone involved." Claudia picked up her mug. "I'm here to learn from you, but also to leave documentation for long after we're gone."

His mother spoke before he could. "If you want to learn from us, practice what we do. It's the only way."

"I don't want to lose time."

Sometimes spitting out the truth feels better than sucking on a lie.

His mom laughed. "Let me tell you something. It's impossible to lose time. I've been trying to shake it for years. Time likes to hang."

Claudia looked panicky. "Creating a record isn't for me. It's about keeping knowledge intact for future generations."

"That's what son's for."

"Yes, Peter is home now. I'm so glad."

Chapter Nine

BULKY PILES WERE stacked against the walls of every room but the kitchen, where the air was thick with bleach. A fetid smell seeped from the black plastic stretched to a chalky gray in places. Peter stuffed clothing into a bag Claudia held open, sucking air through her teeth, her eyes watering. His bandana's trace of cologne could not conceal the stench.

"You remind me of a cat." He laughed. "Staring at nothing. Cats do that so much I end up wondering what they're thinking. Which is stupid, because there they are, looking at a wall."

"Your mom had cats before, I'm guessing."

"I kicked them out when I got here."

"You've made a lot of changes."

"I'm not done making them."

"Did you sort through this stuff before you bagged it?"

"She was in a bad way. I had to work quick."

"Is that what you're doing now?"

"I knew they gave PhDs for a reason."

"You know, there's a show about people like your mom."

"Yeah, she probably watches it. Could tell you the story, season by season. Don't you know trailers come with satellite TVs these days?"

Claudia started laughing and couldn't stop. Went on

and on, coughing, and spluttered, "You can say stuff like that. I can't."

He snorted. "You can say anything you want. We're all alone out here."

"Hey!" Maggie came in waving a dish towel. "What are you doing with those toys!"

"Here we go." His face became placid, almost passive. "Mom, I am doing this so you can live somewhere safe and healthy."

"You want to take over. But you're not ready!" She thumped the wall, scowled and clutched her wrist with her other hand.

"We had an agreement."

"You might need them!" Maggie plucked at her apron.

"If you can't do this, the options get harder."

"Stop threatening me!"

"Peter, why don't we slow down and let your mother chime in?"

"It will take too long!" He shook the bag.

"Give it a try."

"Mom, this stuff's gotta go."

"She knows what you want, Peter. That's why she's upset. Let her explain."

Peter upended another bag and spread the pile of toys and worn books to an even layer, moving through Legos and paperbacks in precise circles. "There! See anything valuable?"

"Peter, these are for your children." Maggie's voice was small.

"I don't have any."

"When you do."

"I don't want them."

Claudia saw a black lump in the untidy sea of red and blue plastic. She leaned closer. Buried in bright Legos and half hidden by a coverless book, it looked like a rock. A turd, most likely. Careful not to step on the mildewed books, their pages waved by years of waiting, Claudia nudged the coverless edition's spine with her toe, revealing a curved black stone in the bed of Legos.

"These are the things you played with." Maggie clasped her hands; from a certain angle, she seemed to be praying. "We were happy?"

Claudia picked up the rock. The stone had been smoothed, had been worked. It was a frog—squat and powerful, with a stern mouth—cut into what looked like basalt. Its big round eyes were starred with crescent moon retinas. Maybe a Makah carving, she thought. But they mostly worked wood. Some shell and bone. Stones tend to be sinkers in Makah territory. I wonder how old it is. The oldest known Makah carving was wood, a two-headed kingfisher dating back some three thousand years and found in the Hoko River.

Pebbled but dull, like surf-tumbled lava, the frog covered her palm. She cupped its haunches, feeling their heft. Wilson Duff made a book with pictures of stone carvings and short analyses of their symbols, more poetic than academic. He asked open questions that showed where his suppositions ended and curiosity began. Duff was considered a genius and a mystic. A tireless advocate for Native cultures, he'd published several books with heavy footnoting by the time he wrote *Images, Stone, B.C.*

Yes, this could be a find. On the page, she could riff on this frog for quite a while. Its mouth was cut wide, big enough to swallow its whole self, like the frog tobacco mortars in

Duff's book. Frog was a favored crest of Charles Edenshaw, a revered Haida artist from Kiusta, a village deserted in the 1850s, one of many emptied by epidemics. When Duff taught anthropology at UBC, he sometimes introduced himself as Edenshaw. "Professor Wilson Duff isn't here today," he told his students, and shortly thereafter, he made it true. A year after *Images, Stone, B.C.* was published, Duff killed himself, hoping to come back as a Haida artist like the carver he so admired—a brown man with blood ties to the culture Duff coveted.

"What's this?" She opened her fingers, holding the frog up.

"Peter's father gave me that." Maggie plucked the frog from Claudia's hand. It nestled in the crook of her palm before she slipped it into her apron. "Peter is a veteran like his dad." Her eyes glistened. "Every Makah who's gone to war has come back home alive."

"Wow! Amazing. Peter, I didn't know you served."

"Army. I cleared harbors in Kuwait."

Claudia trembled, ready to pounce. She'd had it with footnotes. She wanted to divine and portray the meaning of Makah animal symbols using snippets of artwork, song lyrics and personal testimonies, even dreams, along with her brief but compelling introductory essays, insightful but easy to skim or skip.

By itself, the frog wasn't enough for a book. But she could spin off an article. A teaser. Frogs crowded the marshes of Neah Bay, loud as anything on spring nights. Makahs bathe and pray in fresh water. Makah lore teems with frogs. She would figure it out later.

"Maggie, tell me more about Peter's dad."

Peter mounded the pile again. Stepping on the edge of

an empty bag and holding the opening taut, he swept Legos into the hole.

"He was a handsome man." Maggie chuckled. "Especially in uniform. Always chasing tail."

"Mom! Don't."

"What! I was talking about planes."

"Come on now."

"Peter, why don't you let me talk to your mother while you finish up." Claudia pointed at the remainders. Amid the Legos, toy soldiers surfaced, rifles raised.

"Fine. Keep each other busy. I'll take care of everything."

"Sounds good."

He shot her a sordid look and addressed the ceiling. "I'm going for a smoke. Want one?"

Her body screamed yes. "No, thanks."

He left the door open. In everything Peter did, there was some quiet rebellion. Smoke wafted in on cold air from the drizzle. She couldn't afford to feel sorry for him. He was a grown man. This was the life he chose. It was the life he had, anyway. She fought her urge to protect him, to wrap him up in affection and attention. Stop caring for men who refuse to take care of themselves, she thought, pulling the bandana over her hair. Don't be a *mujer*. You're here to work.

"... brought it back from Korea, where he went after a tour in Japan. He managed supplies for the Air Force; they had a base in Neah Bay right outside of town. Where the tribal center is now. And the bingo hall. You know they closed that down. Now isn't that a shame. All the elders loved to play. They put some gym equipment out there instead."

"What did Sam do when he wasn't in the Air Force?"

"He fished. He was a gypo in the off season, you know, cutting cedar into shake. Nothing lasted."

Raindrops drummed the rhododendrons. Peter's back was to them, but he was close enough to listen. She watched him smoke, envious, for a moment too long.

"My son needs someone who understands him." Heat left the room faster now, chasing out the fetid air, a hint of evergreen taking over.

"Everyone does, I suppose." Claudia pitched her voice low.

"Someone who knows what it's like."

"Sure." She rustled a garbage bag, cinching its red drawstring and folding it into an awkward, angular bow.

"Not a white woman."

Peter coughed and scuffed his boots. Both women stopped talking. Head down, he grabbed another bag from the pile.

Maggie yawned. "Time for a nap."

"Already, Mom?"

"We have company tonight."

"Okay. Well, go on to bed."

"I won't be able to rest easy with you two messing around in here."

If Maggie went back into her bedroom with that frog, Claudia might never see it again. "I could wash the clothes we're going to donate."

His glance was a poison dart. "I took that bag to the truck."

He hadn't, not that she'd seen.

"Claudia, you go on home." Maggie stretched her clenched up little hands to the sky. "We could all use some beauty sleep."

Claudia jumped from the couch. She had become too cozy. "Of course, of course!" She extended a hand to Maggie, who waved it away. "Should I come back later?" She collected her purse and coat. I'll have to air this out, she thought, sniffing the lapel on the sly.

"No." Maggie motioned to Peter. "We're having company."

"My cousin." Peter helped his mother rise with both hands and more forearm overlap than she had foreseen would be necessary. "I think you met her husband."

"Oh, really? What's his name?"

"Randall."

"Hmm, when did I meet him?"

"On your way into town? On the road?"

"Oh!" Dear God, news didn't just travel fast here. It teleported. They knew I passed out in my car, she thought, scanning outcomes. They invited me because they feel sorry for me. Or they're curious about my problems. They will tell everyone anything I say. That's why they let me in. Dammit! Did I say anything untoward? "Thanks for everything."

She made her goodbyes and was outside before she pulled on her coat. The wind stole her heat with a sideways stream of air that smelled of the sea. She checked the porch next door—empty, a small miracle, because the last thing she wanted was small talk with Dave. He probably knew that she passed out at the wheel.

Perhaps it was this closeness of information—the press of people, all around you, monitoring your movements— that kept Duff away from Haida Gwaii after his 1950s expeditions to cut down totem poles for display and preservation in a museum. Decades later, by chiefs' orders, the remaining poles were left in situ to molder, a tribute to the villages laid waste by smallpox. Tourists complained about the decay, if not about the dead.

Obsessed with Haida art and culture, Duff never went back, or so the story goes. Better to crave from a distance than be criticized up close, she supposed, and she didn't blame him. Claudia was tired of being tracked. She was about to trundle off when Peter hurried out.

"Stay here. She'll be asleep in no time." He tapped out a cigarette.

"Clearly, I can't do that." She pulled her keys out of her purse.

"Why not?"

"I can't lurk on your porch. She asked me to leave."

"I live here, too." Flames licked the end of his cigarette.

"So you know how it is." She sidestepped toward the street. She was a professional. She would not be sucked into something stupid.

Both their heads turned toward a muffled bump inside the trailer.

"Hold this." The filter faced her, ember cupped in his palm. "I'll be out in a sec."

Say no, she thought. But that's not what she did.

Chapter Ten

IT WAS HIS dad who taught him to watch women, one night when he'd been kicked to the curb yet again. "It don't matter what they say," he muttered. "You gotta watch what you do when they're not looking." He swayed and shook his head. "No, no, that's not what I meant. You gotta watch what *they* do when *you're* not looking."

At the time, all Peter could think was, "How can you watch what they do when you're not looking?" He didn't say much, just took the cigarette his dad offered to spite his mom, and they sat, smoking in silence, until his dad said, "You got to know yourself, 'cause no one else will, and then you got a leg up on 'em."

Maybe his dad drank because deep down, he did see himself and hated what he saw. His jealousy took many forms, making a monster of him, scattering bruises across the two people who loved him the most. As a kid, Peter tried not to take sides unless it got physical, which meant he sided with whoever was talking to him, offering little nods and head shakes so they'd keep talking.

Peter didn't see himself as a broken man. Most days, he held himself apart from the idea of failure. True self-knowledge likes to play hard to get, but whether he wanted to or not, Peter sensed things about other people. Claudia seemed worn so thin by self-denial that she was liable to do something stupid.

At least he hoped so. It took energy for him not to grab her hand and drag her out of the trailer for some privacy. He wanted to ask questions, to learn all about her, but not while his mother was around. He didn't want to waste the potency of that first big talk, the urgency of which led women straight to bed, in his experience. People love to be asked about themselves. He checked his rearview mirror. Yep, she was still following him. Perfect.

Well, not quite perfect. He was having trouble keeping her headlights in sight. Was she trying to pull over? They'd only had three beers each. That was almost an hour ago. She drank the first beer faster than he thought a woman could. Whatever happened tonight, it was better than sitting around a table with Randall's happy family, trying not to stare at Roberta and wonder *what if.*

Claudia crept along. Was she looking at the view? It was a clear night. Aside from bright specks on the Canadian shore, the strait was black as the starry sky. He tapped the brakes, cursing. What an amateur! He hated how women drove. She might as well get out and walk. She was lucky the other cars were heading toward Neah Bay, or she'd get run off the road.

Slowing down didn't bring her closer. She was backing off his tail for a reason. He sped up. So did she. Confirmed. She didn't want anyone to know she was with him. Peter gripped the wheel and pressed back in his seat.

The bar slumped at the bend in the road where Highway 112 crossed Frontier Street, turned from the strait and headed uphill past a co-op, a gas station, an espresso stand in a storage unit, a high school, a church and the turnoff for the corrections center. Streetlights stained everything a rough green. During the day, you could see the bar was blue as a tarp, its corrugated roof the dead beige that used to be called flesh in a box of crayons.

Peter parked in front of the BEER CROSSING sign. The bar windows were lined with plywood and PBR ads to protect the patrons from being seen and those outside from seeing. He watched Claudia maneuver her SUV into a space hidden from the highway by a white van with a faded FOR SALE sign taped to its back window. She hopped out and hurried toward him, still dressed like she was about to go hiking. What is it with white women from Seattle? It's like they all died and went to an outdoors store. But she was pretty enough.

"Not taking any chances, I see."

"You can never be too careful! Thanks for taking the lead."

"After you."

Clallam Bay's only bar was dark, like every other dive in this podunk pioneer town state. Its centerpiece was a pool table lit by low hanging lights that showed the green felt was ripped and rippled in a few places, the ceiling stained with water spots that found their twins on the table, a lifetime of neglect reflected there like clouds in a lake.

Claudia went straight for the bar, brushing past a clump of Indians in sweatshirts and baggy jeans. Exactly what he was wearing. They stared at her and at him and broke into big grins like, "Right on, brother."

He jerked his shoulder real quick, as in, "Shut up about it, I'm still working here." One of them went over to the jukebox and picked "Pour Some Sugar on Me," smirking at his friends.

The bartender was a frosted blonde with thick eyeliner that pegged her as the type who once serviced the best loggers on the peninsula. Soft rolls of skin swelled around her bra strap and waistband.

"What can I getcha?"

"Whiskey."

The second swallow didn't hurt like the first. By the third, Peter wondered why he didn't drink whiskey every day. Deep into their second drink, Claudia's makeup had been pushed into the crinkles beneath her eyes by all the smiles, which was a good thing, he decided. He wasn't as picky as he used to be, or maybe it was that he'd learned to find favor with more faces. How old was she? Best not to ask. Her beauty was brittle, the last blush of fall.

He was looking at her so hard he forgot to talk. Shit. She touched the burn spots on his right hand. "What happened there?"

"Scars number twelve and thirteen."

She snorted. "Why have you numbered your scars?"

"I had to map them for my job."

"Why?"

"So they'd recognize the body."

"How's that?"

"Welding is dangerous underwater."

"You're a welder?" She looked puzzled. More than that. Curious.

"Just because I live with my mom doesn't mean I don't have marketable skills."

She laughed. "I didn't presume . . ."

"Yeah, you did. I quit my job to take care of her. Just so you know."

"How did you get into welding?"

"Don't act like you give a shit."

She looked down into her drink, whether ashamed or calculating her blood alcohol level, he didn't know. He was tired of small talk. For all he cared, she could still consider herself on the clock five drinks into an evening. Not that they timed academics.

He half expected her to walk out and drive back to the rez, but the last thing a woman like her needed was a DUI. She opened her mouth, closed it, took a sip, then another, and tried a smile. "So . . . how'd you manage to count the scars on your backside?"

"Used a mirror." Actually, that wasn't true. He'd used a one night stand. What was her name? He'd forgotten it right away. Took to calling her my dirty darlin', which she liked; she licked every scar, starting with the asterisk on his shoulder blade, where the hook had caught, pulling him overboard the morning he went fishing for halibut with a hangover bigger than he was. He was lucky he didn't drown that day, his body trailing behind the boat like a bag of chum, pulled deeper and deeper by the baited line until he was hauled out by buddies as bloody-eyed as he. His shoulder still burned when it rained.

Claudia got up and, without asking if he wanted to play, tucked a quarter under the rail of the pool table. She plucked a cue from where it leaned on the wall and rolled it on the table; it bounced around like a dying fish. She tried a few more until she found something halfway decent. She wore her wedding band, which he took as a sign that whatever they did wouldn't last. He never got to keep them for long.

Peter took the break, sank a stripe in the side pocket but left a clusterfuck where the triangle had been. She didn't say anything, let him run the table until he was spread too thin to cover the pockets, and then she went to work. She played him like she did his mother, hiding her intentions right up until she had a good chance at getting what she wanted.

He set up their next drinks as she lined up her shots, the other men in the bar paying real close attention as she leaned over the table, hair brushing the felt. Peter saw a dude double check his pockets, come up empty and nudge his neighbor, bumming change to hold the next game. He stiffened his stance in their direction to show who she'd be leaving with, just as soon as he let her sink the eight ball.

Which she did—a clean shot to the corner pocket. She didn't make a fuss about it, which was good of her. Then again, she looked like the kind of woman who expected to win.

She rested the cue on the table. "It's time for me to go."

"Where to?"

"I don't think I should drive."

"Need a lift?"

"People will talk."

"That's all they ever do."

He knew it didn't matter what he said. Whatever she decided, it would be for her own reasons. He waited. He was patient, even as a kid.

"Do you know a place nearby? Could you drop me off?"

The motel was only two miles down the road, but it seemed like a long way, what with her not talking and staring out the window and sighing. Just like a woman to regret a decision as she's making it. She made him reserve the room, waiting out in the truck, half hiding her face with her hand, which was just as well. He got a room whose floors sloped, but the sheets were alright. The harsh overhead light made the bed look like an operating table. He hit the switch, turned on the bedside lamp and hustled out to the truck to lead her up to the second floor, her foot catching once, twice on the stairs. When they got to the room, she had the nerve to ask him where he would be sleeping.

"Don't be naïve, honey. We both know why we're here."

"I don't . . . I don't do this kind of thing."

"I know that." And then he was kissing her neck and taking off her godawful clothes, tossing them into a corner along with his own. At some point, she stopped pretending and stepped into his arms, which held her loosely now that he knew she was staying. She turned a slow circle, his tip bumping and gliding around her waist, leaving a small, slick trail that gleamed in the lamplight, a detail that delighted him, because it had never happened before. A first. He pushed her onto the bed.

Her legs were all angles, her fingers clutching the thin lip of mattress as he gave her the kind of head it took his entire thirties to learn. When he came up for air, breath heavy with her tang, he shoved her face sideways with his chin, whispering, "You taste nice." She looked startled to see him. Before she could say no, or wait, or anything, he pushed inside, watching her face, watching her tits shake, watching her eyes, which had trouble focusing. They settled on staying closed as she clutched his shoulders, her mouth helpless, their minds wandering the darkness together.

The headboard knocked against the wall in an easy rhythm he found soothing, like a train clicking over rails, their cries getting louder and louder until the ringing, high and shrill, became repetitive enough to get his attention.

"'Lo?"

"Sir, we've been getting calls." The clerk's voice was clipped.

"I imagine you would. You're listed, aren't ya?"

"The calls are about a disturbance in your room."

"Disturbance? Is there a force field around here or something?"

"Sir, it's a noise disturbance, from your . . . affair."

"Affair? All we're doing is fucking."

"Please show some respect."

"If you can't fuck out loud in a motel, where can you do it?"

He slipped the receiver below a pillow and got back to it. Someone pounded on the wall from the other room. Laughing, Peter propped himself up and gave an answer with his right fist.

"Hey!" Claudia's eyes were open again. "Down here."

"Oh, I know you're there." He dropped to his elbows, the flat of her belly hot against him. "You're a lot nicer when you have a little whiskey in you."

He saw her face sour, but she let it go, turning her mouth away and arching her back to bare the pale underside of her jaw. He put his thumb into the crook of it, fingers grappling the back of her neck.

Her body torqued as he fucked her, head twisting to one side and the next. She stiffened her shoulders into one axle and drove the pressure down through her hips and into that other mouth, which gaped and begged and was filled.

Chapter Eleven

THE STORY OF Thunderbird and Whale begins with lack, an unfulfilled desire. In a Quileute version, Whale patrolled the deep, devouring. Men starved and prayed. Thunderbird heard them. He winged from his mountain aerie to haul Whale from the water. Thunderbird and Whale battled, flapping land and slapping sea until the earth shook and the ocean pulled back into itself and roared forth. Thunderbird abandoned Whale's body on land to be cut into blubbery strips by survivors.

Many believe these stories memorialized the earthquake and tsunami of January 26, 1700. The Pacific convulsed from what is now Canada to California. Massive tree die-offs attest that a salty wave strafed the coast, scouring the shore of man and vegetation alike. A big surge with no shaking swept nearly five thousand miles west to Japan, where merchants and fishermen logged the date.

Generations later, the 1855 treaty of Neah Bay created the Makah reservation out of ancestral land in exchange for federal promises to preserve the tribe's right to fish and hunt whales forever, a hard bargain struck by chiefs like Tse-Kaw-Wootl, who said, "I want the sea. That is my country."

The Makah tribal logo still shows Thunderbird clutching Whale. In the midst of his people's defense of their right to whale, which was under global siege, a Makah leader told a different story. His version began with a man, hungry and cold. Ice ruled the land. He climbed to the mountains to pray for an end to starvation. Thunderbird heard his cry— but it was Whale who came ashore to warm the land and people's bellies. In this telling, whales beach themselves.

Daylight pressed against her eyelids. A bright smear beamed between her glued lashes. Her head was beyond aching. It pulsed.

The hangover occupied her entire body, spilling off the bed and pooling onto the floor, filling the room. She tipped her face to the window. Curtains parted onto a view of cloudless blue. Her eyes were sticky. So was her mouth. She closed her eyes again; the glare tackled her lids. From beneath, she saw a different planet, a red world veined with mauve.

Birds chirped. A car started. Tires scraped over asphalt. Children shouted in Spanish. A woman shushed them. A car door slammed. She squeezed her eyes shut, scrunching her face. Pain radiated from her temples.

Claudia spread her hands on the bed, patting rough folds of cotton. She was naked and alone but for two crumpled pillows. She reached between her legs. A swamp. Her period? She swiped at her lips and came up with silky black hairs too long to belong to her. Groaning, she turned her back to the window. She was alone now, but she hadn't been.

Peter.

She tucked both hands between her thighs. She'd had unprotected sex with the son of her best hope for a meaningful qualitative study. Everyone would find out, if he felt like making it known. And what man wouldn't. She swung her legs off the bed and sat up. Her headache expanded like a dying star.

A stripe of dirt and flies lined the gray carpet where it tucked into the plastic baseboard. The sound of her own breath echoed in her ears. She was sore. He'd given it to her how she liked it.

The children outside screamed and laughed. A vacuum bumped around the room next to hers. Sometimes Makahs worked these jobs; even if they lived off the reservation, they'd talk. She'd have to erase the evidence. She turned her head toward the door. It was not chained. She always chained the door. That meant they'd had sex here, or at least, come back here. She fought an image of his face moving above her, careening in and out of focus.

Her clothes were doubled over a chair. That's not how she would arrange them. He tidied up. Craning her neck, she checked the other nightstand. Her keys were stacked next to a full glass of water. Had she driven herself here? If not, she would be seen walking an exposed and dangerous stretch of highway that had no other purpose this morning but to shame her. If so, she should already be ashamed. And she was. She had violated every code of ethics she ever agreed to hold sacred, and she did it on a whim, wasting herself on a drunk.

It couldn't be undone. She drained the glass. Water ran down both sides of her mouth. She would have to make herself presentable. Driving down Front Street was like strolling a promenade. Everyone checked you out. If there was a halfway decent chance they knew you, drivers waved or weaved their cars to show you'd been seen.

Claudia stood up to tug the paisley curtains together, wondering if Peter left them parted on purpose. They stuck right where they were, loosing a light flurry of dust as the acrylic shimmied back into place. Okay, no. He hadn't. She scurried to the bathroom, hiding her ass and avoiding the mirror, and checked the wastebasket. No condom, no shiny wrapper, not even a tiny, torn-off corner. Maybe he flushed them. No, that wasn't it, and she knew that already.

She faced her reflection. Her shoulders and breasts bore rough red patches. Claudia pirouetted to check her back. On her neck, next to her spine, four bruises bloomed in a row, purple as pansies. Seeing them alarmed her.

A shower. First things first.

The motel stocked the kind of soap that splits in two when you open the wrapper, and nothing else. It would have to do. Her fingers smelled like cum and cigarettes. She didn't dare take a whiff of her hair. She pulled the curtain and started the water, nearly falling out of the tub when a cold spray sputtered out of the showerhead. Then again, cold water was better for washing off semen, a lesson learned while camping with Andrew. Early on in her marriage, she slept under the stars, unafraid, scoffing at tents, hair full of woodsmoke, inviting dew. Early on, they zipped their sleeping bags together. Early on, they did all kinds of cheesy shit she loved, along with him. When did she stop being young? When had she become used?

She had no choice but to start again. It was that, or die alone. But not this man, a mistake. There was no future here for her, not with Peter. She knew that. She presumed he did, too. He wasn't stupid.

This was not the life she envisioned when she married Andrew, full of admiration for his potential, and her own.

Their honeymoon passed in a happy haze as they cavorted from one meal to the next, marveling at how cheap Mexico was. At least, she marveled outwardly, pushing down disgrace that her homeland couldn't pull it together. The peso would never strike parity with the dollar.

Still, she had fun, draped over the prow of a long boat that lay low in the water, splitting a jungle river at dusk, motoring through the hoots and hollers of howler monkeys, birds flitting by, bats swooping over them, Andrew ducking and laughing. Her smile was so big it hurt. Insects smashed into her teeth.

That night, in their riverfront cabana, he counted her bug bites, trying not to burn the mosquito net as he moved the candle above her. "Only one safe place to kiss you," he concluded. It wasn't her mouth.

Irreconcilable differences.

What does that mean, Andrew? Who is at peace with the daylight between who we are and who we thought we'd be?

She thought they were in it together—no matter what, like they'd promised—but ten years in, his arm across her waist in bed felt heavy enough to stifle.

"I am so close. Just wait."

"We're missing our window." His voice got loud. Indignant. "I feel, I don't know, unwelcome. By my own wife."

The truth was that Claudia was suspicious of becoming pregnant, afraid that Andrew would take advantage of her weakness, her dependence, her need that he see it through. She'd seen it so many times—the humiliated woman discarding self-worth to hold onto her children's wandering father, the man wafting boyish charm and keeping the indulgent affection of their mutual friends, the woman hollowing out, becoming brittle, haggard with work, scorned by those same children later for being weak, when what she'd been was stronger than they could imagine. And if she did leave, it was as a reed flattened by the receding shore. He remarried within the year, and she remained in reduced circumstances.

She was right about that bastard. He'd been boning her sister all along. He must believe Maria's fairytale. Like many single people, Maria cloaked intense loneliness with cheer and disaffection. Her sister maintained the fiction that she was happy, insisting that she loved her life right up to the second she rehauled it, never a bad moment, just transformation after transformation, from painting to ceramics to mixed media, never investing enough time to be taken seriously. Claudia cursed the marital intimacies she shared with Maria out of despair or for a laugh, as though voicing her thoughts would let the wind take them, Maria giggling over the phone, "¡*Estás loca!*"

Maria must have been conscious, then, of her betrayal, feathering her nest with Claudia's sisterly confessions. Or maybe it had been somewhat innocent, until it wasn't anymore. Maria seemed uncontaminated by the striving that seeped into her sister. But when Claudia had something she coveted—a husband just waiting to be appreciated—Maria's ambition unmasked itself.

Maria had been polite, deferential even, asking Claudia about her travel plans for the coming year. Symposiums where she would lecture while others nodded and mapped out their careers, conferences where she would present a paper and drink to forget the work that awaited her—Claudia described it all with the same weary candor, a frankness reserved for people she thought would not judge her. Maria nodded and sipped while they dressed for New Year's Eve dinner. Relieved of the burden of deadlines, Claudia refilled their wineglasses continuously. Andrew had gone to visit Thomas in his study. Let them have their time, Claudia thought. Sisterhood is special.

Later that evening, Maria rolled an empty suitcase out the front door and around the cabin, repeating the names of countries she wished to visit, crunching over snow as Andrew took pictures of the ritual with his phone. In the twelve seconds before midnight, they stuffed green grapes in their mouths, one for each tick of the countdown, for each wish, for each apostle, arriving at the new year with a mouth full of sweetness and laughter, juices spilling over into wet kisses on cheeks and mouths, the whole tradition revived by Maria, who, unlike Claudia, did not eschew her upbringing when she arrived, did not watch and learn and imitate, but instead toted difference like a banner of authenticity. Thomas even threw a bucket of water out the window, a rite he claimed because it required rolling up his sleeves.

No one ever talks about how good it feels to assimilate. It was what I was supposed to do, she thought. More than that, it's what felt right, a refuge from the insistent poverty she once thought would be her fate, fear of which drove Claudia to distance herself from those who had walked across the border. She took a plane. Thomas said it to anyone who would listen, would work it into the conversation somehow with a wry twist of his mouth, and she knew he meant to convey that he took care of her, this girl who was nobody until she became his daughter, erroneous proof that he'd had a life.

In the grand homes of her father's friends, the only Mexicans were there to take care of everybody else. They watched Claudia when she came over, careful not to offer rapidfire conversation until the hosts were distracted, the first shy greeting given as a slight nod of the head, to spare her. They taught her that pure attentiveness requires both an inhabitance and a vacating of presence which is difficult for some to enact without letting erasure dig down to the bone. Those who survived servitude possessed dignity beyond the people who paid them.

Andrew wanted a caretaker, though he would never admit it. No one wanted to fess up. She ran from that life, ran from it like she had never sold roses at intersections—for the church, swore her mom—ran from it like that child wasn't with her all along, observing her fraudulence in real time, knocking on the windshield. If she had to explain why she first withdrew from Maria, why she recoiled whenever she sensed her sister was about to bring up something only they knew in a room full of people, the truth was Claudia hated to see such knowing in another pair of eyes. She wanted to move on.

In bed that night, Andrew fell prone to a long silence Claudia thought was sleep until he spoke. "Why didn't you teach me this stuff?"

"You dislike superstition. Anything related to religion. Remember?"

"Not at all. Tonight was fun!"

By which he meant these customs were so beneath him, so completely and utterly ineffectual, that he didn't mind them. Beliefs that Andrew would have dismissed as backwards when performed by the people of his own country became something lovely in Maria's hands, a novelty. He didn't want an equal. Maybe they'd be happy together.

Claudia peed herself to keep warm, focusing on the shower, which was almost hot. Everything would be okay. Things would get better the cleaner and emptier she got.

She scoured her scalp with shards of soap, moving down her body in brusque circles. The water was cooling. By the time she got to her thighs, it was frigid. She let the icy stream blast her face. Swollen eyes rode herd on a long night of hard drinking. With no conditioner, there wasn't much she could do about her hair.

The towels were the size of tissues and about the same thickness. She dried her hair with unwise flips of her head, reeling against the sink as her brain sloshed back into place. Scrubbing her teeth with a wet towel corner, she rinsed and spat and searched for flashbacks to reconstruct her night.

Kelly green. Yes. It began by playing pool—his bad break.

No, it began with beers on the beach, and the slow creep to Clallam Bay. There were those Natives at the bar. They didn't look Makah. Maybe Elwha. She could play that off, no problem.

Amber light in a tumbler, and another, and another, and another. Had she ordered those drinks? Or did he bring them to her unasked? She couldn't remember paying for anything but the first round, which she did with cash, in case she got stopped. She saw herself sink the eight ball, watched his face sharpen, his smile lines crystalline as he held the door on their way out. Stars tumbling to her right— the passenger's seat. Good, she hadn't driven. Warmth on her body, a hand on her throat, her head against the wall. The clerk's call.

Fuck. They were already famous.

A dark little boy with a cowlick peered into the window. She shook her fist at him, dropped the towel and cupped herself. He howled with delight. Another small, round head appeared just above his. She threw a pillow at them. It hit the glass with a soft whoomph. The boys took off, cackling and waving their hands in the air, running victory laps in the parking lot.

So much for discretion. Claudia sat on the edge of the bed, clothes in her lap, back curved into a bony ridge. She didn't have the energy to be angry. She wanted to have already done what she came here to do. She wanted to run, and to have somewhere to go. She wanted to trade these clothes for a silk dress and a fancy dinner with the man who promised to love her until death parted them. She twisted her wedding ring around her finger, deciding her next move.

She needed to push forward, and that was all. "Put your pants on one leg at a time," Thomas once told her. Claudia mulled over the possibilities while pulling on yesterday's outfit, building herself up again, layer by layer. She would go back to Maggie. Even if Peter told other people, Claudia doubted he would tell his mother. Other people might, though; several hours had passed. He could have put the word out. Most likely, Maggie already knew.

Claudia once read that dementia swept the memory clean, sending brief surges of lucidity downstream, bursting banked trauma at the least opportune times. But it seemed that Maggie's mind rejected things she didn't like, or maybe it was that she failed to anticipate things she didn't want to happen, even when she knew they could happen, or would happen.

Claudia could understand that, having let her marriage, and now, her career, sink into the mire. But Peter was kind of an outsider on the reservation, like her. Even if he did spread rumors, she would deny them. Perception displaced reality so readily.

Wetting a towel, she returned to the sheet and rubbed the stain, her headache intensifying. She was too old to need birth control, right? Forty was the new twenty, but only on the surface; inside, the body aged like always. She lifted the top sheet, snapping it twice in midair before letting it billow over the bed.

Frowning against the cold sun, she pocketed her left hand and edged past a cleaning cart on the balcony. Behind it, a maid stared from the open door of another room just like hers, but with a kitchenette, where the boys played with the faucet. Claudia gave a hint of a nod as she was passing. Maybe she could offer a twenty for a ride down the road.

Her SUV was parked between a blue truck and an aging sedan. Dumbfounded, she opened the door and settled into the driver's seat. It smelled like coffee. The center console held a white paper cup with a plastic lid cool to the touch. And a muffin, which she disregarded, lifting the coffee to read a note scrawled on its side. Thanks! ☺

She took a sip and pulled her wallet from her jacket. Finding no receipts, she counted cash and thumbed through credit cards. Perhaps she'd left one at the bar, or maybe he'd covered his expenses, so to speak. No and no. She felt bad for checking, then irate that she would even consider empathizing with him. He took something from her without asking, when she was in no condition to say yes. But she hadn't said no. Not that she could remember.

She pulled down the sun visor to check her face for clues, yet again. She would go shopping at the co-op and drop hints about her day. Perhaps a walk along the strait. There was so much coastline here. If anyone said, hey, I saw your car in Clallam Bay, she could respond and corroborate. People want to believe the stories they are told.

The pole in front of the co-op was all eyes and grimaces

as she pulled up to the parking lot. She stared at the carvings, trying not to look at the bar across the street, where a man leaned by the door, smoking. She didn't recognize him from last night. At the top of the pole, Thunderbird held his wings wide, chest containing another scowl, the whole of him bursting with ferocity, talons sunk into the teeth of Whale, dangling beneath him, tail curved onto his back like an elephant's trunk. Below the whale was a massive human face.

As she parked next to the pole, trying to be conspicuous, Thunderbird—who brought wind and hail and lightning serpents to steal someone's wife, or so another story goes—well, Thunderbird flapped his wings. She blinked.

That didn't happen. A trick of light, she thought, a shift in the shadows as I pulled up. A matter of perspective. Her mind refused her rationale. Maybe I should eat that muffin. She palmed its buttery dome. The top of the muffin bulged like love handles. She took a small bite. Its cloudlike goodness whirled around her tongue. Her spit kicked into overdrive. She hadn't eaten a muffin in years. She wolfed it down, licking crumbs from the paper and crumpling what remained into a wet ball she dropped into her empty cup. There.

Caffeine, fat, carbs and sugar combined to give her spirit an angle of repose. There were more than a thousand Makahs on the reservation. Although tribal members were connected by blood or marriage, some neighbors didn't speak to each other, carrying feuds begun by those who came before. And so it was everywhere. If it didn't work out with Maggie and Peter, she could move on, and maybe she should, without further ado, knock on another door and start fresh. It didn't feel right, though, to leave things as they were, sullied. She would smooth things over, take whatever she had coming face to face, and, in the process, rewrite the story of what happened last night, reclaim some of her power. She'd lost control, and whether that was his doing or hers, she couldn't say, except that she drove to a bar after splitting a six pack, which told her she was in the mood for excess.

Her left cheek tingled. The sun? She tipped her face from its rays, careful to ensure the driver's seat position didn't leave age spots. The late morning light slanted through the window, hitting only the outer edge of her thigh. She touched her cheek and turned to face the heat's source. A large lidless eye, a black and white ovoid, bore into her. The totem.

The wooden man's mouth was downturned. His top lip cradled a divot much like Andrew's, her mind flashing to the forbidden thought—I would rather him dead than with Maria. A great disaster could befall them both, a chasm, a flood—something terrible and cataclysmic, the kind of tragedy ascribed to God.

The corners of the man's frown tightened into a scowl, his face glowering, brightening the red rim of his eye. I am losing it, she thought. I need a nap. She forced herself to keep looking at the gray curls of cheek and nose, their contours almost fetal between his heavy brow and chin. The air around her grew stifling so fast she understood how their first and only dog died while she shopped for dinner on a fall day. She was distraught for months, displacing Andrew's blameless grief with her own bottomless need for forgiveness.

Don't think about that anymore, she commanded. Get out and get going. On her way into the store, Claudia took a moment to cover the carved eye with her cupped hand, silencing its judgment.

Exactly $237.45 later, Claudia was back in her car, grocery bags nestled in the passenger seat, chugging an organic coconut water for all it was worth. She steered past the Video & Liquor store, wares stacked behind dingy windows that held old "Welcome Home Troops" flyers, and steeled herself to drive past the grocer's hand lettered sign.

LAST CHANCE COLD BEER AND WINE

For the final winding miles to Neah Bay, she kept her wheels on the road's white stripe—so easy to make a hard turn into nothing—and vowed never to touch Peter again, knowing that the thought was a lie, an active and intentional lie, because she hoped it would happen again, on her own terms, as soon as she recovered.

Chapter Twelve

PETER WOKE AT dusk. He checked his phone. 4:30 p.m. This time of year was hard. Just when he got going, the day was gone. He blamed the long nights for his drinking. He knew it wasn't so. His mother was sitting up in the dark when he got home. Dawn wasn't till eight this time of year.

Exhaustion still beat him with big fists. He had let Claudia pass out in the crook of his shoulder. He did not allow himself to rest with her. You should never turn your back on that kind of woman. She had to be observed to act right. He could see that. His buzz slid into a sorry ache as she mewed and breathed heavy beside him. She looked younger asleep.

Spent and near slumber, he felt something close to tenderness, the desire to protect. He eased out of bed, wiping spit off his arm. Pity was a pile of judgment with sympathy thrown on top. He didn't want to take part in such things; once he got concerned about a woman, there was no end to it.

He rinsed his dick in the sink, trying and failing to be quiet. The faucet screeched, loud as anything in the night, water rushing through the pipes like a waterfall. To hell with it, he would not creep. Normal, like a man, he untangled his clothes from hers. He draped her stuff on the chair, trying to make the scene more civilized for her sake. Her keys jingled in her jacket. He would sober up on the walk to the bar. He hoped not to get hit by a drunk. There were some things a woman should not have to do.

His mom did not demand explanations when he walked in the door; she never had. He wanted her to acknowledge his right not to answer her unasked questions. Like why did you skip dinner last night? Our first with Roberta in how many years, and you were where? Maybe she thought he wouldn't come back. Would serve her right.

But when she placed a plate of eggs and bacon and buttered toast in front of him, he ate the bread. The grease and salt worked their way in. It's hard to be bitter while eating. He didn't look up until his plate was empty. There she was again. More bacon, a second helping of toast. She smiled. Her dumpling cheeks swallowed her eyes. He smiled back. He couldn't help himself. That was that.

Through his bedroom door, he heard his mother murmur and pause, murmur and pause. He hoped she hadn't picked up a habit of talking to herself. Old people have so many demons to keep at bay. He doubted Claudia would stop by, given how he'd left her. Maybe Roberta? He hadn't showered. She would know what he'd been up to just by looking at him.

Cleaned up, he strode down the hall and heard a woman laugh. He recognized that knowing, confiding chuckle.

"Son! The most wonderful lady has come for a chat."

Claudia was focused on his mother, smiling and nodding like she was hearing about a child's day at school. Something pinched deep in his stomach.

"Have you met Claudia? I think I told you about her—she visited last summer? We've been telling stories all afternoon. Have a seat."

Claudia's expression was too confident for what he could do to her right now. "Hello." She did not get up. "How are you?"

"Fine, thank you."

"Did you have a good sleep?"

"I was tuckered."

"I'll bet." She gave an open, rueful grin. He would be able to fuck her again, if he wanted to. His whole body relaxed.

"You and Mom were in the middle of something. Should I leave you to it?"

"Take a seat, son. I want you to hear this. I would have told it last night, but you and Roberta weren't around, so I saved it, and then Claudia got to asking about Thunderbird."

Peter tried not to look startled. Roberta sent Randall over alone, with three kids? Was she trying to make a point? Force them to talk? Maybe she saw the window for a rare night home alone—or with someone else, a thought that made him jealous despite the fact that he was sitting next to a woman he just fucked six ways past Sunday.

His mother waited until he got settled. It occurred to him that she might think he and Roberta had been together. Randall, too.

"My great-grandmother came from across. They've kept things going up there. When she told this story, it began this way."

Claudia looked older than she had yesterday, drawn and furrowed, but she bobbed her head in encouragement. Did she know that, in his mother's family, "came from across" meant their ancestor had been brought over the strait as a slave? Or did she know about his dad's side, descended from a highborn tribal member on Vancouver Island, some chiefly Nuu-chah-nulth? Didn't matter. He sure as hell wouldn't tell someone like her. He hoped his mother hadn't either. He wished Claudia hadn't caught her while he was asleep.

"So a bird . . . I can't remember what kind . . . it may have been a blue jay, anyway, Blue Jay hires Kwa-Ti—you know, Claudia, the biggest trickster of them all—well, he hires Kwa-Ti to go get the daughter of Blackberry Bird."

Peter breathed a soft warm scent, a sweet mix of whiskey sweat and soap. His reverie broke when he heard "blackberry bird." There were no blackberry birds in the bedtime stories he remembered. Did his mom mean salmonberry? Her face was animated but closed, black eyes bright and hard.

"And Kwa-Ti, you know, he's always singing, letting people know he's out and about, which is silly if you're trying to sneak around."

I wasn't sneaking, Peter thought. She's the one with a husband.

"But he gets her anyway." His mom clapped once. "He takes her to Blue Jay. Later on, everybody's over at Blue Jay's house, and Thunderbird sees Blue Jay's pretty new wife bringing buckets of blackberries. Every time they'd eat 'em up, she'd go out back and get some more."

His mother was up to something. She knew as well as he did that it was salmonberry bird. And he was pretty sure this wasn't a Blue Jay story, either. Maybe Robin? He couldn't recall. But she wouldn't forget something like that.

"Thunderbird acts like he wants to stretch his wings. He goes out back to watch Blue Jay's wife call blackberries into the bucket. He decides he wants her for himself. He starts flapping . . ."

Claudia shifted in her seat, the first time she'd moved since he sat down. She clasped her hands. Was she nervous? Good. He liked her better when she was off her game.

"He's flapping and flapping. The wind gets going, and it's howling, and there's thunder. Hail starts a ruckus on the roof. She tries to run back in the house. While she's distracted, he swoops in, snatches her up and flies away. He's happy. He got her good. Her house fell down. The hail was big, like boulders, did I tell you that? Everybody else was inside."

From the corner of his eye, Peter saw Claudia jiggle her leg. Did she feel guilty for cheating? Probably wasn't the first time.

"Now Blackberry Bird's daughter is with Thunderbird, living like man and wife. All this time, Blue Jay and Kwa-Ti are trying to get her back, but Kwa-Ti keeps messing it up. Like this one time, they tried to hide as blackberries so she'd gather them up to bring home. Kwa-Ti can't help himself. He just grows so big. Anyone would know not to pick him." She made a circle the size of a grapefruit with her hands. "That's a dead giveaway. Never pick a berry that's too, too big. It may be sweet, but it's hiding something."

And here, his mother paused and looked at him. He sank into the couch. She always knew everything. To hell with it. He rocked forward, ready to fix himself something to eat. Anything to avoid a talking to. He wasn't a teenager.

"Wait, son, I haven't finished." His mom's cheeks crinkled. She was having fun, dammit. "The best part is coming up." She turned to Claudia. "This reminded me of that pole you were talking about.

"Blue Jay gets Kwa-Ti to settle down—not for long, of course—and they make like fish and get themselves caught by Thunderbird. When they're in the house, Blue Jay whispers to his wife, 'Keep my bones. Take them to the water. Wade in.' And she does. She becomes a fish, too. They swim away."

Hands held facing each other, flat as her swollen joints would allow, his mother swayed side to side. Peter saw ripples and tails slipping away in the murk.

"But you know how folks are." She snorted. "It's not enough to get what they want. They want revenge, too."

She bopped the arm of her easy chair. "Kwa-Ti went to Whale and asked to borrow his robe. And Whale told him, said, 'Now don't open this mussel shell until you're ready to put it on.' But Kwa-Ti don't listen. You know he had to take a peek." She cupped her hands together and eased her fingers apart, peering inside. "The whale skin blew up so big, he couldn't get it back in the shell!"

Claudia laughed, a clean peal that didn't sound like pandering to Peter.

His mother looked him over. "Kwa-Ti is sneaky—that's the main thing about him, don't forget that—and he doesn't like to admit when he's done wrong. So he takes some mussel shells and cuts up his own knees." His mother made claws of her hands and scratched at her kneecaps. "He goes back to Whale and says the shell popped open when he fell."

Claudia was still chuckling, low and quiet.

"It goes on like that for a while. Whale gets his skin folded up nice and neat in the shell. Kwa-Ti comes dragging the robe back, letting it all hang out, in tatters. Whale said he'd have to see to this himself."

His mom nodded at him. "It's always better to do something yourself, that way no one can ask you any favors later."

But Whale's the one doing the favor, he thought, and stopped himself. Whale and Kwa-Ti go way back. They must have unfinished business. Why else would you give someone your skin?

Maybe she was referring to how he asked for Claudia's

help. His mom once said that stories reveal the teachings the way light casts a shadow. Maybe she and Randall talked about it at dinner. He flexed his ankles, holding steady, conscious that Claudia had picked up on his discomfort.

"Kwa-Ti and Whale stuff the skin with men and rocks and haul it out to the water in front of Thunderbird's house, real early in the morning, so no one would see them. Thunderbird spots the whale, and wakes up his sons. 'Time to hunt.' They pull on their wings and go outside to get this whale. Man, is it heavy. They couldn't get it out of the water!" His mother hooked her thumbs together and fluttered her fingers, lifting her hands and letting them drop. "But see, the men inside the whale are busy, too. They're binding the feet of the birds, tying them to the whale so they would sink together.

"And that's how the Thunderbirds drowned—every last one of them except their sister, who was out on the beach."

She waited a moment, making sure she had their attention, before delivering the final word. *Shuh.* Enough.

Claudia mumbled at her lap. "Those men, and Kwa-Ti—they drowned themselves to get at their enemies."

His mother clucked. "That's revenge. Always comes back to bite you."

"'Taint not thy mind,'" Claudia whispered.

His mom was quick to reclaim the stage. "Kwa-Ti is always dying, but he comes back. In disguises. He's a weasel... what's the word... a mink. Thick shiny hair just like yours, Claudia." She cocked her head, examining their guest. "It's a good thing you're here. It's hard to get Peter to sit through a story. When he was a kid, I used to have to wait until he was half asleep to begin, or he'd bounce right out of the room."

Claudia left soon after. "I'll be back." Wouldn't stay, even though he asked. "We can start again."

The trailer seemed dingier after she'd been there—stained shag carpeting, piles of bags, even the clean kitchen. She brightened things only to tarnish them.

For a while, he and his mom sat together. Looking at each other. Not looking at each other. A strange crackling filled the silence, full of the pivot and pull of collided particles. He flicked on the TV and scrounged some food.

Chapter Thirteen

WAY OUT ON the horizon, fog covered the curve of the earth, lolling, rolling in, a wall of white swallowing the neighboring peninsula, funneling through its forests to the mouth of the strait. Claudia watched through her sliding glass door. She could no longer see the fence between her and the shore. Soon, her porch railings and picnic table were erased. Into this roiling blankness came the image of Maria and, unbelievable, the deep longing to tell her sister what she had just done. To ask whether she would be forgiven by the Whom she did not know.

Guilt always felt like their mother, watching from beyond. When it got bad toward the end, Claudia convinced herself there would be visitations, clouds of citrus peel and brown sugar enfolding her in the night, which never materialized.

On her last conscious day, her mother held her hand. "Do well there."

A buzz began within Claudia's chest—the urge to scream. "You're sending me *al norte*? With him? How do you know he'll take care of me?"

"*Mija.*" Her eyes were liquid. "You don't know what I know. It's best."

Late morning light spilled through the wind chimes crowding the hospital ceiling. The spirals of sea glass dan-

gled like jellyfish in thick, poisonous clusters. Her mother
sold them before she got sick.

"*¿Y María?*"

"Her father's family will take care of her until she's old
enough. Then Thomas will bring her. He promised."

"Why would he? What do you know? And why just me?"

"*Tus dificultades*. With boys . . . you will drag her down.
Be a good sister."

Claudia watched fluid drip through the IV. Her books
were stacked under the corner table, worn paperbacks abandoned on the beach by hotel guests. A miniature watercolor
by Maria was pinned to the wall. A lobster pot. "What if I
want to stay?"

"Wherever you are, I will be with you. Our spirit is undi-
vided."

Claudia imagined an orange, its bright lunar segments
flying apart at the touch of one soiled finger, her own. She
thought her mother dying was the worst thing. She hadn't
realized how unprotected it left her. She and Maria had never had a dad, it seemed, but in truth, they did have fathers,
only that Maria's walked north for work, and Claudia's had
flown south to play.

Maria escaped the pressures that Thomas heaped on
Claudia as though to make up for never having cared before,
Claudia studying harder and harder, trying to put her wild-
ness behind her as quickly as possible, not knowing that
shame is patient. Her sister arrived years later to attend art
school, of all things, having relieved herself of the duty to be
more than beautiful and charming. Everyone adored her. It
was maddening. Claudia loved Maria—a complex, self-hat-
ing love, but love—and yet being compared at close quarters
made her want to wriggle out of her skin. As children, they

had always been together. Claudia came to measure her own response to the world by how it contrasted with Maria's, never more clear than the first time their mother showed them how to lobster, one of her many lines of income.

"Take the tail in one hand and the head in the other." Her callused fingers traced a striped carapace where the lobster's head separated from its armor. "Twist in opposite directions until you feel the flesh tear." Its guttural cries quickened. "Keep twisting. Pull the pieces away from each other, like this."

Her forearm flexed, its scars lengthening as she turned the decapitated head from one side to the next, pivoting its ochre body for her daughters. Lacking claws, the lobster held her hand in a scratchy embrace, whipping its antennae. Its beady eyes bulged.

Translucent pink meat spilled from the tail. Their mother placed the chittering head in Claudia's palm—its legs crawled, feeble, against her wrist—and encouraged Maria to take the tail. Her sister balked and hid her hands.

Severing her regret, Claudia regarded the interaction at a distance, like a disembodied soul or the anthropologist she would become. She observed herself twisting off five more heads, learning to spot weakness, to find the fissures that widened with pressure. It would come in handy later, in the field.

Managing each brisk beheading, she feigned nonchalance when her mother stopped consoling her sister and noticed her accomplishments scattered on the deck, lifeless. Deep blue water slapped the wooden hull.

That's when Claudia began to live on two planes of existence at once, marveling at their odd angles of intersection.

Still, it's terrifying to see the world with yourself inside it. It scared her into performance, if only for her sister's benefit. Claudia skipped dinner that night. Maria ate her lobster, sopping up the butter with the last heel of bread.

In the states, sisterhood returned with the catty, chatty surety of college friends with a history of long nights and late brunches. Claudia did not question Maria's motives, but she must have felt abandoned, must have nurtured a long aggrievement, for there could be no other explanation for husband theft. Anger entitled Maria.

Claudia pictured her backyard's mossy old maple, branches studded with muttering crows. Andrew took the patio furniture. Maria always liked it, the two of them spending summer evenings with bottles of chilled white wine, grilling and listening to the radio while Claudia struggled through revisions. Maria never dedicated herself to anything but her own pleasure, which made her what Andrew wanted Claudia to be, nothing more than available.

"You're like a guy," Maria once said. Claudia took it as a compliment. Men did what they wanted. That's power, she thought, but it was not true. Power was a symphony of personal bloodlettings. She understood that now. True power was getting what you wanted in the end. It didn't matter what people thought, until it did. Damn her sister.

Claudia pressed her hands and cheek against the coolness of the sliding glass door. Makahs slept near ancestral bones, their blood thick as stone. Every place she lived seemed to crumble out of existence as soon as she left, disintegrating behind her into a pile of rubble.

Maggie was asleep in the big chair by the time Claudia arrived the next morning. Peter saved a plate. Corned beef hash with a twist of orange to the side.

"Let me fry some eggs for you." Peter heated the cast iron pan.

"I'm not hungry."

He cut a hunk of butter. It spread into a pool, edges burbling into the black. "I would have done it before, but old eggs aren't any good."

She twitched.

With one hand, he cracked two eggs and held their shells apart. Chardonnay-colored whites slid out, yolks bouncing.

She picked up the orange slice. Warm and sweaty, it left an oily sheen on the pale ceramic. She bent the smile from the skin and nibbled the protruding pulp—salted, meaty, tainted. Forcing herself to swallow, she plated the rind so its curls spooned, pith to peel.

"You're going to need more than that to get through today."

He tipped the pan over her plate. The eggs tumbled onto the mountain of hash and settled over its crest. Peter pinched some salt from a crusty bowl and threw it on.

She'd resolved not to have any more dealings with him on one level, but beneath it, her body whirred. Sex does that to a person. For a while. Contempt set in once she got to know someone. Carnality ebbs.

The chair creaked. Peter kicked out his long legs. One knee swerved close to hers. "Get to it."

Claudia hated to be observed while eating. She stared at the plate, stalling.

"Is breakfast your only meal of the day?"

God, he was presumptuous. "Certainly the heartiest."

"You only eat when we feed you."

"Don't get too excited. I ate before I came. I'm just being polite."

"Eat."

Claudia watched her hand pick up the fork and slice a corned beef hash patty into wedges. She stabbed and lifted, not looking at him. The state of being thin issued currency that gained value as she aged and her contemporaries thickened in strange places. Men loved women with appetites, praised gluttony as wanton desire, but they didn't linger over its results. She had always felt better being petite, but lately, eating had become horrible to her, proof of her lack of control. There was no real alternative.

The cheap metal fork sent bitter echoes across her tongue. Fried golden brown, the hash was crispy. Its edges gave, smashing flat as she chewed and swallowed. Her stomach woke up. A second bite, full of fat. A third. This time the side of her fork tore through a glossy egg, which collapsed, oozing its yellow load. She shoveled a thick forkful of yolky hash straight into her mouth, doing her best not to look at him. She could hear her own breath.

Stomach distended, she reached for her coffee. He wrapped his hand around hers. She stilled, warmed by his palm, by the mug. Her body softened. She wanted a cradle of arms, the coolness of a sheet. Sleep stirred in her, dreams lifting and clouding like silt.

His hand found the back of her neck. Her head drooped, bringing her forehead near enough for him to kiss. His lips were dry. She heard him smile, heard the wet smack of his gums, felt his teeth hard against the curve of her skull.

"I have to go." She spoke to the smear on her plate.

"Stay." His grip tightened. Lips brushed her ear. "Rest in my room."

"I can't do that."

"My bed's cleaner than the couch." He snuffled against

her cheek, puffing laughter through his nose. She angled away from him.

"That's not what I meant."

"Couldn't sleep?" A hand on her shoulder, so heavy.

"Unlike you, I didn't get a nap in yesterday." She resisted his weight on the nape of her neck, withdrawing slow as a boot from mud.

"You stewing on something?"

In fact, she'd lain prone for hours, tallying her losses, luring slumber only to be rushed from it by a rhythmic rocking, the cabin's, and the sound of wood rubbed with fur, a dry brushing. A bear, no doubt, delighted by this handy corner, scratching its back before a wander down the beach to clamber over the mussel crust of the headlands to the banks of Tsoo-Yess River. Claudia quailed in her bed, cross-examining her own senses, her breath quick and shallow.

"I'm fine."

"I presume you've got things handled on your end."

"What?"

"Are we all good?"

"Everything will be fine."

Peter grabbed the nearest leg of her chair. He pulled her across the linoleum and between his legs, jamming his hand beneath her thighs and scooping her onto his lap to kiss her brow. It could be like this, she a leaf, he the river, gripped by gravity together, bobbing in dappled ripples down to the ocean, who would open, take them into herself, their bodies sounding the deep to emerge as eelgrass, hungry for light.

She squirmed. Peter got to his feet, holding her like a bride, and walked out of the kitchen, passing his dormant mother on their way down the hall. Panicked, paralyzed,

Claudia made furious faces. He grinned and dared her to speak with his eyes.

It was wrong, but they did it anyway, on the floor of his childhood bedroom. The sick dread of discovery chased her into orgasm. They came hard, almost silent, her body shuddering so hard her back cracked.

"Did you hear that?" Her eyes snapped open.

His smile was contented. "Hear it? I was about to hide in a doorway."

Chapter Fourteen

BY THE TIME they unearthed the colorful stacks of paper plate holders, his mother was whipping up batter. Peter felt sick to his stomach, wanted to tell her, "Don't make frybread," but couldn't, not when it would get her out of the way. The cleanup was ticking along smoothly, he and Claudia sorting bags of tchotchkes. True, seeing evidence of his mother's obsessive, disordered mind made him feel like dying. He plunged his hands into hundreds of Neah Bay key chains, colors revealing their era of origin—first the beige and navy of the late seventies, then the fuchsia and highlighter yellow of the eighties, followed by the mauve and white nineties, which is when she seemed to have moved on to other things.

Claudia wasn't saying much as she squatted over the piles, but he could tell she was thinking on something because her brow was furrowed, and she didn't seem to notice the aroma drifting from between her legs, warm and pungent. To be frank, she smelled like raw clams left in the sun, but he forgave her, considering that this was their smell, and the only reason he didn't find it familiar was that he liked to be long gone by this time after a tryst.

Peter watched Claudia sort key chains by color, plopping them into plastic grocery bags, and he didn't bother to correct her obvious waste of time, happy to see her silky black hair fall over her cheek. From certain angles, she looked like she belonged here. If he let himself think that way, it would be something to settle down with such a pretty lady, even if she was on the skinny side. A man didn't need much more than a truck and a woman and a place to park them both. They could buy a new house and set it down where this brokedown old trailer was, as soon as it worked out. Guilt broke in. He was daydreaming about his mother's passing, and there she was, in the kitchen.

Luckily, Claudia didn't seem interested in sorting the fried food baskets by color. She stacked them off to the side, the puzzled look on her face being replaced by something more, a gradual dawning he wished she would share.

"We should throw this shit away." He kicked at a pile. She winced. "Recycle it. Donate it. Whatever. There's nothing useful."

"I think she was saving it for a reason." Claudia traced the thin grid of a plastic basket designed to hold a square of paper and fries, something crispy and delicious, but which had instead for years held its dusty twin. Claudia inserted her fingers into the lattice, lifted a few from the stack, let them drop.

"I'm sure she thought so, but we know better." Peter grabbed the bags of key chains. "It's gotta go. This place is a firetrap. You should have seen the newspapers. The phone books! She couldn't even move around. And it smelled! There's no plan here."

Claudia did not answer him. Instead, she undid the knot of another bag, pulling from it four blankets, the kind Peter remembered from every couch of his childhood but last saw at truck stops, thick velour in royal blue and crimson, covered with airbrushed wolves howling at the moon and eagles with outstretched wings. His mother's bed had nothing but a thin duvet cover with no down comforter inside it; she didn't like to sleep hot, she said, but it bothered him, how she stinted herself while keeping blankets for beds that had never been made, never been slept in.

She was a goner. She'd been long gone by the time he got back to her. He didn't know what he was hoping for when he bagged this shit in grief and desperation, troubled by her repeating mind, her addiction to worthless household items, the acquisition of one, then the other, and another, never satisfied with what she had, already fixated on the one coming down the pike. Kind of like his serial fuckery, but there was no mass grave of past lovers to shame him. And yet, here was hers, disinterred.

"Let me talk to her." Claudia wiped her palms on her knees.

"This shit has to go."

Claudia leaned in the doorway between the living room and the kitchen, where his mother had surrounded herself with a heaping bag of flour, a can of baking powder, a large cup of water and a shaker of salt. Beneath the old dish towel she used to cover the mixing bowl, batter was rising, pushing the faded gingham into a conical dome that sloped off to one side. She was about to make Indian tacos, his favorite before the night his dad died, before he smelled batter and oil and blood as one, the memory a warm penny in his mouth, always. He had never been able to eat frybread since, never been able to go to a powwow in some distant city when he was missing home without staggering out, tears streaming from the oil and flour smell that hovered over the fairgrounds, the stray ladies in the parking lot thinking he was just another sad drunk who shouldn't be around children.

A shiver in his chest shuddered up to a tic in his left eyelid. He couldn't stand a repeat of this morning's battle. A hard-won calm kept his mom in its grip while the drugs lasted. Serene, she moved like she was in water, wading from counter to counter, humming.

Peter stepped into the damp cold, leaving the door open as he braced himself with deep gulps. The more he inhaled, the more air he wanted, his chest heaving, lungs singed by his struggle to give himself what he needed. He could not get enough, could not fill himself up, but he kept trying, bending over to prop himself against the trailer, huffing clean mist until his teeth buzzed.

Calm down, he commanded. Calm down. Trying not to hug himself in case the neighbors were watching, he boxed the air and spun a tight circle like he was exercising. Any man needed to step out sometimes. After he'd thrown enough punches to heat his cold sweat, running in place, feet thrumming like the wings of a hummingbird, he was glad to find a forsaken cigarette behind his ear and a lighter in his pocket, and that burnt taste was never so good, he took it once, twice, three times, the ember hurrying toward the filter.

Now he was relaxed. Now he could listen.

"Mine never turns out that stretchy." Claudia was such a kiss ass.

His mother must be pulling the batter apart. "Never knead frybread. That's a mistake." There was the thump of dough falling onto a floured countertop, like the old days.

"I'll remember that." Claudia didn't sound fake, like he

thought she might. Maybe she could learn something. But then, "So, Maggie . . ."

He heard bubbling—his mother always dipped a wooden spoon in the oil to make sure it was hot enough—and her silence. She could wait anyone out, a trick Peter used on his bosses, who filled his lengthy pauses with chattering, depleting their own power, unused to his peculiar form of nonresponse, which could be mistaken for politeness.

Claudia cleared her throat. "So, Maggie . . . I was just thinking about the wonderful things you've been gathering over the years. And I can't help but notice that a lot of them seem like gifts."

Did she say gifts? Claudia's voice was softer; he backed toward the door, cocking his head to one side. The first piece of frybread went into the cast iron with a frenzied rush of hot froth. The sweat that had risen and vanished from his forehead was replaced, replenished by a line of beads across his brow. Stay put. His heart was speeding. Stay put. "I've seen those kinds of gifts before, at that potlatch we attended on the Quileute Reservation. Remember?"

Another ball of dough sent the oil into its fury. He had to admire the sheer cussedness of women. They were squared off now, but his mother had pulled out her stoic Indian act, and was quiet.

The smell of frybread was sucking out the door and glomming onto him. His heart ricocheted around his chest, sweat running down his cheeks; his back against the wall, he slid down, covering his eyes, keeping his ear as close to the doorjamb as he could stand, turning his head every once in a while to catch a fresh breath. He heard a paper towel tear. The bubbles were still, oil dripping; he imagined the frybread being lifted onto a plate, soaking the paper. Saw blood, too, the stain spreading across his mind.

"Were you planning a party?" Claudia's voice was sweet. "Were you planning an Indian party for Peter? Did you want to have a giveaway to pass on some things? Like maybe his Indian name, and family songs?"

He heard a creaking wheeze, shattered coughs, a suppressed wail. Peering over his right shoulder, palm pivoting on the dirty concrete, he saw the dark crown of Claudia's head bent over his mother's small coiled braid, saw her hands pat his mother's heaving back, saw his mother encircle this stranger like she was a buoy, like they were saved from drowning, the two of them sobbing together—Claudia, that pantomiming cunt—the two of them sobbing together, and him outside, dying alone.

Peter covered his face, smelled Claudia on his fingers, flung them away, stomach heaving. He crawled to the edge of the concrete pad and buried his hands in the sweet loamy grass till his nails were black and dirt traced every ridge of his palms.

"Gardening?" Dave's voice was cheerful and loud from his perch on his porch's folding chair.

Peter willed his eyes not to spill. "Not in the mood, Dave."

"Why don't you come over here and tell me why you're crawling around on the lawn?" Dave's cackle rattled, raspy.

"I told you. I'm not in the mood!"

"Can you drive me into town?" Dave's smile was casual, but his eyes were fixed on Peter's face. "My grandson has the car, and I need to pick up a few things at the post office. I got a check coming."

Peter unclenched his fists. A breeze cooled his forehead.

He saw—as if for the first time—the tall cedars, how their limbs danced in the wind, how a light rain put a shine on bicycles tipped over in the long grass down the street. He did not want to accept the weight of that entire stinking trailer on his back, on his still young life, the burden of their shared past too much for anyone to bear. He'd stayed away for good reason. The shadow of his father's death made him crazy.

Dave stepped toward him, beckoning. "Come on over here while I get myself together."

Peter felt his legs moving, heard his loud steps through the soggy grass, his body on autopilot, thoughts dragging behind like a bunch of cans.

"Atta boy!" Dave held the door open. Dull smells—musty smoke, ripe dishes—wafted out. "I won't be a minute." He shuffled to the back bedroom, shouting, "I'll take a quick piss, get my coat, and we're off."

Peter sat down on the couch, reminding himself not to shake hands later. He doubted Dave was a hand washer. It was clear to him that Beans was living here most of the time now. Though they hadn't spoken, Peter saw him escorting a pudgy—pregnant?—young woman into the trailer when Dave was down having lunch at the senior center. It wasn't for him to say anything; for all he knew, Dave agreed to it. Maybe Dave was tickled to know there was life left in this dated furniture. Something more than waiting for the end.

Peter checked his pockets, grateful he kept his wallet, keys, smokes, lighter and a knife on him at all times. He would not have to go back to that house for at least an hour. Let Claudia deal with the bullshit she'd been trolling for all along. He would have nothing to do with it. His Indian name. Please. His mother didn't speak a word of Makah.

Never had. Neither had his dad. She was turning Indian in her old age like she'd turned to the church when he was a teen, hoping something would take away the anguish. Nothing could do that but death.

Dave was taking his time. It's not easy having an old pecker. Peter's eyes wandered over the newest things in view. A flat screen TV took up one corner—timber money must have come in, either that or Dave's son had coughed up some fishing cash, what with his boy crashing there—and, below it, a gaming system curled in its cords. Would a good father buy games when what his son needed was a car of his own and maybe a computer?

Peter could never spend more than ten minutes with his own kind without criticizing. That's what his mother accused him of as a boy, when he still listened to her because he thought she had something on him. What she wanted was a pallbearer for her pain. He wasn't having it.

"Ready?" Dave stood above him. How long had he been there?

Peter tried not to be obvious about helping Dave into the truck, but he held the door and an elbow and kept close behind him to break the fall, if it came. No busted hips on his watch. When he started the engine, a shadow flitted across his peripheral vision. His mother and Claudia, their arms around each other, standing behind the screen door. His mother's hand was on the screen—don't push too hard, I just replaced that, he thought—straining the mesh into black folds radiating from her small palm. Her mouth opened and closed. Was she calling to him? Their faces were swollen, watery behind the crosshatched wire, and they looked unsurprised to see him leave without saying goodbye. He'd felt that expression on his own face more times than he could count.

The truck was rocking. Dave waved with both hands, in a frenzy. "Those two are getting along. Claudia's been coming out for a few years now. Hasn't stopped by my place this time." He fumbled with the seatbelt, the metal tongue missing the slot, eyes and hands moving at cross purposes. "I hear you've been keeping her pretty busy."

Peter's foot twitched off the gas. They coasted downhill. Dave slapped the dashboard. "Say, this is a nice truck."

The post office couldn't come soon enough. When they got down the hill, Dave cranked down the window, leaned out and called "How's it hanging?!" to every codger he knew.

He knew everybody. Peter arced left between the clinic and the Presbyterian Church—"the rock and the hard place," his dad used to call them, his mom shushing him—and hung a right along the waterfront. A line of flags flapped in front of an open building, a beamed structure with a peaked roof.

"Seen the new veterans memorial?" Dave blew on his hands. "Your dad's up there."

"Fancy."

"That's where the Spanish built their fort back in the day. There's a write-up in there. Doesn't say we chased them off."

"Figures."

"Want to stop by?"

"Maybe later." Peter sped up once the road straightened out.

"Slow down here, kid. Let me introduce you around." There wasn't much for Peter to do but what he was told. That's how he ended up in front of the senior center, swarmed by elders who squeezed his forearms and patted his shoulders and haha'd in his face once he stepped out to give an old girl the hug she demanded, claiming to be his great auntie. She probably was, too. Her face sank to the bottom of a sea of wrinkles that moved when she called him handsome, pinching his biceps with her tiny hand.

If they hated him for leaving his mom, they didn't say so. They were all long-toothed smiles and not too many questions, which he liked. More shuffled down the long wet ramp from the center's side doors, overhung with big beams that would look at home floating in the flat gray bay. Peter wanted to tell them to go inside. It was too cold and close to Christmas for them to risk their health. He stood, grinning like an idiot.

Trucks and SUVs slowrolled the scene, drivers and passengers angled toward him, zeroing in on him and saying things he couldn't hear. They didn't look friendly but didn't seem mean, either, their faces set to a weary suspicion he recognized in himself. Peter shook hands, wishing he had washed up and cleaned his nails, careful not to crush bones in his sudden eagerness to be accepted. His great auntie latched onto his arm.

"Married?"

"Not yet." Peter was stunned by his own answer. Not yet?

"Kids?"

"No, ma'am." None that he knew of.

"Job?"

"I'm a commercial diver. A welder. But I quit to come take care of Mom."

A mild stream of approving murmurs gurgled around him, accompanied by bobbing crests of wispy white hair. A thin, straight-backed man stepped up. "Will you bring her down to see us? It's been a while."

"I'll tell her you asked after her."

Dave broadened his stance and lowered his head like a bear, his face not as friendly as it had been. "We best be going. We got a lot to get done, eh?"

Kissing his auntie's hand for good measure, Peter backed toward the truck. He felt the warmth of the engine block and slid toward the cab and into the front door, making sure not to insult Dave by spotting him in front of his peers. Dave hoisted himself onto the seat and arranged his legs, pulling his knees into proper formation one at a time.

"Was that so bad?" Dave stuck a hand in front of the windshield to waggle his fingers at a guy forklifting pallets of nets by the marina.

"You got more family reunions planned before we get to the post office?"

Their eyes met. Peter's mouth quirked. Dave laughed and waved him on. For now, that was enough.

Chapter Fifteen

ATOP THE KITCHEN cabinets, plastic plants sprouted from dusty baskets. Claudia made out woven patterns darkened by a thick film of smoke and oil. Her hands itched to hold them, to stroke their sides and cosset them, the yearning almost physical, the way she presumed most women felt about babies. She would never hold her own baby. The realization sounded a strange keening through her bones. She would not get another chance at that life.

Still, Claudia was proud of herself. It was she—who was not from here, who had no business asking such questions, according to Peter—she who divined the source of the hoard. After he left, tension thickened the air like rain steaming from a sidewalk. As the day wore on, Maggie's movements grew lighter, her talk brisk and easy like the conversations they once had. Peter still hadn't come back.

Claudia glanced at the sticky notes covering the cabinets in bright orange and purple. TURN OFF OVEN. TAKE MEDS. Maggie had managed to keep it together for this long, but there was no guarantee. Claudia needed to get to work.

"Peter doesn't understand. We must have witnesses, or the song won't belong to him." Maggie buttered frybread and spread a dollop of jam over its cratered surface with the back of a plastic spoon. "His cousins on his dad's side have been bringing out the song at parties. In other villages, of course. Couldn't get away with that in Neah Bay. They think I don't have people. But I do. I have people. I know what they been doing. Songnappers."

Claudia giggled in spite of herself. Songnappers. But this Indian business was serious. True, they were called parties, but potlatches propped up Makah society, indeed, tribes all over the Pacific Northwest. Each song was a map of blood claims to big chiefs. Potlatches had kept tribes together for millennia. Makahs who survived the ravages of smallpox resisted federal policies to instill individualism and property accumulation. Refusing to be controlled by prison time, they paddled across the strait, where fearful whites did not venture, to hold potlatches in their summer fishing and whaling camp on Tatoosh Island, drumming and singing and dancing during big giveaways for the ones who mattered.

There was only so much status to go around, especially now, with tribal members multiplying, and with them, competing rights to the same old group of songs. Anything claimed by one was lost by another. Family came first. Before the tribe, before anything.

"Better eat while it's hot!" Maggie buttered another piece.

The frybread greased Claudia's hand. Working with these people was going to make her fat. Even their name—Makah—was either a mangled Salish term that meant generous with food, or a Clallam word for never leaving without being full, depending on who was asked. She took a bite. Butter slid down her wrist. By eating Maggie's food while hearing her story, Claudia vowed fidelity to her version of events. Fair enough. Her right hand squeezed, instinctive. Oil oozed onto her fingers. "What do you plan to do, Maggie?"

Maggie's eyes flickered over the bite-scalloped frybread in Claudia's palm. She dumped a spoonful of jelly on what was left. Claudia smiled and shoved more into her mouth.

Maggie waved a strip of frybread in the direction of the bags lining the living room. "Peter wants these things gone. But I didn't save them for years to give them away in a jumble. It's bad enough he burned my papers. And oh, my directories. He'll never learn those names."

"You know, if you wanted me to hang onto some of these gifts for you, to give Peter some space, I could do that."

"Would you?" Maggie looked close to tears.

"Of course! It would be no trouble at all!"

Maggie's mouth puckered.

"There's a loft in my cabin. I'm not using it. Really."

They kept chewing.

"Let's start with a car load." Claudia patted Maggie's knee; it twitched beneath her touch. "See how you feel."

Maggie's eyes were glassy, pupils dilated, lips widened like those of that lost frog, which was not lost to her, but only to Claudia, who had found her way out, her way through, and would find her way back to the ivory tower.

"Maggie, it's your show. What would you like to do?"

"I want to have an Indian party." Maggie pinched off another corner. "I want to do it right. All we have to do is get people together for a few dances and a big meal. Dave can help. He owes me that much. Roberta and the girls, too. Randall and Beans can back Peter up on drums."

Claudia fancied herself a strategist, but really, it was Maggie scheming a coup all along. Interesting.

At first, Claudia hoped to keep her work on the reservation off the radar and, hence, apolitical, a plan made easier by the fact that she followed the pattern of interlopers and wolves, picking off fringe members of the tribe when they were at their weakest. Maggie's plan upended that notion.

"How many people do you want to invite?"

"As many Makahs as will fit in the community hall. And certain families from the Nuu-cha-nulth, from the Quileute, from the Hoh. We need folks to go home and tell others what they saw."

"The hall will be packed."

"We better get hopping."

It was only with the third "we" that Claudia realized Maggie was referring to her, Claudia, as an active organizer. "I think it's a wonderful idea."

Whenever she tired of the grind of academia, which was often, Andrew offered the same counsel—"If you can't get out of it, get into it."—and for the first time since she walked into their emptied home, which after all wasn't so long ago, she was grateful to him. She swallowed. "Let's get started."

Claudia needed to be gone when Peter got back. With Maggie's things in her cabin, she would have a reason to return—proof they forged an agreement. Some decisions were made safe by the passage of time. She was here to do her work, and that meant helping his mother preserve and pass on what she knew. Or at least part of the story, the sanitized version, for ceremony's sake.

Commitment made Claudia panicky. She would not be able to stay in the margins. Not for long. Anything public was political in Indian Country. You can always leave, she told herself, quieting her rattling thoughts. Like right now, get up and go.

Claudia stood, knocking back her chair. She felt feverish.

"You okay?" Maggie frowned.

"Um. Yes." She righted the chair. "I—I should leave."

"We're just getting going!"

Claudia sat, drumming her fingers, and sprang back up. "I'll load my car." She was out of the kitchen before Maggie could protest, the air outside welcoming her with evergreen and a hint of brine as she scurried down the path, garbage bags in each hand.

When Maggie hauled the mask from beneath her bed, Claudia felt as she hoped she would when she decided upon anthropology in college. Thrilled. She was awed by relics of true belief. That certainty had always eluded her, yet she was triumphant. After years of work, she had been granted access to what Maggie had been withholding in the hopes that Peter would care before it was too late.

It was no surprise that these people shrouded their tribal knowledge. They had learned as much during centuries of persecution that left them little enough that those who survived fought over what remained. She believed Maggie knew less than those who came before, and they less than their grandparents, and so on, the entire generational line leaky as a sieve with giant holes left by the twin epidemics of smallpox and federal policy. Less, but also more. The elders now were not the old-timers who remembered life in the longhouse, as they attested whenever they stumbled over a story. The eldest of the elders now were the once-resentful children of those shipped off to boarding schools to be stripped of their native language and family bonds. Of their old ways, but not their homing instinct. Maggie came back for good after carousing spells in satellite cities up and down the coast, into the Midwest and clear across the

Atlantic and the Pacific, following her enlisted husband's deployments.

She had convinced Maggie to bring out her regalia by offering to make invitations for the potlatch on her laptop, using photos of Maggie at the beach with the gifts she planned to pass on to Peter. Maggie warmed to the idea of proving her family wealth and lineage to everyone invited, rather than just those who came or heard about it later.

On their way out to Hobuck, they watched a bevy of swans glide into Wa atch River. "It's so beautiful." Claudia sighed. "You live in paradise."

"It is beautiful."

"I can't imagine what it's like to look at this for as long as you have."

"The thing is, you and I can be looking at the same thing, but we see two different things. You come out here, and it's like a picture. What you see is right in front of you. But I look at it, and I see a lot of places in time, all wrapped up in one, you know? I see the stories my parents told me, and their parents, like how the sea covered this prairie for four days, back when the waters rose and sent our canoes every which way. And the whole time I am remembering, you're thinking about birds."

True.

"Like Dave." Maggie snorted. "You look at Dave, and you see an old man. Dirty, maybe, but safe. But I seen what he used to be. I know what he used to be, and he knows it, too."

"What was he like, when you were younger?" They came up on the quarry. Claudia kept her eyes on the road. The lines blurred and doubled.

"Dave? He was dangerous. Didn't know how to control himself. Got people in trouble."

Claudia slowed. It was a short trip from one end of this reservation to the other. She wanted this conversation to roam. "Let's drive out to the hatchery."

Crossing the low concrete bridge, she kept left at the fork to stay on the paved road through a patch of replanted forest.

"Did he ever get you in trouble, Maggie?" Claudia braked at the first speed bump, creeping along. A basketball hoop and a faded goalie net wobbled at the edge of the road. Behind them, a house hugged the edge of a clearing. Tall grasses were reclaiming its shed and woodpile.

"Well, he used to drink pretty hard. And he chased women. They outran him most of the time, but he tried. He and Sam were drinking buddies. They would run over to Forks or P.A. Sometimes clear to Bremerton or Tacoma or Seattle. Just to have a good time, you know. Acted like they had business. What business. They always came home broke. Brought bum people back.

"Probably seemed like a good idea at the bar. By the time they got here, at least one of them would have gone sour, usually the person they brought. They wouldn't notice, you know? Because that person was probably like that before. Probably had them figured from the start."

Maggie's watery reflection was pasted on the glass, superimposed over the dark trunks flashing past. The trees opened onto a weathered gray barn and a house. Between them, a thick carved pole crested with abalone eyes that glittered green. A long curve of whale bone crushed the grass at its base.

"I don't understand." Wind swept through the lush prairie on either side of Tsoo-Yess River. She kept driving, listening to the slick hiss of road.

"I could tell you everything, and you still wouldn't get it."

Well-kept homes commanded open views of the valley and, farther west, the Pacific. At the gleaming mouth of the Tsoo-Yess, crosscurrents formed small scuds of waves where the river emptied itself against the sea.

"When he was a teenager, just a kid, Peter came home one night to his dad lying dead in the kitchen."

"What?"

"I couldn't tell him what led up to it. I just couldn't. I didn't want that man."

"What man?"

"They're the ones brought him."

"Who's they?"

"I never should have went out that night. Dave talked me into it. And then he took matters into his own hands."

"Maggie, what are you saying?"

"Dave was arguing with Sam about this law in Canada—it's off the books now—that kicked women out of their tribes if they married a white man. He said we should do something about it. Sam said it served those women right. I don't know how they got into it. They were supposed to be playing cards. That's why they invited that guy. To stake the game, you know? They were going to play all night. After they got into it, Sam went to get more cigarettes. Least that's what he told me later. He was gone an awful long time. I never got to ask him. Not that I wanted to know."

"What happened?"

"I'm getting to that. Pull over a minute."

Gravel shimmied and popped beneath Claudia's tires. Maggie looked out at the flat grays of the horizon, the sea changing with the sky.

"So anyway, Dave was drinking—it's what we did—and he says to Sam, 'You looked in the mirror lately? You're kinda pale.' Sam jumped up. He and Dave were swaying over the rest of us like trees left by a clearcut.

"I was keeping my head down. Don't know why I went out that night. Dave was bothering me about being a shut in, but I didn't like to party if Sam was drunk when I got there.

"So I look up, and there's this white guy. He'd been staring at me all night, and he gave me a sideways V with his fingers, you know? Pointed to the door. A smoke, I thought. A way out.

"He and I pushed our chairs back at the same time. Sam was all over it. He says to me, 'Stepping out with our new friend?'

"And I looked around, waiting for someone to jump in and defend me. From my own damned husband, but still. Some laughed and shrugged like, 'Hey, these guys'll say whatever. Don't mean nothing.' The others held still, waiting for the party to start again. Dave kept quiet. So I left.

"The white guy followed me. It was a nice night. The stars were out. It wasn't raining, for once. I was feeling sick, I was so mad.

"He offered me the pack. I was going to say no. I wanted to go home. I could hear them inside, and it got me, you know, them inside, and me out there. He asked me to take a walk. I said yes. We didn't walk very long. Far enough, I guess.

"A car passed. The taillights were shiny, like rubies. I remember that.

"He pulled out a flask. Offered me a swig. I said no.

"I wasn't even looking at him when he hit me the first time."

Claudia's silence met the rise and fall of Maggie's voice, old truths dropping like stones in a river, the windshield fogged with breath. She started the car and shifted into drive. Movement was the only possible response, a self-protective measure she couldn't help but use. She had no idea what to say.

"What I remember is his breath. Spoiled."

They passed through the long metal gates of the hatchery. Low blank buildings rose behind a paved series of pools encircled with chain link.

"Did you tell your husband?"

"I didn't have to. He knew just by looking at me."

"What happened to him?"

"I was faithful. Even after all Sam did to me. Things I never told Peter. He loved his dad. I never wanted to say something that hurt him just to make myself feel better, you know?"

Maggie never told her son about the sour smoke in that man's mouth, the scrape of stubble and cold mud, a star exploding on her cheekbone, his one hand at her throat and the other on his buckle, her kicking and bucking until he slammed forehead into teeth and she lay still, gasping through pain while he finished what he came for.

But she told me, thought Claudia, who circled the parking lot while Maggie relayed the story piece by piece. She could not stop seeing Maggie as she must have been, eye sockets swelling, jeans dirtied by her long crawl to get home.

"Drink made Sam sick. Brought out the worst in him."

He was like a baby, helpless against his own urges. Maggie absorbed it all, her calm a pillow he beat to pieces, searching for the center. That night, shaken, fearful, she did what she could manage, mixing up a batch of frybread to blot the alcohol, an offering, a distraction. There wasn't enough concealer in the world to hide her bruises. When Sam came home, he went after the only one in sight.

"He wasn't himself. Said I must have wanted it. I got to hollering, he was after me so bad, and where was he when I needed him? Dave must have heard it going down, because he came in and got between us."

And then Maggie was alone, as she would remain.

"Dave always said he didn't mean for it to happen. I swore to God I'd call the police if he didn't get out right that second. I wasn't thinking about what I had coming. Just crazed, you know? My kid's dad was dead. I live with that. Every day. That's how I come to peace with it. For a long time, I looked your god square in the face and dared him to judge. He couldn't look at me. I got old, waiting. Wised up just in time."

The trailers Claudia passed on her way back to the beach were lit from within by a flickering blue whose deepest hue found its echo in the dimming sky. They would have to hurry the photo shoot. The light was falling, but maybe she could frame Maggie with the sunset. Tires thrumming over rain-pitted asphalt, she assessed the damage she could do by aligning herself with people marginalized enough to need her.

Felons, if unconvicted. Maggie said no one went to prison. Claudia couldn't find a way to ask what they'd done with her husband's body, whether they went to the police. Maggie shook her head when asked what Peter did after he found his dad.

"He took off." That's all she would say.

Just after her son left, Maggie started keeping things to call him back. Or to provide a hiding place for her husband's spirit. Who knows. Maggie said the dead don't know how they affect those left behind.

Maggie's boast—"I have people"—ricocheted through Claudia's gut. Maggie's husband was in the grave and her son most at home on the road, but she belonged. My own people are gone to me, Claudia thought. They grew past me, pushed me out. Knit together. They're stronger now, like a scar.

If Maggie really had people, she would not call an outsider into family business, Claudia decided. But this was her way in.

Everyone is related here, she reminded herself. It's a matter of degree. The blood tributaries of the tribe were charted in the memories of those who attended potlatches held to set the record, the prerogative of the rich in any society. The hosts paid the most important partygoers with Pendleton blankets and carved paddles and twenties, if they could afford it, but a dollar per guest would do, and they'd even give out quarters, like at the potlatch Claudia attended with Maggie the previous summer. Claudia made a makeshift altar with the gifts she received for chauffeuring an elder—a beaded olive shell necklace, a pounded cedar bark rose, a plastic napkin holder—but what she truly cherished from that night was a scathing analysis shared among the smokers outside. Claudia was close by, having left to see the night sky. She couldn't sit still for ten hours like a Native. She almost nodded off during the namegiving— the name belonged to a great-great-grandfather who was a hereditary chief, according to the emcee. The coffee had worn off. She was heavy with chowder.

A squat woman coughed a laugh into her fist. "Please! People are pulling some bullshit now that the elders have passed on. His great-great-grandfather wasn't no chief." The others nodded, plumes of smoke writhing into a ball whitened by the gym's floodlights.

Maybe she kept that moment close because it meant the whispers of her childhood did not set her apart. Here was no different. No matter where you were, people held each other down. Or, to be more anthropological about it, freewheeling gossip was the most accessible form of self-governance.

Claudia could only imagine the stories that had flown around Maggie since her husband turned up dead. Would the tribe turn out for Peter's party?

Camera slung around her neck, Claudia held Maggie's elbow until they were past the dunes. A line of clouds sent gusts to tug Maggie's button cape toward the forested hills. She insisted on carrying the mask herself.

Snipes scurried beyond reach of the waves, only to dart back in tandem, pecking and pulling. Rocks below the tideline held in their wakes braided rivers of outflow whose patterns replicated flood-furrowed land east of here, ravages of the last ice age.

Claudia positioned Maggie against the distant outline of a sea stack. Her focus shifted from Maggie's face to the heavy mask in her hands. "Put it on." She raised her camera.

"It doesn't belong to me." Maggie frowned. "I just take care of it."

"For the picture."

"Only Peter can wear it. When we do the giveaway."

"Can you hold it up? Close to your face. Closer."

Carved from a solid piece of cedar, the mask was a wild man with open eyes, his mouth a grimace, brows and cheekbones arched to the same height, accentuated with bars of red worn thin at the edges. A large charred circle crowned his forehead; on either side of his hooked nose, phased moons orbited his hollow cheeks, meeting in a pair of singed crescents at his chin. Twisted ropes of pounded cedar feathered from a topknot at the center of his hairline.

Next to the mask's geometric grandeur, Maggie's face seemed small and wizened, yes, but more alive, too, her eyes brilliant. She did not smile. Claudia stepped back to frame the bird-shaped rattle in Maggie's other hand, noticing the trembles—cold? fatigue? emotion?—when she zoomed in.

"Want to go inside?" She lowered her camera. "Warm up in my cabin?"

Claudia had stopped getting cold as of late. A distant part of her brain knew she should feel chilled—it was December—but her body felt at peace with its surroundings, if not her thoughts. This woman did not need more pain. Peter hadn't yet agreed to play his part, and without him, there could be no potlatch. Claudia may have gotten ahead of herself when she proposed the photo shoot for the invitations. She would have to talk to him. Convince him to make good.

Through the lens, Maggie's shoulders were narrow beneath her red cape. "I'll hold these out." Her blue polyester pants ended above dark socks, exposing a small strip of dry skin. "I can't keep this up. Take the picture!"

The digital camera sounded out a shutter click.

Chapter Sixteen

THE ROCKS SIZZLED, gushing a large cloud of steam that sent Beans to the bottom bench. It was hot as hell, but that was the point of a sweat. Peter couldn't see anyone but for a faint red sheen along their paunches. Dave sighed. "That's good."

Plywood creaked and groaned under their weight, the corrugated roof rumbling with rain that hadn't let up for days. The door opened. "Who's that?" Dave craned forward. A figure appeared in a blast of cold air and rain. A white guy. What the fuck? Dave bumped fists with him. "Come in!" Peter kept his silence. Dude offered a hand before the door swung shut. "Dwight."

"Dwight, this here's Maggie's son Peter, the guy I was telling you about."

"Nice to meet you, Pete."

"It's Peter."

"Nice to meet you, Peter." He sat, blowing out his cheeks.

"Dwight cooks for the tugboat crew. Tanker breaks loose, they're on it."

"Big job."

"Long day." Dwight propped his elbows on his knees and hung his head. "Ready for it to be over."

"We're just getting going." Dave shoved another log into the stove. Peter split wood all afternoon. Dave said he had to contribute something, so there it was, a nice wall of firewood from telephone poles being replaced somewhere outside of town. Forget the creosote, Dave said when Peter brought it up, but he didn't want to be in here when the first treated log went nuclear. He stocked the sweat with old cedar and stacked the new stuff out back. "I'll do the prayers tonight. Don't nobody open that door."

Dave rummaged beneath the bench, coming up with a bulk bottle of oil. He sprinkled a few drops on the rocks and turned a faucet next to him; water shot through a pipe onto the rocks. Peter sat back. Steam so loud it hurt his ears. Eucalyptus stung his nostrils. "Didn't know they used that stuff in a sweat."

"Smells good." Dave laughed. "Unlike you."

"Not what I was expecting."

"This is Plains Indian technology, son. Might as well spruce it up."

Beans snorted. "You want something traditional, take a swim."

"Grandson's right, that's what Makahs did. Still do. Nothing like it."

"Me and the boys thought we'd try a dip off the bow." Dwight slicked his hands through his hair. "My balls just about crawled out my mouth."

"Been wondering what happened to your face, buddy." Dave hooted. "They got stuck in transit."

Peter decided against commenting on the dunk tank set up outside. A food bank bin. You cannot make this stuff up. You would be accused of something. He always said that to people, when they asked him about rez life, but they didn't get it. Resilience was unrecognizable to those who had never needed it.

The fire popped. Rain smacked the roof. Each breath brought the steam deep into his body. Sweat rolled from his face, arms, chest and legs, splattering his feet. At some point, he stopped thinking. Sweet relief. Sweat and breath.

He heard Dave pull a rattle from a plastic bag with a hollow clatter that sounded like shells, sending Peter back to sitting cross-legged at his grandmother's feet as a kid, listening to the dry clap of her hands as she taught the family—work that was his granddad's, but she was the one who stuck around—his mother making salmon hash, his dad's favorite, and listening from the kitchen because these songs didn't belong to her, a bystander. Before the fall, before the flight, before the world split into glare and murk, there had been that, a room full of people making music like the ones who came before, the reel of years too long to hold in his mind. When his grandmother still asked her son to show up, he made Peter a drum, giving him something to do, and he did it, pulled the boom from his heart, over and over. The drum sang its way back to him, always welcoming, no matter how hard he hit it.

"Thank you, Grandfather Rocks." Dave shook the shells, and shook them, and shook them, and shook them. "We thank you for being here with us today to show us the way."

What followed was a long string of words Peter could not understand, chanted again and again until it was the cadence that counted, the swells carrying him into something he could not name, like going back in time and finding himself before he fucked up, and discovering it was still him. When he couldn't take the heat anymore, he stayed put and kept sweating. His vision grayed around the edges. His ears popped like he was underwater. He would not get up before the old guy. Dave didn't move. They sat, liquefying. He would not get up before the white guy. They sweltered and dripped, and no one made for the door.

By the time Dave sent his prayers to all four directions, Peter was clutching his own real true self, right there, bear hugging it like the best friend he never had.

Beans was the first to break, but it was a bumrush after him, men bumping into each other like boys as they poured into the rain, heads steaming, Peter first into the pool, his whoop louder than rain, louder than fire, louder than the voice that had been riding him for years, that liar.

Stretched out on a beat up old lounge chair, Peter and Dave sat and smiled and didn't have much to say. They watched Dwight pack up his things in contented silence. Beans was gone as soon as he touched his phone and found the world rushing by without him. Thumbs flying through replies, he waited at the wheel of Dave's car, face aglow, stopping once when Dwight rapped goodbye on the window.

"Kids." Dave nodded. "Don't know how to live with themselves."

"Hard thing to do."

"You're telling me." Dave sucked down a soda. "Spending a lot of time at the beach, eh?"

"I can't stay cooped up. It's bad enough being on land this long."

"Been keeping warm in Claudia's cabin, I imagine."

"Don't start dirty daydreaming on me, Dave. I'm not having that."

"You're so sensitive these days. You probably use conditioner, too."

"What are we talking about here?"

"Keep close to good people. Stay away from bad people. It's that simple." Dave burped into his fist. "Some people, they can't help themselves, they're all tore up inside. Bad energy. Their spirit is sick. And you know they got good reasons. But you, you got your life to live. Surround yourself with good people." He took another swig. "I'll give you an example. Being with someone with bad energy, it's like singing next to someone who's off key. Yeah, you keep singing. But you have to filter out what's coming from them just to hold your line. And that takes energy. Costs you. They're not trying to hurt you. They just don't know what else to do.

"The good part of you, the part you're trying to grow, wants to help them out. And you should. The thing is to live right, to be able to look in the mirror without judging yourself and to know that you are living right, honoring your obligations, doing right by other people. It all comes back. But at some point they need to get to a good place inside of themselves. You need to see that's where they operate from. Or at least that they can access it. It's too easy to get blown off course. Some people don't want to get better. And watch how they treat other people. They'll treat you like that one day. Believe me. I been there.

"So yes, help people. Give them a hand, give them a lift. But seek out the folks that make you feel good. Seek out the folks that know how to make themselves feel good by walking around, looking at the trees, the mountains, the water, breathing the air, feeling the sun, feeling the rain. Those people—those places—are good to be around."

"Is there a point in there somewhere?"

"I know you know things." Dave clapped him on the shoulder. "That's why I'm telling you. Pass on what you know. That's your part in this. You will have work to do when we're gone." He put a plastic bag of green leaves into

Peter's hands, some shaped like ovals, others like crooked hearts.

"What's this?"

Dave said a word he could not understand, full of soft *has* and *shs*.

"What?"

"Snowberry. Good for the spirit. And the pecker. A twofer!"

"I don't need this."

"That's strong medicine, Peter. Wash with water steeped with these."

A car with subs on full blast pulled up. His teeth buzzed with each beat.

"That'll be the next shift." Dave uncrossed his legs. "Back to work."

"Guess I'll be going. And thanks, Dave. That sweat did me good."

"Any time, son. Any time."

Dressed, his towel and trunks slung over one shoulder, Peter made his way out to the truck, avoiding the younger men who gathered around the trunk of their car to stare into the sound of blown woofers. He didn't recognize any of them. He might have been able to guess their families if he got a good look at their faces. Not knowing felt wrong in a way that betrayed every choice he'd made since he was their age.

His truck smelled like old smoke, and so did his clothes. He patted his pocket, out of habit, and instead rolled down the window and stuck his head out, mouth open, to taste the rain on his way back home. But at the base of Diaht Hill, he veered left, not quite ready for another night with his mom, watching TV and not talking, communicating instead with little grunts of acknowledgement, him waiting, just waiting for her to bring up the Indian party so that he could light into the idea, expose what a fraud she was.

Just after his father died, on the day she found him crying in the bathtub, scrubbing blood from his boots with the toothbrush his dad wouldn't be needing anymore, his mom drove him to a Shaker Church on another reservation. She'd never been a Shaker. She laughed at Indians convulsing and speaking in tongues and laying hands like they were Pentecostals. But when she found him freaking out, her face went grim. She took him by the hand to his bedroom and watched him lace up his sneakers before leading him out to the car.

They said nothing during the hours to and from the church, his question—"What happened?"—met by her silence, and, finally, "It was an accident." Not knowing hadn't protected him, not from the nightmares, nor the self-recrimination, nor the anger, nor, for that matter, the flashbacks, which showed up on the day of the Shaker ceremony and never left.

The plain room was lined with rough pews. Candles sucked the air. Everything was white but the people with metal bells in their hands, and they were clanging and clanging, and he was back with the lolling buoys, the nets splaying like wings around the corpse of his father, who rolled to face the deep. The people were told nothing by his mother but that he had a demon inside, and they were shaking and clustering around him, words flowing from their mouths, heat pouring from their hands, which were all over him, and him feeling nothing but cold, trembling with anger they confused for holy spirit.

Months later, when he was alone in the garage billed as

a studio apartment in the classifieds, he got the feeling that someone was trying to shake him awake. He took to drinking before he went to bed, just to sleep through the night after his shift. Soon enough, he lost the garage, and when he did wake to a hand on his shoulder, he was on a couch. He should never have played along with her schemes.

Tonight, though, tonight a potlatch didn't seem so impossible. He didn't want to get snookered into something by one good sweat. He turned up a logging road before the Pacific appeared on the horizon, his hand steadying the wheel as his lights washed over a blue and white sign, a stick figure running from a wave. His truck shimmied up the muddy gravel to Bahokus Peak, swinging its backside every time he hit a rut.

Crushed cans and cigarette butts splattered from the base of a huge boulder scrawled with graffiti. Peter pulled over and huffed up the sloped path to the top of the rock. A dog barked in the distance, setting off its neighbors crisscrossing the hills from the clamshell-shaped town to the hidden maze of houses. To the west, lit by the moon, gray clouds toppled over each other, pushing up the sky and leaving a band of night on the horizon. The coast scalloped into sand and sea foam that erupted into sea stacks at Shi Shi Beach. Peter focused on the far sound of breaking surf. The cloudbank leaked a light rain that thickened, snuffing out the separation between sky and sea, the squall line moving ashore, swallowing the earth. He was buffeted by a burst of wind. He liked being close to the ocean because the elements of survival were clear. The punishment for not paying attention was immediate, irrevocable.

He'd been up and down the west coast, anywhere there was a port and people willing to pay for progress. Seattle.

Coos Bay. Grays Harbor. Longview. Portland. Oakland. Long Beach. San Diego. After years in the Gulf of Mexico for oil and gas, flying to foreign seas for deepwater jobs if they'd have him, he chose to hug land. From offshore oil rigs, he turned to dams, locks, bridges, nuclear power, shipping and docking facilities. No job was beneath him. Employers were the sole architects of his time, which he hated, but he liked barnacling barges and pilings with anodes one day and, the next, welding steel members on bridges and platforms and powerhouses.

In the end, no one saw his work, but everyone depended on it. They only came for him if he fucked up, which satisfied his inner nihilist. He wanted to be left alone.

His dad was like that. During the six and a half hours it took to motor the *Magdalene* to their fishing grounds, the waves foaming over the prairie in big rolls, the boat getting beat up and them with it, his dad wouldn't say a damned thing. If Peter wanted to talk, it had better be before the trip, when they'd fix what needed fixing and bait two hundred, maybe two hundred fifty hooks to a tub, depending on who was packing. By the time they got through putting the gear together, his hands felt like they'd been out for six days.

Peter hadn't fished since. His dad was gone. Being here changed nothing. He was in Neah Bay to get a job done, so to speak. Get his mom on her feet. He wouldn't stay long. The gathering storm calmed his thoughts. His next gig was lined up. A jetty down south, beginning in spring. He'd been let go from his last contract and the one before that and the one before that. He didn't like making allies. Got the best pussy in Portland, all the same. City ladies were desperate for a decent lay.

There was a city lady close by. He didn't want to face his mom just yet.

Claudia paled when he asked her if she wanted to do a sweat with Dave. Didn't seem like such a big deal, and he was pretty sure his neighbor would help him out, seeing as it was for the best cause on earth. Getting laid was almost a vocation for Peter, and had been for Dave, in his day.

"It's not Makah. I mean, it is now, I guess. Didn't used to be. You'll like it."

"Are you close to him?"

"Me and Dave? Oh yeah, we go way back."

"Do you have a cigarette? I'm in the mood."

He didn't want to smoke, not right then, with his body swept clean, but he did it to be with her. He gave himself the pleasure of lighting both cigarettes with the same flame, their foreheads close enough to touch, the heat on her cheeks and his own, and relished her wry smile as she rocked back, satisfied, to lean on the wall of her covered patio. Smoke took root in his lungs, sending its tendrils from his tip to his toes. The Pacific churned and roared.

"Dave's been helping your mom out over the years."

"Yeah, you could say that."

"Are they together?"

"What? No. He keeps an eye out for her, that's all."

When all was smoked, and some whiskey too, the sweat seemed like it happened to another man. Him, but not him, a shadow he, a parallel man best left to the past. He kissed her. The smoke and drink had varnished their tongues, but he kissed past the taste, kissed through the taste, until he couldn't sense where his ended and hers arose, their mouths made one soft and soiled place.

She pulled away. "Why did you leave like that?"

On the morning his mom stunk up the house with frybread, around three o'clock, so real early that morning—what used to be night when he had a life—his mom was agitated, kept saying, "It's coming!" Wouldn't say what "it" was. He thought a nice big breakfast would calm her down, but she insisted on coffee, too. The last thing he wanted before dawn was a cracked out old lady, but he brewed a fresh pot. Dignity meant choosing her own destiny sometimes.

But not all the time. The coffee kept her hopped up, raving, "It's coming! It's coming!" He couldn't reason with her harsh eyes, that stiff mouth. She bumped into the piles, raking her arms against the unseen weapons of frayed baskets and fistfuls of pens. He bandaged her twice before he offered a sedative.

Scratching and pacing. Scratching and pacing. At five thirty, he flat out ordered her to take a pill. He insinuated that his command came with doctor's orders. "She gave them to you for times like this." He wanted to summon the "Because I said so" but couldn't make their inversion of roles irreversible, irrevocable. He wasn't ready to come full circle. He thought she would balk, but she didn't. Seemed relieved when he brought her a glass of water and the vial. Hell, she'd eaten, he told himself. He saw to that, first thing.

He hadn't meant to drug his mother so he could fuck Claudia in the next room, but that's what happened. And then Claudia had to go and plant ideas in his mom's head, to justify her sickness, as if her hoarding had a purpose. He wasn't to blame for what she became. He wasn't about to reveal his mother's trickery, how she'd never been interested in Indian things when he was growing up, except for bone game and the basketry, she always did that, and she knew how to make the old school stuff—buckskin bread, halibut chowder, salmon every which way—and she'd harvested clams on the regular. But she also went to church, and made him go. If she and Claudia wanted to come up with some kind of conspiracy theory, fine, that was on them. He would get his.

"I gave my mom a pill to help her sleep. That's why she was passed out when you came. Groggy. I wouldn't put much stock in whatever she told you."

She gasped.

"She's been having bad dreams. Wakes up crying. You should have seen her at four in the morning. She was all over the place." He squeezed her arm. "Hey. I didn't have a good option."

"Do you think she knows about us?"

"I'm guessing you didn't share that in your little heart-to-heart." She was all up in his family's business, but she had yet to learn that tit for tat was the key to this place. What would she call that? Reciprocation. He'd mention it later. After. "I haven't told her." The nasty side of him, the side he had a hard time controlling around women, the side that was good at keeping power when others wanted to make him feel disposable, added, "Yet."

A long while passed. "Are you going to?"

"Hadn't planned on it."

He knew better than to ask about her husband, and whether he knew about what she was doing out here on the edge of nowhere, as far as most people were concerned. The last thing he ever brought up before banging another man's wife was her marriage, though it was the damnedest thing—they usually did afterward, when he sure didn't want to talk about who got first dibs. Stay single long enough, and you see the full spectrum of humanity. But Claudia wasn't talkative, except when she was on the job. He liked that about her.

Her bed looked like a dog turned circles on it, an oval at its center and thin blankets heaped at the edges. With a knee on the edge, he leaned her into the center, pulling off her coat, leaving himself enough room to crawl in. He felt her watching him unlace his boots, the knots fighting him, his jerking movements shaking the bed.

"I know about your dad."

He flinched. "Do you now."

"I do."

He lit a cigarette, tried to drop the match into the empty glass on her bedside table, missed. The ember burrowed into the laminate. "Does that change how you feel about me?"

She propped herself up on one elbow. "Why would it?"

"I don't know. What I did."

"Doesn't seem like you had much choice."

He studied her face, memorizing the set of her mouth, the calm shine of her eyes, claiming this moment within the enormity of eternity. "I been carrying that a long time."

"So has she."

"I don't want to talk about her right now." He ashed in the direction of the table. Gray specks fluttered to the floor.

"She needs you to do this thing. For him."

"Why do you care?" He mashed the cigarette into the glass.

"I just do."

He didn't know what to say, so he spooned her, resting his chin on the crown of her head, his ear on his arm, which bent up and away, sure to fall asleep. She twined her toes around his calves and wiggled her hips into him. They lay listening to glass rattle with rain, to patters on the roof, to gutters gurgling. They were breathing easy, chests rising and falling as one. Finally, the solace he'd long needed and never given himself—to be seen, for who he was and what he'd done, and accepted.

But of course it had to come with a price. Nothing was free for the taking, not with women around. If he and Claudia kept on like this, he was going to fall asleep, his right arm already on its way, the deep tingle working from bicep to forearm despite slow clenches of his fist, and that's not what he had in mind when he got himself worked up to come over.

He started out like he wasn't in a hurry, kissing the closest bare stretch of skin, her neck, and eased his arm from beneath his head, the burn shooting through it like a vise clamped him from wrist to shoulder. Stroking the clenched cords of her throat with closed lips, he retraced that trail with his tongue, body looming, trying not to crush her, though it was inevitable in this position. He gave up on spooning and slung a leg over her, working himself up so his weight was on his knee. He had her where he wanted. His arm was almost back to normal, his hand feeling like it belonged to him. He touched her face. Most women like that. It makes them think you're paying such close attention that you might fall in love with them while the smarter part of you, the part that knows better, is off duty.

Claudia shook him off like he was a fly. "Fuck me like you mean it."

He caught hold of her shirt below her collarbone and tugged downward, ripping the fabric, popping buttons like bottle caps. She watched him, steady and still as though he might hurt her, which he liked, and the liking of it made him go into a quiet place he reserved for being alone. That's how he felt on top of her, taking off her pants so she was naked, and him still in his shirt and jeans. Alone.

Her hips were bruised. Had he done that? Maybe she had another man here. Maybe someone else fucked her in this bed. He took off his shirt, deciding not to care. Her gaze told him nothing. She was otherwise pale, with brown nipples that hardened as he brushed them with his teeth. He didn't remember their color from before. He worked his way down her ribcage and stomach, tracing her shadows with fingers and tongue, checked her smell—no one had been here—and dipped in, tasting nectarines at low tide.

Her breath caught. He cupped her hipbones with his palms, held her flat. Her back was arching. It was time. He cradled her quaking shoulders, clasping her face between his hands, and kissed her, keeping a knee wedged between hers as he rose up and unbuckled his belt.

She opened her mouth, her eyes focusing, narrowing like she was about to say something. He covered her lips, the thick side of his palm against her nose, and she didn't shake her head, or scream, and so he went inside with his other hand, three fingers curling back toward him, the base of that palm against her clit, grinding back and forth, and her mewling and worming around on the bed until he couldn't take it anymore, his ache contracting into pain he pushed inside her, over and over, oh my god, oh my god, the sight of her sharpening in his vision, raindrops on her breasts. Was there a leak? He checked the ceiling. Nothing. That's when he knew he was crying. He almost turned and ran but there were her hands on his back, her legs locked behind him, releasing him and bringing him in, and now he felt her let go, felt her convulse around him, and she was conning him into falling for her, goddammit, he was careening down into her, and that's when he took both her legs on his shoulders and drove his dick straight into her ass, and now she was screaming, now she was crying for real, and he was inside her as far as he could go. There was no stopping this, she could not stop him, but there was her hand sliding on his chest, her locked arm propping him back and her other hand on herself, caught between them, fingers moving frantic in tiny little circles he crushed against her, and she was still screaming but it was different it was building and that was his voice he was roaring she was begging oh please oh please they were shuddering, echoes of aftershocks, and he was gone, legs and arms collapsed, sweating, spent.

She pressed the heels of her hands to her lids, once, twice, and wiped his face, palms wet against his cheeks, pushing his shoulders back and working a foot between them until her sole flattened against his chest. She shoved him off, wincing as he withdrew.

From opposite sides of the bed, they stared at each other. He tasted salt that might not be his own.

Chapter Seventeen

"CLAUDIA!" DAVE LUMBERED over for a hug. "Where you been hiding?"

"In plain sight, I guess." Laughing, she maneuvered out of his embrace to give two boxes of chocolates to Maggie. "These are for you." She didn't say Merry Christmas Eve, unsure whether tonight's dinner recognized the holiday's Christian origins, or if they used having tomorrow off as an excuse to get together and stuff themselves, disregarding the church's gilded history of expunging Native cultures, like most people.

She wanted to say ¡*Feliz Nochebuena!* but somehow her Spanish had become mixed up with the pain and confusion of missing her mother, or at least that is what she told Maria when her sister asked to speak in their mother tongue. Claudia declined. She needed to stay far away from who she'd been. And now the ache of Maria meant she might avoid Spanish for the rest of her life.

Maggie handed a box of chocolates to Dave. "Enough for everybody."

"Hi, Beans." Claudia waved in case he still wasn't into shaking hands, like last summer.

"Hey." He was taller, with a wispy mustache and a sleepy look to him. Maybe he'd been out partying with the crew reunited by winter break. Older kids drove in from community colleges and state universities in Oregon and Washington—she alternated between hope and fear that a Makah student would take her class—and this year, a coup all the way from an Ivy.

Peter came out of the kitchen, drying his hands on a towel. "You made it!"

He gave her a quick kiss on the cheek, his breath hot on her ear as he drew back, her slight sway toward him imperceptible, she hoped. His presence pulled at her like sand tugged in surf. She clenched her toes and planted her feet, trying to stop the erosion. Here was not the place. "Thanks for having me."

Everyone was quiet. This was not going to work, not even a little bit. What had she been thinking. She smiled. "Happy holidays!"

"Let's eat!" Maggie motioned them into the kitchen. A small mercy. They had pulled out the leaves on the breakfast table and brought more chairs and even turned off the scanner for the occasion. The kitchen sparkled. He must have scrubbed it down. In fact, the walls gleamed around vanilla scented candles that covered the bag-filled corners in shadows.

The table was set with glasses of ice water, a plate of buckskin bread, a butter dish and a jar of jam. Maggie ladled chowder into bowls she passed to Peter, who placed them in front of each guest. Claudia kept quiet, listening. Makahs tried on multisyllabic words like a tight sweater, emphasis poking through first vowels with the force of an errant elbow, followed by a shimmy through the rest. The one exception was hello.

Dave filled Peter in on his daily rounds. "I wasupatthe

FISHhouse YESterday andsawyour COUSin. Hetoldmeto-
tellya helLO and tocomebytheboatsinceyou'rein NEah Bay."

The run-together syllables didn't imply that Dave spoke
quickly. Like most Indians she met—didn't matter from
what tribe—he didn't. Time and time again, Claudia re-
strained herself from trampling on the ends of their sen-
tences, holding her silence with her tongue pressed against
her upper teeth just like when she was young, ignoring her
mother's warnings that it would make her bucktoothed, by
which she meant ugly, unwanted. Maybe the Makah way of
speaking related to their original tongue, a lower Wakashan
dialect full of words that went on like rivers that had dried
despite the tribe's diligent efforts, despite the schooling and
the certification of new language teachers, despite the habit of saying *Kleko, Kleko* to thank each other for each and
every little thing. She wished more towns spent as much
time on conservation of resources as this village, which was
overseen for too long by Indian Agents who arrived with
the federal edict that the native language was to be extermi-
nated along with the values it conveyed. When Makah kids
returned from the boarding schools they'd been forced to
attend, their mouths were still bitter with soap their teachers used on students caught speaking anything other than
English. Most couldn't understand the elders, and many
didn't care. That generation was gone now—not up in trees,
laid out in canoes with holes poked in the bottom, like in
the old days—but buried in the ground.

Claudia's spoon dove around soft yellow globes of butter
and cream to surface with a single kernel of corn, a cube of
potato, a flake of fish.

"This chowder sure is tasty." Dave dipped a square of
buckskin bread in his chowder. "Who brought the halibut?"

"Son's cousins." Maggie looked dour. "Trying to buy me off." She folded her arms, clasping her elbows, and settled back in her chair.

"Now, Maggie." Dave lifted the dense, dripping biscuit to his mouth.

"Don't 'Maggie' me. You know what they been doing. Parading our song around."

"They kept it going." Dave slurped some soup. "Isn't that something?"

"They stole it. Had the nerve to claim the song was on loan to Sam. Lies. As if getting his boat on the cheap wasn't enough."

Peter reached for another square of bread. "Let it go."

"Do you know, they asked your dad to sing at your grand-dad's deathbed."

"That seems appropriate."

"You don't know anything! You can't bring the song out after that. They wanted to use his father's death against him! Just so they could come up."

"We're having a nice dinner."

"Don't you change the subject. I know what I'm saying. Tell him, Dave." Maggie shook her finger at him.

Dave put up his hands. "Don't shoot!"

"Now's no time for jokes."

Claudia's head pinged back and forth between them. Next to her, Beans hung his head over his third bowl of chowder, scooping one bite after another.

"Mom, that was a long time ago."

"Your future depends on it. You're a big man here."

"I'm not staying."

Rain rapped the windows. No one spoke. Beans finished eating. Claudia couldn't put her spoon down without a clatter. She held it aloft, awkward, and glanced around the counters. There, in the flickering shadows, was the pan, its black lip lustrous. She closed her eyes, saw Sam come at Maggie, Dave gathering a wild swing with one hand, the pan sliding off the oven, spilling hot oil and frybread, dipping and going aloft like a bird in an arc that stretched from his shoulder to the sick crunch of Sam's temple.

Saw Peter, so young, come upon his parents, or what was left of them.

I shouldn't be here, she thought. But where? Even now, Thomas and Andrew and Maria would have switched to cognac, its honeyed amber rusted to russet by the fire, woods deep in snow around them, discarded skis spreading puddles in the mud room.

"That song is yours." Maggie smoothed and refolded her napkin. "Claudia is going to help me. You never got your Indian name. We could bring out the song."

"Since when do we speak Makah?"

Maggie nodded at Dave. "You'll be there, won't you? I need an emcee."

Dave put down his spoon. "On one condition."

"What's that?" Maggie scowled.

Claudia held her breath.

"That we quit talking. Let's have a good time. Roberta's going to stop by after she puts the girls to bed."

"I want nothing to do with this." Peter pushed back from the table.

"Listen, we'll do a warm up party at my house," Dave said. "See how it goes. All you have to do is show up."

The front door shook in its hinges.

"That'll be Roberta." Peter, Beans and Dave were out of

their seats so fast the table swayed. She and Maggie were left blinking at each other.

Claudia reached over and took Maggie's hand, not knowing why, only wanting to erase this old mourning from that crumpled face, its wide cheeks fallen in folds. "I'll speak to him."

The first happy greetings sounded from the group at the door. "Merry Christmas Eve!"

"Sorry I'm late. I had to get creative with the hiding spots this year. Randall's home with the girls. They'll be up before the crack of dawn to check under the tree."

In the small lull that followed, Claudia cued in on Maggie, who had drawn Peter close as Dave paced their periphery. "You're going to wear out your tires."

"I have to get back to work. Besides, you used to travel."

"When?"

"Come on! You and Dad drove all over for bone game tourneys."

"That's a great idea!" Dave clapped his hands. "Let's play." He took Peter by the shoulder. "Help an old man carry his drums?"

Beans looked at his phone. "Marissa and I were supposed to hang out."

"You'll be wanting my car."

"Yeah."

"We'll win quick. Help me scare up the sticks."

Claudia excused herself to go to the bathroom. How would the university react if she called off her research? A meeting with her department chair. Questions upon questions. Institutional review boards. She would lose standing. Would she also lose her funding? There was no way out but through.

When she crossed back over the border to study *recorridos* for her dissertation, it felt like everything was possible. She would make sense of the society that spurned her and come to some sort of peace. The country people she met were impressed—one of their own made good—hosting meals and song circles for her benefit, eyes shining as they introduced their children with exhortations to follow her example and study hard.

Maybe she could find that feeling again. She just had to make this work.

By the time she walked into the living room, the men were back, smelling of wet ashtrays. Beans carried a folding chair. Claudia wanted a cigarette more than she ever wanted anything.

"Maggie, you and Peter and Claudia are a team." Dave rubbed his hands. "Me, Beans and Roberta will play against you."

"What are we playing for?" Peter took a drum from a canvas bag.

"Let's see." Dave turned out his pockets. "Got cash?"

"For an old codger like you? Maybe." Peter opened his wallet and thumbed through a thick line of bills.

"Wow!" Dave grinned. "Let me hold that."

"If you run, I'll have no choice but to take you down." Peter cracked his knuckles. "I might like it."

Dave flapped his face with a fan of ones, fives and twenties.

"We've got a newcomer. Let's stay on budget." Peter plucked two twenties and two fives from Dave's hands.

"Don't let Dave hold your cash for too long." Maggie folded the bills into a bandanna she deposited into her apron. "He'll make it disappear right quick."

"Cash? What cash?" Dave twirled his deerskin drum by the twisted rawhide crisscrossing its back. Holding a beaded drumstick in his other hand, he opened his fingers to show no bills hidden there.

"Check the drum." Maggie pointed. Sure enough, once Peter managed to pry the drum from Dave, there it was, a neat roll of money wedged behind the wavy lip of hide.

"It makes the drum happy!" Dave touched his heart. "You want it to sound right, dontcha?"

"Just for that, I'm going to trade you Claudia for Roberta."

"One pretty lady for another—how could I go wrong?" Dave motioned to Claudia. "Come on over to the winning side. We'll show you how it's done."

"Don't worry, you can't mess this up." Peter tickled the roll of cash from its hiding place. "It's fifty-fifty every time."

"Unless you got mad skills." Beans put on a pair of sunglasses.

"Ever played?" Dave tucked his drumstick into the rawhide handle.

"No."

"It's real simple. We got two sets of bones." He opened a carved wooden box at his feet and held out four short lengths of barrel-shaped bones. Two were inlaid with a thick dark stripe at their center. Reaching into the box, he lifted out a carved killer whale with matching rows of sticks bristling from its back. "We divide these ten sticks even steven between us. I brought my old yew wood set—I know you're into that kind of thing—but these aren't the ones I bring to tourneys. Those I got made special, with fancy beading and whatnot."

Dave pulled a longer stick with a figure clinging to its top from the blowhole—"this is the kick stick"—lingering as he laid it in Maggie's palm. "I'm giving you home court advantage because that chowder was so good."

Maggie looked pleased, and for a moment, a small glow lit her and Dave. Claudia wondered whether she could ever show so much grace. Anyone who wanted a family must forgive. Just the thought of her sister made her sick.

"Okay, so when we're playing, one team will have both sets of bones at a time. A set is an unmarked bone and a marked bone. We got six people, so both teams will have a drummer. The other two will each be holding a set. They'll mix 'em around behind their back or under the scarves—that's Maggie's favorite way. Keep a good eye on her. They'll be singing and kind of dancing in their seats, if they're feeling lively. Taunting, you know. Don't let it get to you. The pointer decides which hands the unmarked bones are in. Guess right, get the bones. Guess wrong, give up a stick. It goes on like that. The game will end when we have all the sticks. Maggie's holding on to the kick stick, so I'm guessing she's the pointer for them. Kick stick's the last one to go."

"Who's the pointer for us?" Claudia hoped against hope it wasn't her.

Beans slipped his phone into his big untied sneaker. "Me."

"Do you ask us where we think the bones are?" She smiled, watching her teeth flash in his sunglasses.

"He'll take all the help he can get." Dave nudged his grandson. "Sit between us, Claudia."

Once she was ensconced next to Beans, Claudia drew close to his glossy ear and whispered, "If I see which hand it's in, I'll tap that foot, left for left, etc. One tap for the person on the left, two taps for the person on the right."

Behind his shades, Beans arched an eyebrow.

Peter positioned the chairs so his team's back was to the kitchen. The lights shimmered around them. He conferred with Roberta, her long hair swaying against his arm as she angled her head to take in what he was saying. The other drum twirled in his hand. From where Claudia sat, his face was in shadows. He had never been so attractive. Jealousy compelled her like gravity.

She cradled her set of bones, stroking the slight ridges at the edge of the inlay, holding the pair up to the light to study the hollows eroded by sweat and time. Beans cleared his throat. She hid her hands behind her back, using her fingerpads to ensure the marked bone was in her right hand. Dave started drumming, his voice deepening as he sang out a series of vowels she was pretty sure didn't add up to words. When she brought the bones back out again, she clutched her right hand for all it was worth. The veins and tendons rose along her forearm. She glanced to her right once or twice.

Maggie guessed wrong. The unmarked bone showed in Claudia's left hand, which bumped up against her partner's open right palm, also holding an unmarked bone.

"An inside job." Roberta's mouth twisted as she handed over a stick.

When their turn came, Peter drummed, a deafening monotony of strike after strike, Maggie and Roberta dividing the bones between them, laps covered in scarves, wailing, "Hay yay yay yay ya-ayyyyyy! Hay yay yay yay ya-ohhhhhh! Hay yay yay yay yaaaaaa! Hay yay yay yay yohhhhhh!"

Claudia was distracted by Peter's determined look, how he picked up the drum like he never put it down. Was belonging like riding a bike? It wasn't until Beans leaned forward to glance at her feet that she remembered she was supposed to be doing something. Maggie and Roberta were zeroed in on her face. They know I fucked Peter, she thought. Alarm bloomed in her stomach. She concentrated on the drums, allowing the din to drown her thoughts.

Beans took his time to make the call. Maggie and Roberta held their closed fists out, fingers turned toward their own faces, moving back and forth in rapid bicep curls that kept beat with the drum.

Before she could stop herself, Claudia tapped her left foot once and her right foot twice. Without acknowledging her, Beans made a *V* with his thumb and forefinger, the rest of his fingers curled into his palm. Roberta and Maggie shrugged and showed their hands—she was right!

Bones and sticks passed from one team to the other, a steady stream of handoffs that ebbed and flowed for hours, Maggie rallying with a few good calls. Like birds, the flashy piece was male and the unmarked piece, female. They flew from hand to hand in secret courtship. Everyone pursued the women.

In the end, it was a drubbing. Beans hugged her when they got the kick stick. Dave's cheek, when he kissed her, was wet with sweat. "We can play together any time."

"Here I am, the boy who slept under folding chairs, the powwow broke kid," Peter shook his head, "and along comes a white woman to sweep the game."

His admiring gaze—he wasn't looking at Roberta now—almost covered the slight. A white woman. *Soy mexicana*, she thought, but that wasn't really true anymore. She'd become American, like them, whether anyone liked it or not. She blushed.

"Broke is right." Dave laughed. "Another? I'll throw our winnings in."

"No thank you." Peter stood. "Consider that my Christmas gift."

It was nearly Christmas when she left, begging off from more food, waving away Peter's offer to follow her home to make sure she got there safe. Her weariness went down to her bedrock, but it almost felt good, almost made her nostalgic for Christmas in Mexico, where women exhausted from working all the time went into hyperdrive on the holidays, bustling through big meals on weekends and evenings, anything to enliven time with family.

By the time *Nochebuena* rolled around, everyone had already spent the last eight nights out and about, following around the lucky pair who got to dress up like María and José, knocking on doors like they had been forced to do in Bethlehem, looking for a place to sleep, the name of the ritual—*Las Posadas*—referring to the shelter that was repeatedly denied, a failure of hospitality that, millennia later, looked like a bunch of dressed up children carrying candles, careful not to spill wax on their Sunday shoes, singing songs back and forth with whomever opened the door, the call and response akin to the negotiations that must have happened before the birth of Jesus.

Or so Claudia had been told, but she had stopped believing so long ago it was hard to remember what faith felt like, a forfeiture that led her farther and farther afield, seeking authenticity in the rituals of others. Maybe it didn't matter if Peter believed in the song or what the potlatch represented. It seemed to Claudia that believing culture was important had replaced actual cultural belief among most of the peoples who still claimed to have a culture of their own. Among the Makah tribe, there were grave reasons for that—among them, persecution and genocide—but the only way she could understand it was through the lens of her own lost Catholicism. The wafer never became flesh in her mouth. Though she took communion for social purposes and a shot at redemption, she didn't believe. But she missed the *tamales*, the *pozole*, the *buñuelos*, the whole charade of *Las Posadas*. She missed feeling like part of something. Nothing awaited those who fled the church, that's what her mother always said, and Claudia supposed she was right, even if the hereafter was a hustle to colonize people right down to their very souls.

Christmas had begun by the time she got to her cabin. What was she to do with the rest of this accursed day? Work was the answer, the only solace she knew for sadness, though she'd been glad to ward off professional duties with a "vacation" message.

> *I am on research leave until summer quarter. If you have pressing concerns related to the university, please contact the Department of Anthropology at . . .*

The emails loaded in a trickle that widened to a cascade, the list scrolling so long that Claudia almost closed her laptop. Instead, she browsed, letting the names wash over her without stopping to satisfy them with responses. They would pity her for attending to emails on Christmas.

But there, nested among the endless words crowding her screen, a blank subject line, and beside it, her sister's name, the letters burrowing into Claudia's eyes. She clicked.

> *I did the unspeakable. I know that. It's not fair to want you in my life, but I do. Sisters are para siempre. That's what Mamá told us. Please be my family. I miss you.*

Fuck her. It was beyond forgiveness, what she did, and Maria hadn't even asked for absolution. How dare she? Out to swallow whole lives. To take everything, right down to the marrow. Not if it were her last day on earth would Claudia welcome her sister back into her life.

What awaited her in Seattle? Proximity to a person she would no longer claim as blood, the chance of stepping off a city sidewalk and seeing the husband who had chosen wrong and made a correction.

Maybe Claudia could just stay. Sell everything and call it good. Claim immersion as an anthropological practice. Remain involved.

Who was she kidding. There was no future here for her, no job she could do without remorse. Not only had she bedded a community member, but she was now accessory to an old murder. Her only defense, if it came to light, would be to deny everything, which wouldn't have been hard—Maggie had dementia—except for Peter, who could ruin her. It would come out.

She had just torched her career, the one thing she truly cared about, the prospect of mattering a bright star she had followed since she came to this country. And for what. A lover who lived in a trailer with his mother and didn't own enough stuff to fill the bed of his truck. Tenure had brightened her future like a beacon, a steady job teaching students she could scarcely bring herself to consider, but also the platform to publish her own theories to mild acclaim and the occasional invitation to join a panel, and then to annihilate the sorry soul inside her intellect with enough wine to choke a pig.

There was no salvaging her life. If she wanted to disappear, she could park at the Shi Shi Beach trailhead and hike the steep headlands on the way to Cape Alava, where few braved bracing themselves with knotted ropes that dangled down the trail. All she would have to do is let go. The rocks would do the rest. The sea would take her, before long.

Stunned by her own certainty, she went straight for the shower, trying and failing to avoid the mirror, where she saw a petrified woman with hair plastered across her forehead, a double who was not her, an impostor—don't look at her, she's staring back at you, don't get closer, she'll hurt you—but already her fingers were on the mirror, and now they were touching, soft as glass, their hands streaking down the reflected world, where the towels and the tile were all the same, but she was not me, and never would be again.

Chapter Eighteen

A STORM WAITED off the coast. From the first overlook on Cape Flattery, Peter watched the rain. Fall streaks grayed the sky over the mouth of the strait.

The sea surged to shore. Dark water broke over mussels and rocks, draining white foam, rising through green curls of kelp. Waves boomed through sea caves that riddled the sandstone cliffs, shuddering the earth beneath their feet. An eagle wheeled overhead, keeping watch. Otherwise, they were alone.

When he showed up at her cabin this morning, Claudia acted like it was just another day. Which it was, he supposed. At least he had something for her. Whiskey and cigarettes, the last of his stash. She was not as cheerful as he'd hoped, but he tried to rally. "It's a joke. You know. Get your own?"

"Shouldn't you be with your mom?"

"She's at Roberta's. The girls are opening presents."

"That's what I mean."

"I thought we'd go on a walk."

"Peter, what do you think we are doing?"

"No one will be on the trail. It's Christmas."

Claudia ignored the view and studied the carvings on the overlook's fenced deck, her fingers caressing gouged hearts that spread like spores across the damp wood. Squared initials and cupid's arrows repeated on the handrail and bench.

Peter was fairly certain that the only place his name would appear would be his tombstone, if someone went to the trouble. He tried to imagine Claudia as a teenager whose boyfriends sawed tributes into trees and tables.

She dawdled at unexpected intervals on the trail, wearing a listening look. Runoff from the morning rain gurgled through culverts. She brought her ear real close to a tree, face awash in wonder. Urban women.

He didn't worry until she stopped where a sudden creek had washed out the trail. She didn't respond to her name. He hopped over, picked her up and carried her across. "You're not made of sugar."

She crouched, hands wrapped around her knees, rocking and staring at a banana slug oozing its way across the forest floor.

"Hey." He pressed her with the side of his leg. She did not look up. "I said, 'Hey.'" Another nudge. "Let's go."

Thick fog clung to the trees. Needles condensed the mist. Rain dripped on them both. He followed her zigzag off the path. Forest duff thickened the topside of crumbling nurse logs. They walked over spongy carpets of moss. Sword ferns tickled their waists. He was soaked.

They made their way down the hillside, her steps cautious across stumps and roots. She pawed the air as if blind. No branches spanned their path. He kept her in front of him.

The next lookout jutted toward a sea cave like the prow of a ship. Thick-bodied birds flew into the maw, turning sideways to skim its striated surface. A teacher once took him out here, before there were boardwalks over the boggy areas, before signs were written to explain things to people who didn't know how or whom to ask for knowledge. She was teaching them something while he let the tide of his boyhood friends sweep him into a giddy lack of attention that marked most of his teenage years, before life pulled the rug out from under him. What was it? She said that Neah Bay was rising and moving northeast at the rate of more than an inch per year. "Making a break for Canada," Peter joked before she shushed him. "Going to visit our cousins."

The class lesson was about the earth's plates. They covered cardboard with peanut butter and slid a bunch of other cardboard pieces around on top, showing how the earth's crust moves on molten iron. She pushed one piece beneath another. "That's what happens here, offshore. Sometimes a piece of the earth's crust gets stuck as it slides below its neighbor. It builds up pressure." Her hands stopped, trembling in place. "Guess what comes when it pops loose and dives down? An earthquake."

The best part was watching girls lick the cardboard clean.

Claudia hunched over the corner of the platform, ribcage wedged over the top rail, feet off the ground. It was hard not to plant a hand on her shoulder. He shoved his fists in his jacket pockets. She could look after herself. He scanned the forest above the cave. A tree leaned into the wind, roots snaking down the cliff face, exposed. Below, any rock that escaped the restless water was streaked white with guano. Two thin gray figures wriggled on the highest reaches. Holy shit. Sea otters! They humped and scowled.

"Somebody's getting some!"

It was unnerving to be around a woman who didn't talk. Let him drift in her presence. Before his dad died, Peter spent his days scrambling around and cliff jumping with Randall, who hadn't yet sought a uniform to let people know his judgment mattered. Everywhere they jumped, rocks hid beneath. Even if it looked clear, they'd go in only to realize they could have died right there. Never a good place to pull out. Shoals cut their hands and chests. Their moms found out by doing their laundry, though Peter always blamed the blood on fish guts.

When Peter jumped from his favorite high spot, his arms and legs flared when he hit the water, flipping him upside down. It seemed natural to swim in the wrong direction. The sun was rarely out. Randall taught him to spit air and watch where the bubbles went. Follow your breath, he said when they surfaced, and it saved Peter a few times.

The temperature was dropping. It was near freezing, his favorite weather, the kind that let you know where you ended and the world began. Clouds rose from his mouth, mingling with fog feeding the trees, heading upland. He hurried down the path after Claudia.

Beyond her, the Pacific buckled into white caps all the way north to Tatoosh Island and west to the horizon. He could barely see the lighthouse. Mist veiled the low line of mountains on the far side of the strait.

Bypassing the raised wooden platform, she sidled up to the cliff's bare dirt lip. On the tree next to her, branches pointed east in deference to sea winds. During the summers of his childhood, Peter lay down to stare at the seals and sea lions and puffins zooming through the water. Later, he had a hard time finding a good spot. Too many legs shuffling into semicircles. Like Claudia, he often leaned out and hoped a sudden gust didn't come, knowing from the torque in his stomach that he'd be a goner if it did.

Looking at her was like peering over a cliff, something his mom used to yell at him for when he was a kid, before the tribe put a platform at Cape Flattery for the crowds that came to claim the northwestern corner of the lower 48, not knowing it was on another cliff. The tourists—white people, mostly, but Asians, too—chattered the reservation's unfamiliar name. "MAKah. MakAH. MaKAW." They flocked to peck at the view of Tatoosh Island and its lighthouse, hoping to take something home with them, if only a nature shot, soft focus and sepia toned like pictures they'd seen of Indians back in the day.

The toe of her left shoe hovered in space. The wrongness of this moment—it's happening now, he told himself, you must act—haunted him, as though he was already looking back with regret, peering down at them both, dizzy with vertigo, which, in the end, was a sick love of falling. He spoke her name. She did not answer. He stepped toward her, quiet.

When he was close enough, he bent his knees, leaned back and took her by the shoulders, clutching her to his chest and backing up, her feet dragging, her body limp in his arms.

He pushed her up the ladder to the relative safety of the enclosed space and side rails, her weight slack over his shoulder. Panting, he slung her onto the deck. "There's a better view from here."

She inched away from him until her back was against the banisters. Black hair blew around her face, her collarbones sharp beneath her skin, fragile as a downed bird. Her distant expression made it easier for him to feel something, to impose an emotion she might otherwise reject. He studied her pale skin, the dark shallows beneath her eyes and cheekbones, giving way to her stark beauty, which was unforgiving, that of bleached shells, the crisscross of branches in winter.

She knocked the back of her head against the railing.

"Christmas is hard for everybody, sweetheart."

Again. Again.

"Take my mom. First thing she did this morning was wander out of the house. Before it was light. She made it all the way downhill in the dark. No sidewalks. People on the road that early are just getting home. Not fit to be behind the wheel, you know?"

He waited. Waves splashed and crashed against rock, wind whittling pine needles off burl-knotted branches.

"I wake up, and she's gone. I jump in my truck. She was past the museum, nearly all the way to where the road climbs up 200 Line. In the goddamned rain!

"She says she can hear drumming. I don't know, Dave said there's a lot of spirits here, everywhere. 200 Line is one of the strongest places. Because of the creek that runs there. People used to hike up there to bathe. Purify themselves, you know? So they would be given a song."

Claudia stopped rocking.

"I guess two medicine men went up there one time. They fought. Only one came back. Plus when the small-pox came, people went up the creek to die. That's why it's haunted, Dave said, but I don't buy it. All the beaches here would be thick with ghosts. The whole goddamned place. Who knows.

"There's a bunch of housing built up there. The tribe is moving some services to higher ground. In case we get a wave, like Japan. But people keep hearing drumming and singing. Dave said he goes up there to clean houses. I asked him what that means. He said you have to be there."

Her eyes were open now, if not focused.

"Dave said I need to prepare her. For death. Asking her what she knows. If it's always been this way or that way in our family, and learning it.

"When she heard I was going to see you, she said it was okay. She thinks you'll convince me to go ahead with this party. And I don't want to, you know? She can't fix me. The things I want to learn, she doesn't want to tell me. About Dad. She shouldn't have been the one. I wanted to, sometimes, after he roughed her up. I had my reasons. Like you. You have your reasons why you're not home with your husband. You don't have to tell me, if you don't want to."

She squeezed her eyes shut like she'd been kicked.

"I'm talking too much. I just want you to know I understand. I know you hurt inside, like me."

Her mouth moved, soundless.

"Dave says we need a healing. I hate how he thinks he knows everything. Maybe he's right. We could try the warm up. Bring out the song. Even if it's just for us. Maybe she would get better."

Her shoulders were shaking, her lips a square, her head wilting on its stem. He gathered her into his arms. "It's gonna be alright, I swear."

He held her hand the whole way back. Welding taught Peter never to pull away too quick. Leaves holes damned near impossible to repair. He hadn't known that when he fled Neah Bay, full of self mastery, taking GED classes at community college, clearing tables, sleeping on couches when he got behind.

But the thing is, it's hard to fix someone else's weld, to get it to lay down nice and smooth like it would have if he'd been there from the beginning. To fuse steel, he learned to make a hole and let the liquid metal fill it, not too fast, not too slow, the arc so short it blurred into a halo. His shield went black when sparks flew. Only happened if he backed off too much. He couldn't help watching, though he saw spots the next day. His teacher kept potatoes on hand for people like him, with no self-control, who stared at the tiny sun of their own making. He sliced the spuds— that's what he called them—and put them on Peter's eyes with a reminder. "Next time, look away." Most of what he remembered from his apprenticeship flickered between the smell of matches and the sight of his neighbor's boots in a shower of sparks. His earplugs made everything sound like he was underwater. So that's where he went. There was work for those willing to risk their lives.

He always thought he would end up blown to pieces or pinned in silt. Crushed. Electrocuted. Running out of air before the topside crew figured out what was happening. That kind of thing. On good days, he didn't give a fuck about anything but getting it right in the cold wet dark. He felt then as he felt now. Emptied, relieved and at rest. Neutral buoyancy. Nowhere to go but up.

Back when they used to fish together, his dad talked about being on the boat—when the lines were set and their minds smooth as water, waiting for the fish—as being ready for anything but not in a hurry. That's how he felt. Prepared for what would come.

Peter locked the truck's doors as soon as they were inside. Cedars closed in around the road, jade branches laden with rain that splattered the windshield. Between their trunks, the sea flashed silver and pearl. The blur of pavement calmed him, as did the handlettered sign on the way to Hobuck.

HAVE COURAGE TO CHANGE

He felt peaceful, like a storm had cleared the air. The worst possible fate had washed over her and receded. Leaving its wreckage, true, but now all they had to do was pick up the pieces. He was good at that. At least he could try.

Peter didn't want to leave Claudia alone in her cabin, but he had promised to pick his mom up from Roberta's, and he couldn't stand to hear about another thing he hadn't done for her. It was dark by the time he pulled up to their curb. He beeped the horn so he wouldn't have to hear the happy shrieking over presents, wouldn't have to see the mosaic of family pictures of Sarah and Layla tumbling over each other with gap-toothed grins, John in a serious face and shorts that hung to his skinny calves, the entire family lined up, nice and neat, in front of changing backdrops—the marina, Randall's patrol SUV, a green mountain, a brick wall— Roberta looking the same in each photo, long hair draped around her, hands placed on a kid's shoulder or around Randall's broadening waist, the main indicator, aside from the children's heights, of the passage of time. He couldn't stand to watch Randall swagger like he owned the place, which, of course, he did. Peter's father never acted like that. By the time Peter started noticing those kinds of things, his dad treated his wife like she was a schoolmarm.

After they got his mother bundled into his idling truck, Peter turned on the radio, scrolling through AM's long fields of unused frequencies, hurrying past the distant voices of religious fanatics and the empty rush of news to land on a country music station. That'll do. He turned it up, static and all, and settled in for the short ride home, thinking on

Claudia, which had become a bad habit. There was the moment on the cliff. He massaged it in his mind until she was being incautious. He pulled her back to protect her, it's true, but only from a sudden gust of wind. When he held her, he could feel her need, its gravity, their friction, the pressure building to something more than a fuck buddy, for once.

She must be lonely, so alienated from her own life that she would choose to spend it with strangers. And wasn't that what he had always done. On the years when he weakened and accepted an invitation to spend a holiday with the family of some guy he met on a job, regret slapped Peter across the face as soon as he walked into the happy home, regret at being there, regret at not having this, regret at remembering the good times of his childhood, and the bad. Pulled up to their table, seeing the silliness of the kids make its way into adult faces, Peter saw how much he'd been holding in, and for how long. It was that, or a bar. Plan B became Plan A on the same day, more than once, but it seemed that was expected of roustabouts.

He used to keep a girlfriend for such occasions. Not the kind of woman you marry, but it was easier to put up with entitlement than to waste time bedding a new one with dinner and drinks. For a while, he got off on spending money. Every shore leave, he bought something—clothes, electronics, a little blow, if he felt like it. Living that life was like climbing a wall of butter. He grappled with every day and ended right where he started.

He got back here, and what had become of his mother? A hoarder. Shit stacked up to the ceilings. It felt like punishment for everything he hadn't become.

"Son."

"Yeah?"

"Watch out for these people."

A family of six waited next to a minivan parked at Ba-hobohosh Point. He braked to let them cross and leaned over the wheel to scope the beach. Great powdery gray billows rose above the black shore. People in jackets and hoodies and jeans stood in semicircles around clumps of smoke. He heard popping, flinched but broke out grinning as a giant flower cracked green fire across the sky. The night boomed, sparks streaming yellow and pink followed by rounds upon rounds of red, white and blue, leftovers from last summer.

Skyrockets screeched at the moon, spraying sparks that swirled up and shot off glimmering flashes. Willows and palms whistled and bloomed with bright splashes that burned out in long trails, going dark just above the heads of children who ran with sparklers, chasing each other in lines of sizzling light, their faces ashimmer with smiles. His mother laughed and clapped her hands beside him, their windshield twinkling red and green.

He saved his mom's gift for when they were alone at home, watching the Christmas specials. First he chitchat-ted to make sure she wasn't off somewhere in her mind. He had to watch it around her. Even so, the vaguer he tried to be about something—like, say, his future—the sharper she got.

Well, actually, she was the one who brought out a gift for him first. Made a big deal of it. He could see why. She wove him a hat. Not just any hat, but a big conical cedar hat with a knob at its top to show anyone who knew anything that his family was a force to be reckoned with since way back.

"For your big day."

The brim shaded his eyes and ears. He had to stand up straight for it to set right. He remembered tromping through forests when he was young to help her gather, peeling strips from cedars on the right day of the right season, the whole year a wheel that turned in her mind like shadows around a dial.

He knew her wrists hurt when she opened a jar or the fridge or anything. How many turns of the wrist to make a hat.

When she stopped crying and rubbing his back, Peter pulled out his wallet. Ignoring her grumbles about not wanting to be paid, he thumbed through bills. There, tucked in the fold, the only picture he ever kept, the one that survived. Her albums were black with mold by the time he opened them.

The photo was yellowed and rubbed white at the crease. The edges were soft and bent. Her bangs were curled into a halo above wings of feathered hair. She wore a thin striped sweater and flared jeans. One arm was blurred. The other held the handle of a pan. By her shiny smile, a drawing he made as a kid was tacked to the cabinet—their boat with a bunch of birds behind it. A hand towel was slung over her shoulder. There were wet spots at her hips. She used to let him wear her apron before his dad said the boy was too old for that shit. Behind her, his dad sat in his chair, laughing and pointing to something off frame.

"You kept this."

"I did."

"Don't you want it?"

"I know it by heart."

Chapter Nineteen

CLAUDIA FIXATED ON the chip in the windshield, forgetting her purpose until her tires grazed a rumble strip. Once she made it to her cabin, she stashed the pregnancy tests below the kitchen sink along with two boxes of condoms. She would get ahold of herself. Whatever that meant. It was bad enough asking the clerk to unlock the clear plastic case shielding the pregnancy tests. She made herself drive to Port Angeles for that pleasure, rather than risking it in Makah territory, but she couldn't go through with the ritual just yet, though it was familiar to sit, frozen on the toilet, stick in hand, staring.

She kept going back to their hike at the cape, the wind and waves droning an incantation that soothed her, quieting her mind to a single purpose, guiding her forward to what she must do, whispers converging into a wrathful symphony that turned discordant, the sweet lure of the cliff a lone oboe pulling her through. Just when she gathered her courage to step into her fate—to plummet—there was Peter, dragging her back.

She had wanted to taste the ocean and would have too, had it not been for Peter. Being with him was distracting. It was hard to hear the cedars rustle their warnings while he watched, making untimely disclosures, staring at her with carbon eyes whose color deepened the longer he looked at her, as if that were possible. She could see it in him, the attraction to her vulnerability, the need to cosset, to protect, when what she wanted was to be free, and fierce. It was all she could do to inhabit this body. His hand was slippery in hers, too hot. She had wanted to take off her clothes and roll in the moss.

Claudia couldn't eat, gripped by nausea that appeared upon waking. It was just what she deserved. She was disgusted by her own weakness, and yet she knew she should be asking for help, should be returning to Seattle for evaluation and treatment. Her sight had crystallized. Fractals spread across her field of vision like frost on glass, patterns repeating in trees, waves, blades of grass. There was no one she could tell who wouldn't create an echo chamber of rumors she could not afford.

Work would save her. It always had. She opened her laptop and, shying away from the Internet and its cruel tidings, began to type.

My arrival to Neah Bay coincided with the holiday season. Christmas is celebrated by many Makahs, even some who profess to hate Christians, and with strong reasons. The contradictions here are too numerous to be named, but they speak to selective adaptation of cultural practices as a way of exercising personal agency over assimilation. I began work right away, reconnecting with a prior research participant named Maggie, an elder with strong ties in the community. Joining us for the first time was her son, Peter, recently returned after a long and unexplained absence. Maggie had become a hoarder in the interim decades since her husband's death and her son's departure.

With the support of her son, I agreed to assist Maggie in sifting through what she had saved. It was my hope to salvage, repair, and catalogue any cultural materials we found while creating a safer and more pleasant environment for her to live in. Unfortunately, before I arrived, Peter burned all of her papers—directories, news clipping, photos, and who knows what else—which he claimed, perhaps accurately, were destroyed by mold and urine (Maggie has a fondness for cats). My rapport with Peter and Maggie was greatly aided by support of this large effort, which put us in close contact and allowed for intimate conversations about cultural preservation, tribal traditions, and familial loyalties.

Someone knocked. She tensed and checked her porch steps through the window. Peter. She was more thankful for his presence than she would have liked, but she kept her smile frosty. She owed him her life.

"I wanted to come earlier, but Mom's been on a rampage."

"I was just getting to work."

"So you're glad to see me."

"It's surprising how well you know me, considering."

"You're not as hard to figure out as you think." He stuck his hands in his pockets. "How's it going?"

"I'm alright."

"Been thinking about you. Can I come in?"

"I don't know. Any more choice comments to share?"

"You're doing better than I hoped." He tapped the riser with the steel toe of his boot.

"Thanks?"

"Come on, don't be embarrassed. Let me in!"

"I'm not embarrassed."

"Sure you are." He stepped up the last stair and hugged her. "But you shouldn't be."

She pulled him inside the door to protect herself from peeping eyes, but it wasn't paranoia that made her bury her face in his neck, tug off his smoky jacket, and guide him onto the couch, where she lay on top of him, glad for the long shifting warmth of his body, for his hands on the back of her head, on her waist, beneath her thighs, for his fingers finding the crease of her knees and drawing them close to his ribs so that, without meaning to, she was straddling a man who was moving and grinning like, how about now? What relief to be outside herself, if only for a moment, in his company.

Peter hovered behind her open laptop, sipping his coffee. "What are you doing?"

"Drawing up my fieldnotes. And some participant observations."

"What?"

"Fieldnotes are my account of my time here. A personal narrative. And the other stuff is more formal—observations about your family."

"Here." She heard him set his mug down behind her. "This should refresh your memory."

She faced the screen, resolute. He was not trained to leave her alone when she was writing, as Andrew had been. Something soft and damp pressed her cheek. She smelled ballsweat.

"That's it! Out!"

Laughing, he left with a kiss to the part of her hair. "See you at the house."

> As it happens, I was able to identify Maggie's intent in saving these items. While she disclosed to me during a prior interview that she had gathered materials for her son's review, that was not the whole story. In fact, Maggie had been buying and saving items for a potlatch that she wants to host for Peter, who she believes is in line to receive a song that proves chiefly

lineage and an accompanying dance, together known as his tupat, along with a mask and a rattle. Complicating matters is a competing claim on the song from Sam's brother's sons, who Maggie says have been performing the song without permission on neighboring reservations. In contrast to his mother, Peter does not seem to be bothered by the actions of his cousins.

While it remains unclear to me what brought Peter back after an absence of more than twenty years, it seems likely, from casual statements that he has made, that he will not stay for long, perhaps waiting for his mother's death before he departs, perhaps not. I believe the prior abundance of materials obscured the hoard's purpose from his view, and that his mother's hope for him was too closely guarded to be revealed before its time. During the fraught process of revelation, I agreed to assist Maggie in putting on the potlatch, which requires the accumulation of many gifts and foods, the invitation of hundreds of Native Americans, including what seems to be the larger part of the Makah tribe along with representatives of the Nuu-chah-nulth, the Quileute, and others. Peter is going along with the effort but seems ambivalent about his mother's plans for his future here.

I acknowledge that my participation politicizes my presence here. Perhaps fortunately, I have decided to refocus the terms of my inquiry to a qualitative study of this one nuclear family unit. There will be longstanding social, cultural, economic, and political repercussions—alliances both forged and riven—depending on which families decide to support Peter's claim. If Makah oral history is any indication, these consequences will play out for centuries. But that is outside the terms of my research.

There. She left out their affair, but it was a start. What did John Whiting say during a lecture, when he was too old to care what anyone thought? Oh, yes. "An observer is under the bed. A participant observer is in it." She doubted he foresaw her situation. Then again, she would not be the first, not at all. Besides, she told herself, everyone edits their own narratives. It didn't matter.

That was a lie. The stories we tell each other matter, but the stories we tell ourselves about ourselves matter the most. We lie so we don't have to change. She could look no further than her own life, but her shame was too great, so Claudia preferred to study Maggie, who trusted that her failings as a parent could be rectified if she pulled off this potlatch, and Peter, who thought running from his past would free him to be a better man. Neither story was true, but they were believed, clung to, a faith that carried mother and son through lives that were never what they wanted. Of all the practices Claudia had come to study, this basic element of survival was the most essential, a triumph of endurance beyond the scope of whatever remained of her research objectives.

She had bought the pregnancy tests as assurance. Not from true doubt or fear. And so it was with shocked awe that, having peed on the stick and her hand with it, she watched one line appear and soon enough, another alongside, saturating with blue as she rubbed her eyes with her dry hand. She hadn't been so unlucky. Strange that she felt more than fortunate, fingered for some higher purpose by a wise and mirthless judgment, made to pay and redeemed all at once. She was wild with joy and terror. There was no going back. She would keep this child.

Lights blinked along riggings throughout the marina. In the early fade of evening, they glowed into their satiny reflections. Claudia parked in front of Washburn's and girded herself to buy groceries and mingle with her new kin.

The store bulletin board was thick with advertisements

for electric lawn mowers, lost dogs, afterschool tutoring and computer repair. The overhang kept the rain off the welcome back signs for war heroes and the handmade posters for Baby Makah Days Queen and Makah Days Queen, the lucky names outlined in puff paint and covered in glitter, photos curling in humidity that persisted until August, when Makah Days came around again and the title passed to the next well-connected family. As with Claudia, eyed by other Latina panelists for her pallor, the girls in the photos didn't always look the part, blue eyes peering beneath woven cedar headbands, olive shells shiny in hair the color of wheat. Claudia's favorites were the babies with brown eyes and big cheeks.

In the three years she had been coming here, Claudia once saw sisters take the twin crowns of baby queen and queen. During the parade, veterans leaned out of trucks. A short prayer was said to bless the American flag since Makahs earned the right to vote in 1926. Claudia watched the sisters and their mother pass by in regalia that didn't match but echoed, the mother's fringed shawl trimmed with mother of pearl buttons that also traced the outline of her daughter's red cape and dotted the cedar barrette on the baby's downy crown.

Claudia's mother had dressed her and Maria alike for church until Claudia grew old enough to complain. After that, it was complementary, the navy blue of Claudia's striped shirt finding its way into her sister's shorts and their mother's headband. Her mother kept a hand on both daughters and smiled, munificent, at each person who passed them in the aisle. Later, examining the only photo she packed for boarding school, Claudia moved the flashlight over the faces of her dead mother and distant sister, their eyes seeming to squint against her examination. It had been a bright day. The sun was behind the camera. Only then did she realize that this small vanity, a monogramming of sorts, signaled to strangers that their trio was related.

No longer. Maria would not know she was an aunt, if Claudia could help it. She would protect herself this time.

People filed into Washburn's, hurrying to buy whatever they forgot to pick up on their last trip. Chips and salsa, soda, an extra steak, maybe some ice cream. A laughing couple ducked inside, hand in hand, trailing wet boot prints, the woman's belly ballooning well into the third trimester. In front of the soda machine, Claudia pretended to fumble in her purse for change. She could practice living here, though becoming part of this place, subject to its laws and customs, was daunting. She would have to take care of herself, no matter where she ended up. Thomas had no time for failures.

Maggie was halfway to the kitchen by the time the door swung open to the smell of melted chocolate and butter. "I have to pull these out or they'll burn!"

"Hi!"

"He's next door." Maggie's words were muffled by the interior of the oven, where she was stooped.

"I'm here to visit you." Well, not entirely. A fresh test prodded her thigh through her pocket. She wanted to be ready to tell Peter if the right moment appeared, and to furnish proof, if he doubted her. Though she hadn't decided whether to tell him, she was curious to see what he would say. Likely he would recall a clinic somewhere and offer to split the cost of a procedure he would assure her was simple and painless, so she could write him off forever, like she wanted. Beneath that whispered the hope for a witness to her unfurling. "I brought some tea."

Maggie slipped her spatula beneath rows of cookies, one after another, transferring them to wire racks that lined the counters.

"I've been writing up my notes." Claudia leaned close to a cookie and inhaled. Heaven. "I hope you'll be proud of the work we've done."

With a swollen knuckle, Maggie pressed the center of the nearest cookie. "I'm too short on time to sit with you today. One more batch to bake. Go see if the guys are finished? Take a few of these with you!"

"I'll just leave this tea on the coffee table."

The living room felt empty. Well, there was furniture, but nothing wedged between or around or beneath or behind it, each piece a goodly distance from its neighbor. A normal place to live, if you were poor. What joy her news might bring to this home. What sorrow, too. Claudia knew she wasn't what Maggie had in mind for her son.

Drumming shook Dave's house. Claudia neared his porch, her blood pounding. His door was closed. Whistling began, high and wild. She stopped. The Wolf Ritual? She had read about it thanks to Alice Henson Ernst. She'd never seen it. She regretted not cultivating Dave, though it was hard to look at him with fresh eyes, knowing what she knew.

Back in the day, Makah ceremonial leaders claimed the right to kidnap or kill anyone who intruded on a ritual or even the warm ups. She wavered. She needed to talk to Peter. Fear of being rebuffed—albeit by a gruff "Get out!"—kept her from drawing closer to the door.

Chapter Twenty

SEATED ON DAVE'S couch, his mother wrapped her lap with blankets, looking so Indian it confused him. Peter stooped by the TV, shuffling through stacks of games, imagining future evenings away from her newfound interest in sharing the teachings. His sassy mom, the social drinker and daily smoker, the tight-jeaned lady of his childhood had become something more, but also less, somehow. He missed her brassy self.

"We've got to get you prayed up and ready." She rustled through a plastic bag and withdrew a rattle shaped like a bird, its fat body and long wooden tail worn shiny by generations of hands.

"Ready for what?"

"Ready for your power." She tapped her foot and called at the hallway. "Dave, you all set?"

From the bathroom, Dave shouted, "Give me a minute!"

She fidgeted with the rattle, patting its feathers.

"Aren't we going to wait for Claudia?" Peter left the door open to the rain, in part to clear the smog of nicotine and tar emanating from the yellowed walls, but mostly to hear her car. He regretted not having picked her up.

"Peter, I asked you a question." His mother shook the rattle at him.

"Don't call the ancestors on me."

She looked askance at her hand, soothing the bird with a few strokes to its head. "Good, you haven't forgotten."

"About what?"

"The songs, son, and the dances."

"When would I have learned about that?"

"Your dad used to dance you as a baby. His mom came over and sang, too. We took you everywhere. Remember?"

Peter thought back to cold nights in the car, waiting for his parents to come out of a party, wondering who would drive, or if it would be his lucky night behind the wheel, which he loved but pretended to resent because it gave him something over them. Better to recall the dented legs of folding chairs, the understory inhabited by children during bone game tourneys their parents played for full days and nights, pausing for sips of Pepsi and bites of frybread and burgers, buoyed through hunger and exhaustion by the prospect of winning the pot, up to tens of thousands of dollars, a fortune. And him passed out, arm curled around his dad's ankle, until he got old enough to sneak smokes outside.

"I remember you gambling."

"You saw places, met people. Be grateful."

"I saw a lot of gyms."

"You met girls!"

"Them, I do remember. Thought you didn't notice."

"Why do you think we brought you?"

They laughed.

"What about the Indian parties?" She was persistent, if nothing else.

"I've tried to forget about your partying."

"You know what I mean. The potlatches!"

"When you used to make me stay up super late and bring

coffee to all the oldtimers? And sometimes the emcee would give me a quarter, and you'd make a big deal of it?"

"Yes! You danced."

"That was a long time ago."

"You're not so old as me, to have forgotten so much. Come sit."

Dave walked in with a drum in his hand, another hanging from his shoulder in a canvas bag. "Let's get down to business."

It was settled. The sharpness of his mother's eyes was such a comfort after the dense haze that he sat down at her feet with his legs crossed. Her dementia faded into the background now that she had something to pursue. But no—her derangement, her terror—they were different from her hysterias when he was young, which were desperate, to be sure, but tinged by reality. His dad did drink like it was his job, and he was gone a lot, and they were hard up.

"This song was given to your father by his father, long before you were born. You need to remember where this song comes from, and why it belongs to you. Your grandfather was given this song by his uncle . . ."

Dave broke in. "My granddad's brother."

". . . who only had daughters, during a big party in Neah Bay. There were lots of witnesses. His uncle got the song from his grandfather's brother."

"So the song came from my grandfather's uncle's great-uncle."

"This song made your grandfather a big man. It came with this rattle and a mask to go with the song. It was a pair of songs, actually, but one's been lost. There was a curtain too, but your dad got ahold of it."

"What did he do with it?"

"Sold it to a collector for next to nothing."

"What about the other stuff?"

"I kept them hidden. This here's the rattle. He was real mad about it."

"Where's the mask? I haven't seen it around."

"Learn this song, and I'll show you. One last thing. When your dad still spoke to his brother, he gave him permission to sing this song. But he took it back."

"Over what?" Peter was fairly certain it was about her. His mother was beautiful, once, and much sought after. His uncle's eyes rested on her whenever, wherever. He relished every chance to tell her how Peter was seen doing something he shouldn't have. "What he needs is a strong man to look up to," he said once, within earshot. She folded her arms at the door, withering her brother-in-law with quiet, until he finally left, and she broke her own rules and went for a cigarette in the bedroom her husband hadn't slept in for days.

"He started singing at out-of-town parties. Your dad wasn't going. And I couldn't go. I had to work. He was supposed to check with your dad each and every time. He didn't. If I had been there, I would have stood up and said something, paid him in public. Shamed him till he stopped.

"Your uncle claimed he was keeping our culture alive, making sure no one else laid claim to it, but he was staking out our song. Always changing his story—one day, he'd tell someone Sam gave him the song outright. Another day, he'd say your grampa made up his mind to take the song from Sam and give it to him. Or he'd say his father gave it to both his sons. Anything. He'd say anything. His sons have been up to the same bad business."

"Mom, I don't mind if they share a song with me."

"Peter, you've got to know what's yours." Dave leaned forward. "Your cousins use that song to get privileges. They've taken status from you."

"Okay, I get it. What else?"

"There's a story that goes with the song. For people who know, the song kind of cues you into the story. And if you don't know, you don't need to know." She straightened. "The story begins like this.

"Way back when, the men in your dad's family were whalers. If you'd been here fifteen years ago, you could have been one, too. There's still time. But like I was saying, your ancestors hunted whales. The man who wrote this song was the bravest one in the canoe. He would get in the water after they harpooned the whale. It was his job to sew up the whale's mouth so it wouldn't sink."

Dave leaned forward. "They tied seal floats to the whale to tow it in."

"Shh, I'm telling it. Can you imagine that, Peter? The whale's tore up. It is big, and bleeding all over. He dove into the ice cold water and looked it straight in the face. He kept his back to the whole ocean! That's in your blood, son.

"And he's doing it, he's using some innards to sew up the whale's mouth. Along comes a seal. Playful. At least they can be. But there's blood in the water. Makes animals aggressive. People, too.

"That seal keeps bumping the back of his head. Believe me, he's trying to hurry up. But you can't rush good work. Sewing is tough! Easy to lose your materials. Especially when the waves are going every which way. He's kicking to stay afloat, trying to stay with the whale. No idea what's beneath his feet.

"Every time he came up for a breath, the seal did, too. Darned thing wouldn't leave him alone! But he's almost done with his job. One part of it, anyway. They still had to get the whale to shore."

"It could take a week, pulling day and night, if a storm came up."

"Dave, I said, 'shhh!' I'm telling it. The seal noses him in the back of the head, and he turns around to poke back. And that's when he saw them. Killer whales knifing through the water. Straight at the whale. Straight at him.

"He just about died. But what he did was, he got in the canoe, quick as could be. The seal flew through the air. Flung up, you know. He figured he'd been saved by it. Warned."

Though he once watched hundreds of hammerheads pass over him, their shadows dappling his mask, Peter never saw a whale below water, let alone a killer whale. He had always been grateful for the latter, but right now he felt cheated. He wasn't given the chance to test his mettle like the old ones. Or, more like, the things he was tasked to do would wear anyone down. Where were the spectacular high water marks he could brag about later? Nowhere to be seen.

"This song came to him. About his tumanos. Do you know what tumanos is?"

"Don't act like I didn't grow up here." Peter stood. "I need some air."

"Alright." She looked down at her hands. "I could use a break, too."

"Mind if I join you for a smoke?" Dave was already getting up.

"It's your porch." Peter stepped outside and tapped a cigarette from the pack. He heard his mother shuffle to the bathroom and turn on the faucet as soon as she closed the door, a sure sign she was crying. He wanted to get away.

Dave's lighter rasped. "My back is aching. You ever had a

hurt back? Never leaves you alone. Just like a woman, always telling ya you should be doing something different."

Peter eyed his neighbor. Cagey old codger. Together, they puffed and watched wind move through the branches of cedars along the horizon.

"Peter, I done things I'm not proud of, things I would change if I could. But you can't go back. We can only move forward, and that's what I want to help you and your mother do, move forward. Honor the past, of course, but keep it moving. It's too easy to get stuck in time." He nodded toward their home. "You see where that gets you. Addicted to the pain. I been there, going back to pain like it keeps giving. All it does is take."

Peter listened for Claudia's car. He was in no mood for lectures.

"You two done yet?" His mother pounded the door from inside. "The day is getting away from us."

From the edge of the coffee table, Peter kept an eye on the street. His mom clapped her cupped palms crossways in tempos that quickened and slowed in strange places. In bone game, the main speed was 'let it rip.' Dave picked up the beat right away, the soft head of his drumstick finding a worn spot on the face of his drum. Peter waited, listening.

"They sang this in the canoe. We'll do it again. I'll sing." Her arms swayed back and forth over her knees. "Tumanos wo hey a hey hey, tumanos wo hey ahey o ahey o." Her voice sunk low, ascending as she repeated those words, the melody shifting beneath her like water.

It had been decades since he heard someone sing the Makah way—husky, open-throated, so unlike the strident, piercing Plains Indian powwow songs. Makah songs boomed like the ocean in a cave, waves that crescendoed and subsided, echoing in his chest.

"Hear that drum?" She clapped when Dave's steady dun-dun switched to dun-dun-dun. "Time to change your steps. Back in the day, they used to sing it through five times. We'll do two or three because the dance is so hard. You'll be down real low."

He would have to dance. In front of everybody. Of course.

Peter found a rhythm with his mother. They got small things done in near proximity to each other, their gradual circumnavigations forming slow constellations in their home, where he promised himself he'd never live again—a trailer, yes, a doublewide. When their eyes met, it was with the agreement that they would not argue, their loose layer of friendliness like loam over hardpan.

He stopped waiting for Claudia to visit, went instead to check on her, and more often than not, found her in bed, where they ended up staying. She was listless, said she didn't feel like drinking, no matter what he brought over, so he made his way through the whiskey he gave her. She hadn't been saying much, but he told himself he was tired of talking. It was nice to find a reprieve.

But her silences were worrisome, if his life experience was any indicator. Women pipe down when they're planning something unpleasant for their partners. Which he was, he supposed. He was her partner, at least in putting on this potlatch. That was not nothing. They could build on that. The best cure for the blues was something to do.

He reached down to clasp the arch of Claudia's foot,

startled at his own smell, theirs together, a rich musk tinged sweet by rutting. "Let's take a shower."

Peter held her hand down the hall, held it when he reached in to start the hot water, held on while she stepped into the shower, their knees bumping against each other as they shifted beneath the spray. The water wrapped them in warmth, holding them together, glistening.

"Why haven't you come over? Mom's been telling stories. I thought you would like it."

"I need time to myself. Christmas knocked me off guard."

He ran his thumbs over her eyelashes, cheekbones, lips. It felt like he'd never been this close to anyone, but that wasn't enough. She was closed to him, a black box. "Why are you here, Claudia?"

"I fucked up. I'm trying to make things right."

"We all feel that way."

She kissed him, water filling their mouths wherever they parted, his soapy fingers slipping down her back and around her thighs, working the suds over her, into her, back and forth, her hands clenching his shoulders, body curling toward him, breath loud in his ear.

Too good to last. He knew that. He knew it when he toweled her hair, knew it when he pulled her close in bed, knew it when the first light of day silvered their bodies. She had a husband, a whole life. And what do I have, Peter thought. If I died right now, I would leave so little behind, even less than my dad did. Just this body, and a mother with not much time to grieve.

A dream sprang from the depths of his slumber, winding and curling around the swirl of his thoughts until, one by one, they succumbed.

Chapter Twenty-One

THE CARPET, WALLS and kitchen tile were a light dull brown, punctuated by dark laminate bookshelves crammed with baskets and carvings. An autobody repair shop calendar, out of date by more than a decade, was pinned to the wall.

The old man held up the invitation. "Coming up quick. That's a pretty tight turnaround." What was the man's name? Frank, she thought. And he was. Most people would keep their mouth shut until you were long gone and others were sitting where you had been.

Maybe that's why they came here first. Maggie insisted on delivering some invitations in person. She and Roberta divided the list into visits and stamps before Claudia arrived with the invitations. She didn't get to hear them map the tribe's hierarchy, their loyalties laid bare. Instead, she stuffed envelopes, shaky, dipping a sponge in water to wet the glue.

Roberta shrugged. "No one has anything planned that weekend—and the Devils don't have a game—so."

Printed on the best paper Claudia could find, the invites sucked all the ink from her cartridge, twice. Returning to P.A. for supplies had depleted her, controlling the car's working parts and lights and beeping noises almost beyond the energy she could marshal. She collapsed onto the couch with her feet up when she got back, dragging herself to her task hours later, her printer soon zipping along, layering colors, the mask emerging, over and over.

Maggie was happy when she first saw the invites, but maybe Claudia should have ordered something professional from a print shop. Makahs pay attention to things like that. Frank ran his fingers over the photo. No embossing here. Claudia felt like someone should say something to him, but supplying the paper did not buy her the right to speak. Since they got here, Roberta had been the only one talking.

"We've been prepping for years. Can you make it?"

All three women held their breath. It was just as well. The air stank of a long solitude. From the walls, Frank's face beamed next to a woman's, their white hair tufted into powdery clouds.

He rubbed his hands together. "Who's running the mic?"

"Dave," croaked Maggie.

"Ah." His expression pulled into itself. "That's good." Claudia surmised he thought he would emcee, run things his way. Propriety depended on perspective. Any family slighted—by the order of introductions, the lineup of dances on the floor, or the value of gifts—would criticize. Everyone else fell in line depending on blood, politics and business. Maybe Dave would run the floor right. Or maybe he'd finish what he started decades ago and run this family into the ground.

"We are so glad you'll be there to represent your family." Roberta smiled.

These pilgrimages to power centers across the reservation would take weeks. Across the street, a woman cut her lawn, circled by a muscular black dog that played with the mower, closing in on its leading edge and bounding away. In a frenzy of barks, the dog peeled off to lope alongside a passing car, biting the tires. The house next door had grass to its eaves, tufting around its trove of rusted boats and cars. The rest of the block was uncluttered, if weatherbeaten.

Stroking the frayed armrest of her chair, Claudia glanced out the window at the blustery length of Wa atch Beach, picturing what she had almost done, their child a silent partner to her free fall, a hummingbird stilled in a cocoon gone cold, gone the precise temperature of the ocean, gone. This baby needed another protector, but she couldn't bring herself to tell Peter. He might want to correct the flaws of his parents badly enough to become a father. He would have a claim. This child belonged with these people.

She needed to decide before she started showing. At the rate she'd been tearing into bread late at night, shoving doughy handfuls into her mouth with one thought—baby needs carbs—she would pop soon.

"Claudia." Roberta's voice was sharp.

"Oh, sorry. You were saying?"

Frank snorted. "I knew I was boring! Finally, an honest woman!"

Everyone laughed. Maggie looked embarrassed. You and me both, Claudia thought. "I'm so sorry!" She flapped her hands like a seal.

Roberta asked after some distant cousin, and they were off again, sharing stories about the fortitude of Makah canoe families at last year's gathering of tribes. Coffee cans brimmed with eagle feathers around the room. Claudia paced to the nearest spray of plumes and traced the wavy edge of the tallest one from the metal lip to its tip.

"You like those, huh?" Everyone was looking at her. "I was quite a hiker when I was young. I walked every ridge of our U and A, from Ozette to the Pysht."

She picked up a small cedar canoe atop a bookcase full of baskets. A lightning serpent wound along its side to emerge with oblong eyes and bared teeth as the prow.

"My son's a carver. He's working on the full size version for Tribal Journeys. That's just the model. Showed me his vision."

"Come sit. You're making me nervous." Roberta held out a cracker. "Worse than my girls, getting into everything!"

"She's alright. Besides, I got an appointment."

"We'll get out of your hair." Roberta rose to help Maggie. "Thank you."

"No hurry! Thank you for this Indian tea." He patted a plastic bag of spiny green leaves. "The wife always hoped it would soothe my bellyaching."

The corduroy chair creaked and rocked in his absence. He shambled over and reached past Claudia to pluck a downy feather from the can.

"Come by anytime." He pressed the quill into her fingers. She embraced him before she could stop herself.

On the way to their next stop, Roberta's eyes rested on Claudia in the rearview mirror, questioning, assessing. Tsoo-Yess Prairie rippled by. Makahs used to set fire to rare swaths of flat land to keep back trees and encourage cranberries and elk to return, season after season. What were her mother's last words? Moments of seeming devastation are your greatest opportunity, she'd said. When all's been laid to waste, pick any direction and start walking.

Tsoo-Yess River appeared, flat and gray, its mouth hooked like a salmon's. She rolled down the window to hear its rushing gurgles and with them, slow murmurs, riffles of conversation swelling into a cocktail party. She never disclosed rivertalk to anyone, least of all Andrew, who chose riverbanks for campsites on the regular, before they only said "I love you" to get off the phone. Would he be surprised to learn how devastated she was? How she'd tried twice.

She picked at a shiny red stain the size of a dime on the seat next to her. Melted crayon, by the looks of it. She slid a nail around its edges and lifted until she heard the velour tear. She switched to fiddling with her wedding ring, which cinched her swollen finger.

"Where are we going?" Maggie fidgeted in the front seat.

"We're going to pay a visit." Roberta patted her shoulder.

Claudia rubbed her open hand on the velour. Her sweaty palm left a dark damp trail on the fabric. She was running hot these days.

"What's the big occasion?" Maggie jiggled her leg.

Roberta flexed her hands on the wheel. "We are dropping off an invitation."

"Whose party?"

Roberta's eyes sought Claudia in the rearview. "Peter's."

"When's he coming home? I miss him." Maggie played with the plastic bag in her lap. "Sometimes I think I'll die before he gets here."

Roberta glared at the road, forehead wrinkled like a walnut, and eased her car onto a gravel shoulder. To their right, a long beach held back the gray water, unbroken but for a smattering of sea stacks offshore. Up ahead on their left, a freshly painted home advertised its front yard as a 24 H MONITORED parking lot. Just beyond, two hikers with towering backpacks tried to thumb a ride down the road to the Shi Shi Beach trailhead.

Roberta checked her watch. "You know, auntie, I forgot. I have to pick up my girls. Maybe we ought to do this another day."

"Oh, sure, sure." Maggie pinched her pants and rubbed the fabric between her fingers. The small scratch of sound filled the car. This was her child's grandmother. Maggie deserved to know, even if she wouldn't remember.

Roberta made a U-turn and rolled back through the prairie. Wind flattened the grass. They plunged into the forest and back out onto the bridge. Wa atch River dimpled beneath a sudden rain.

"You know, one time this land was covered in water." Maggie swept condensation from the window with her sleeve. "Cape Flattery was an island. Can you imagine that?"

"It's not hard to picture." Roberta cleared her throat. "Scary, though."

"The water left. Four days later, it came back. Swallowed this whole place. The only ones who survived had canoes. Lots of them died, too. The water went out again. Their canoes came down in the trees. Others drifted north and started a new village."

James Swan recorded a version of this flood story in his diary. Quileutes say that long ago—but not so long—their people saw the horizon blot out the sun. They tied their canoes together and anchored them to trees. Some lines broke. The wave swept canoes to the other side of the peninsula. Survivors founded the Chimakum tribe in and around what is now Port Townsend. Similarities between the otherwise linguistically isolated Quileutes and Chimakums bore out the story. Chief Si'ahl, Seattle's namesake, led a raid to wipe out the Chimakum, hardly the pacifist that whites made him out to be.

Others told of people climbing mountains when the rivers turned salty and the rains began. To no end. Drowned. They told of sea beasts stranded by the receding waters. Of a mighty battle between Thunderbird and Whale—or was it Kwa-Ti? Of Thunderbird's rage. Of Whale's demise.

"Where'd you hear that story, Maggie?"

Maggie turned toward the back seat. "Who're you?"

"I'm Claudia." She blushed. "Your friend."

"I don't think so."

Roberta stroked Maggie's hair. "You're just worn out, sweetheart. Putting on a big event is stressful."

They passed under the alders and headed up Diaht Hill. Maggie kept looking at Claudia in the side view mirror, suspicious, probing. Roberta cast apologetic glances over her shoulder. Claudia shrugged and winked like it didn't hurt. Maggie forgot Peter was back. Best not to feel wounded.

I am carrying your future inside of me, she thought. We are family, bound by blood.

Ostensibly she was in Neah Bay to research a book, but what she wanted to know was how belonging somewhere—really and truly belonging somewhere—formed people and their worldview. Being here only served to remind her of how orphaned she felt. How very much alone, until now.

Could she take root here? There were a lot of Mexicans married to Makahs, multicultural Latinos whose families believed in being Makah, and it was that common faith—and selective claim—that sustained the song system, which joined them as a tribe in thought as well as blood. Peter's family was a link that would remain broken until an event of epic proportions resurrected itself from the times when those things were believed possible. With this potlatch, Maggie was reaching for eternity.

What could the city offer this baby by way of a future, and not just the gratification of material needs? Urban dynasts redistributed wealth in small, tax deductible increments exchanged for the recognition of donor lists. While Claudia wanted to believe the Makahs were better, somehow, it was just difference, and everything good had its downsides. As compromised as her ambition could be, upward mobility was only available in a society as voracious and forgetful as mainstream America. Makahs were anchored by oral history but also burdened by gossip, and if there was one thing she wanted, it was to forget.

So maybe it was the scale of the potlatch, and not its principles, that distinguished Makahs. You could give it all away, but collective memory was long enough for bounty to come back to you and yours long after this generation was gone. It wasn't a group of people warming up a big hall in a small town on the far edge of a continent. It was a place in time, flowing backward and forward, without end.

Chapter Twenty-Two

THEY REPEATED THE song. Again. Again. Until Peter could beat the drum without faltering. Until his arms buzzed long after he stopped playing. He was singing, and his mom was singing, their voices in unison but octaves apart.

The drums sustained him like coffee, except the effect didn't wear him out. Like cigarettes, without clouding his breath. Like whiskey, if you took out the hurt. Like nice cold beers on hot days, minus the gut.

No, that wasn't it. The drums were like water. Downright necessary. Like sex, if the world weren't so fucked up.

Claudia showed up in the open door, blocking the light, her face rapt.

Dave patted the couch. "Join the party."

"Please don't stop for me." Claudia stayed put. "That was great."

Peter turned to his mother. "Why are there so few words?"

"When you know the story behind the words, it doesn't matter how many there are. Each word brings the story back."

"Will you tell the story, Maggie?" Circling around Peter, Claudia sat between his mother and Dave.

Dave rubbed her leg. "Good to see ya, Claudia."

She patted his hand. Peter's chest compressed with one thought—look at me. He liked her better when they were alone. When she was his.

"Son's grandfather died before he could pass on everything."

"I'm sorry to hear that. Will Peter be named for him?"

He cut in. "We haven't discussed it."

"Oh, sorry . . . um, were those vocables at the end there?"

"What?"

Dave answered. "Vocables sound like words, but they don't mean anything. They help carry the song through where words used to be, parts that have been forgotten."

Peter said nothing. He hated looking stupid.

"I told you to come over more, didn't I?" Dave dropped Claudia's knee and pulled the drum over his lap.

"You never ask me over." Randall's voice rumbled from the doorway.

"Doesn't stop ya." Dave laughed. "I guess you better come in."

"Sorry we're late!" Roberta piped in from behind Randall. "It took a while to get the girls out the door."

"Did you bring them?" His mom craned to check the area around Randall's knees, pushing to get off the couch.

"Nope." Arms spread wide for a welcome hug, Roberta flitted around Randall, wet hair sticking to her button-down shirt. "We took them to his auntie's house."

"Too bad."

Roberta gave a quick, pained smile. "We have a lot to go over."

He couldn't stomach another session on protocol. "Mom, why don't you tell a story we can all enjoy? I need a break."

"Happy to. I have just the thing."

Randall set up two folding chairs to face the couch. With a grandiose sweep of his arm, he pulled one back for his wife and settled in as Maggie began the story.

"The people had no light. They didn't even know what light was. They lived in the dark. They were cold. Kwa-Ti went to find light. He was bored with all the shivering and the moaning and the hunger. He walked and walked. He climbed mountains. He crossed rivers. After a long time, he came across a house. There was a big pile of mussel shells outside." She traced an arc with one hand and smiled.

"He was so hungry. He sat a while to see if anyone was home. It was quiet, but there was smoke coming from the house. He crawled to the pile. He hid in the bushes and snatched whatever was closest. He sucked the juices from the shells at the very edge.

"Well, you know Kwa-Ti. Before long he forgot about hiding and started clawing his way into the pile to get more. He rolled around and grabbed big handfuls. Shells tumbled off the heap. They made a big clatter.

"It wasn't long before Moon came out of the house. She stared at Kwa-Ti. Her eyes got smaller and smaller until they were bright little slits. She called for her dad. He came outside and hauled Kwa-Ti by the fire to get a good look at him. Kwa-Ti said he was too hungry to remember where he came from, but he would work if they gave him mussels. Moon was tired. Her hands were rough from scrubbing and cleaning. She looked at her dad with all that tiredness in her eyes until he said okay.

"But he didn't trust the newcomer. Kwa-Ti worked in that house for a year. He chopped wood. Cozied up to Moon. She glowed and grew big in the belly. Still, when she and her dad gathered mussels, they left Kwa-Ti at home.

"At first, Kwa-Ti didn't mind staying back. It was warm by the fire and cold and dark outside. But he got antsy, like always. He remembered why he was there."

She looked at him. "Why was Kwa-Ti there?"

Peter sighed. She made him feel ten years old. "He was there to find light for the people."

"That's right." She nodded. "One day, Moon's father was busy building a new house for his daughter. Moon was getting rounder and rounder. He told Kwa-Ti to help her get mussels. She led Kwa-Ti to the cove where they kept their canoe.

"Kwa-Ti paddled along the dark shore. How was he supposed to see the mussels? He kept quiet. Soon enough, Moon pulled out a small leather bundle. She unwrapped it. Inside was a very old mussel shell. It glowed. Rays of light came through its cracks.

"Moon opened the shell. A sunbeam shot out. For the first time, Kwa-Ti could see the black rocks were covered in orange and purple starfish. Something fierce woke in his heart. His chest squeezed. He tried not to breathe too hard. Moon opened the shell all the way. Day leapt from her hands and onto the green land and blue water.

"Kwa-Ti almost died, he was so happy. He played it cool. They tied up to a big stump. Kwa-Ti held Moon's hand. He steadied the canoe when she stepped out onto the rocks.

"'I'll show you how,' Moon said. 'Hold this.' She picked up a cedar basket and handed him the shell. The mussels closed up tight onto the rocks. She bent over—it took some doing because of her big belly—and scraped mussels into her basket with a clamshell.

"When she turned back to the canoe, Kwa-Ti was a speck on the horizon. He'd cut the line and never looked back.

"That is his way. He has always been this way." Her eyes flickered to Claudia, who was looking at her own hands.

"He left the shell open so Moon could find her way home. That's what he told himself. But really, he liked seeing everything. He didn't think about their baby or how the rocks would cut up her feet. He sweated and pulled. His greedy heart thumped in his chest. He looked at the big bright world."

Foreboding hung on Peter. Was his mother accusing him? Of what? Out with it.

"Moon was so mad at herself. She didn't even take time to cry. Ran home right away. She slipped on the rocks. The mussels sliced her feet to bits.

"Her dad knew when he saw her run up the path. Red footprints followed her. He went to ask Rainbow to bring Kwa-Ti back. Rainbow stood on the horizon and stretched his arms far as they would go. Kwa-Ti's canoe was beyond his claws.

"And so it was done. The people got the Day. That is the end of the story. *Shuh.*"

Everyone clapped but Peter. He didn't want to give his mother the satisfaction. He felt implicated, somehow, for something he'd done or hadn't done or was about to do. His mom ladled unwanted instruction over what was supposed to be a welcoming moment. She was sneaky like that. Always had been. She couldn't be trusted. Then again, no one could, not in the stories she'd been telling him since he was a kid.

Love is a kind of home. Later that day, shifting close, chest to back, he wrapped Claudia's ribs with his arms, chin topping her crown to rest on her forehead, legs folded loose over hers.

Their shadow was soft on the sheets. He was nostalgic for this love even as he lived it. He couldn't say why he cracked open when she came into his life, why it had to be her, why it happened at this time and in this way, but it happened. It was happening. He wanted her. He had never wanted anything so bad. He pressed his dick between the swells of her ass and filled his lungs, ribs bowing into the arch of her back. His legs were sore from dancing. He felt like a man. When they were lying in bed, he didn't have to worry about the future or mull over the past. He could just be. If they stayed here, entangled, dewy where they overlapped, their world of two felt real and true. Realer and truer than anything.

Submerged in bed, she kept his attention, slowed his breathing, stilled his thoughts, narrowed his senses to a steady state, focused on thin blade of shoulder, pale crook of arm, valley below cheekbone, sharp ridge of lip. He wanted to bathe in her, wanted to toss their togetherness around in great handfuls. Wanted to eat the light on her skin, drink her sheen of sweat. Wanted to smoke the smell of their sex, roll it up and set it ablaze.

Wanting was not the same as having. She'd been acting distant. Preoccupied. Wouldn't drink or smoke with him. Women were like that. They'd do outrageous things then turn on you for nothing. When she split, he would, too. He didn't expect to go with her. He couldn't picture a place where they belonged, couldn't see her by his side in front of changing skylines. His daydreams came back to them, right here, naked. Stark. No debts, no claims.

Maybe they'd see each other. Maybe. That's what he told himself to ease the desperation. They didn't owe each other anything, but they could build a room like this someplace else. They could choose to be reborn into an unknown better than who they'd been, what they'd seen. A big, bright, blank future.

He nudged her. "You awake?"

"No."

He cupped the pooch of her belly. She sucked in and held still, her body taut, unmoving. "You don't have to, you know. It's cute." Women were always so worried about their bodies. He didn't know how to make her accept herself, and he never would. That's not something you can do for another person. Some women had done what they could for him, and he tried not to remember them when he was lonely, tried not to remember how they had opened themselves to him, shared the sadness no one saw, too distracted by the nice body and shiny hair that were, to be honest, what attracted him in the first place. At least he didn't tell their secrets. Women put up with serious shit from an early age, is all he would say. But Claudia, she could put their whole lives in her book. And it wasn't the facts he minded so much, but her power, how she could place his family on a grid and insert the pin. People would believe her words because they were printed, or worse, gone viral, preserved online in perpetuity. She held their story in safekeeping that felt more like custody.

Weeks went by without his mom wandering, but it was bound to happen once he'd let down his guard. Of course, it was Roberta who noticed, charging into Dave's house, distraught and full of accusations. "She's gone!"

Peter and Randall quit drumming as one, but Dave kept on for a few more beats, sweat running from his forehead. Peter put his shirt back on and headed toward the door. Roberta stepped into his path.

"Claudia didn't notice your mom had left." She brushed off Randall's hand, her eyes fixed on Peter. "She was sitting in the kitchen, rubbing a basket, while your mom wandered off."

Peter stopped. "Where is she now?"

"Which one are you worried about?"

Dave picked up his keys. "I'll get Maggie."

"No, wait." Peter remained planted. "I should go."

"What's one more time? She expects me." Dave was out the door, just like that. Wobbling down his concrete pavers, he called through the rain, "We'll keep at it when I get back."

"Hold up, Dave! I'll go with you." Randall pointed at the door. "This is what I'm talking about. For years, Peter. Years. And when you do show up, you're half checked out. That woman is here for her career, Peter. Not because she cares about you, or Maggie, or any of us. You watch. She won't come back here but once a year, if she's feeling generous."

Roberta waited until the car left to lay into him. Tapping her foot in anger, just like when she was a girl, she looked like she was going to start hopping around. "What is going on with you?"

"It's going to be fine. We were next door."

"Why is she here if she's not going to look after your mom when she's right in front of her? That's sick."

"She probably thought mom was in the bathroom."

"Your mom is old, okay, and it's cold and rainy outside. Something could happen to her. She could slip and fall. She could catch pneumonia. She could get hit by a car. Don't you care?"

"Why are you yelling? This has been happening, Roberta. My mom wants me over here with Dave. I'm doing the best I can."

"You're barely trying." She tossed her purse onto the couch and strode into the kitchen.

He heard her run the faucet, the familiar clink of plates in the sink. Roberta was so good all the time. It never occurred to him to do Dave's dishes. "You're upset, and I understand that. But Mom asked for Claudia's help." Her back to him, Roberta shifted from one foot to the other. "I know you did a lot."

"Every time I come by, you're someplace else." She plunked a soapy glass upside down on an old dish towel and plunged her hands into the sink, rustling up a handful of forks and knives. "With her."

"She's got nothing to do with this. Besides, we've both been working our asses off to make Mom's place fit to live."

"Here it comes." Sponge in hand, she scrubbed and sloshed. "You think it was easy to bring my kids there? We brought her food. We kept her going."

"I said, 'Thank you!' How many times do you want me to say it?"

Roberta dried glasses with a towel, working them over like she could rub the shine off them. "You have so much growing up to do. There's not enough time in the world. We've done everything for you. You act like it's nothing."

"Why are you pretending like you're the only one who feels anything? I came back. It wasn't easy. It's not like I left for no reason."

"Don't even try that, Peter." She slung cutlery into a drawer with reckless clangs. One after another, knife followed spoon followed fork. "Do not go there."

"Can't we agree to get along?"

"What is it, exactly, that you think I've been doing since you got back?"

"Waiting for your chance."

"Oh, you little . . ."

Super quick, like when they were kids, Peter put Roberta into a headlock and noogied her head. She swatted at his fist, slapping his arm. "Stop that!"

"Not till you say 'Uncle!'"

"Peter, no! You can't."

Her rapid blows became an occasional punch. He knuckled the bumps of her skull. Her hair rasped. "Relax, Momma Bear. Everything will be fine."

"My daughters have better coping skills than you." Her body became womanish beneath his palms, warm and soft and solid. He let go.

"I've looked after myself my whole life."

The deal she proposed was simple. After the potlatch, Peter could leave knowing his mom would be cared for—if he let them sing his song, bring it into their family, which after all was a blood connection, not too far back. He didn't know what to say. He knew his mother wouldn't approve. So did they. He didn't have a better idea. "I'll think on it" was all he said to send her home.

"We'd keep it going." Roberta tried to meet his eyes. "It's still yours."

The sour part of Peter wanted to believe this was why they'd been looking after her. Wanted to believe that inside, they were sad and selfish, too. The rest of him knew they had him figured. They didn't want to see good wisdom go to waste when he died alone in some apartment. And they were right. He would leave. Tooling through town in his truck, he could smell it on himself. Restlessness. He needed to make a beer run, but strangely, he didn't want to. Or he wanted to, but the wanting was separate from who he was. He could see it from afar, the wanting. He held it at arm's length for the first time in a long time. It was weird. This ability worked on him like guilt. Another thing to add to the list.

Of course, Dave kept nagging him about staying sober. Said it was part of the journey. Thing is, some people can drink, and others can't. It's not fair who gets to be what, but there you have it. Dave couldn't drink because he did fucked up things when drunk, to hear him tell it. But me, I'm different, Peter thought. I don't have to drink. I drink when I want to.

Ray's was right there. Better yet, he could go to P.A. and stock up on some 24 packs. He was tired of running out. Maybe he should pick up Claudia, take her with him. She was probably holed up in her cabin. What did she do in there? What could she learn from a laptop? A road trip would do her good. They could crack the first beers on their way back. He pulled a U-turn in a driveway as soon as the thought hit him. He cruised past the beaches along Front Street, past the senior center full of elders eating lunch.

Inside the breakwater, the bay was calm. On the far side, the sea heaved skyward. Waves tossed foam to the wind. Clouds hurried from Vancouver Island to cluster over Neah Bay, backing up over the strait, where they darkened, gathering force. Just before the bend in the road, a culvert emptied onto the beach, seagulls standing in sentinel formation around an overturned trike, one handle's silver streamers flowing with the current toward Waadah Island, the others dangling limp in the rain.

At the fort's semicircle of flags, Peter pulled off and ran into the shelter, breathing hard. Between pillars of smoothed trunks, historical explanations went on and on in Spanish and English next to plastic reproductions of line drawings. Chiefs and old maps and ships. Peter shied away. He drifted towards the memorial for veterans. Rain shined the black rock, names chiseled there for anyone to see.

His father's name dropped into him like an anchor. He never got the chance to ask his dad about being in the service, never got the chance to compare notes on the shitty food and the stupidity of sergeants. Never got to say thanks for serving the good old US of A, those bastards. Never got to hear it, either. His name wasn't up there, among them, his brothers, the warriors who all came home alive, if not well. Who came home.

That's what happens when you go MIA on your family. No one celebrates what you've done. All they can do is mourn your memory. Right here is where he belonged, and he damned well knew it. It burned him that his dad's boat— his boat, by right—belonged to his cousins. Maybe he should pay them a visit, like Dave said. Maybe he could get on their crew. He couldn't imagine pacing her deck, taking orders from someone his own age. But it got him thinking on the good times, that last fishing trip his folks took as a family, a memory he saved for special occasions, so he didn't wear it out, him with his dad on deck, shouting, "Get up here, it's nice!"

"I got something going on the stove!" Mom was always busy.

"That can wait!"

"I seen it before!"

"Not like this, you haven't!"

She trudged out, wiping flour onto her apron, her face glossy red, and stepped into light that glowed blue. His dad pulled her to him, and Peter, too, that arm's weight so welcome on his shoulders, the smell of meat and butter drifting from her, his stomach, his whole self come alive in the cold cobalt sky. Seawater swallowed the last shine of day. Wheel well glowing golden, the boat slapped and pitched through an ocean of sapphires. From far above, they must have looked like a star.

Chapter Twenty-Three

DAVE'S CANVAS DRUM bag slid off his legs and bumped into the coffee table. "I'd watch it around the drummers. You done this before?"

"I'll make you look good." Claudia zoomed out until the pores disappeared into the brown shine of his nose. "Don't worry."

Randall guffawed. "She's got your number."

"Don't get too many ideas. They'll ruin that pretty face." Dave grunted and picked up the strap with a hand on one knee.

Beans checked his phone. "Can we get started?"

After Maggie was settled with a pillow behind her back, Peter pulled the coffee table to one side and sat on it. "Roberta! Out of the kitchen! It's time."

"Oh, sure." Roberta dried her hands. "Whenever you're ready."

"He didn't mean it like that." Maggie patted the cushion next to her.

Claudia hit the record button just as Roberta snuggled in to kiss Maggie's cheek. And so their video began with sweetness and shifting around in seats.

Peter addressed the camera. "That thing on?"

She gave him the thumbs up.

"If you're watching, you better be Indian."

Beans laughed. "What about her?"

Peter's eyes found hers through the lens, somehow. "She's different."

Dave banged his drum. "For posterity. We are honored to be with Maggie and her son Peter as we prepare him to receive his song. On the couch next to her auntie, we have Roberta, and this here is my grandson Winston . . ."

"Call me Beans."

". . . and Roberta's husband Randall, helping out on drums. I'm Dave. Alright, fellas, let's start."

Maggie clapped her hands. "We're singing, too."

"That's right." Roberta smiled. "Get with the program, Uncle."

"Yes, ma'am." Dave saluted. "Never cross a woman. She'll make you pay."

"Any more advice, Grampa?"

"Stick with family. They're all you've got."

"Okay, now." Peter cleared his throat. "Let's begin."

Drumbeats rolled, big and low, rumbling through her body, which held still, a miracle, her lens poised on the music makers.

"Tumanos wo hey a hey hey, tumanos wo hey ahey o ahey o." Peter's voice swelled above the others, passing through her. "Wo hey ahey o ahey o."

Claudia moved close, slow and sure, pausing on one knee to pan over his mother and neighbors. These people were family. Their song filled the room, surely uncontained by its walls, surging onto the street to meet the rain and wind, carried through cedars swaying above the sea, ceaseless from here to where the west meets its end.

The room thundered. She put her hand on her stomach to smooth her breath, felt a flutter inside, the quickening like a fish grazed in a dark lake—Can you hear this, baby? Are you taking a sound bath?—the love coming on like longing, her heart open, flayed and flooded. When the tears rose, she refused to sniffle. She let them run, wetting the viewfinder along with her cheeks. Steady, now. Steady.

Dave's eyes were kind as he ushered her out, hours later, after many rounds of stories and coffee she had a hard time refusing. "We've got to get to the good stuff." He winked at her. "Go over a few things that can't be overheard."

"Especially not by a white lady writing a book."

Beans was direct. Claudia appreciated that about him. He made things clear. No one spoke. Roberta showed Maggie pictures of her girls on her phone, not looking up. Claudia forced a laugh and reached for her purse while slinging the camera around her neck. "I suppose I'll accept the 'lady' part but, just so you know, I am Latina. Or Latinx, I guess. The names keep changing."

"First I've heard of it." Smiling, Peter punched Beans in the arm.

Dave held the door for her. "Sounds complicated."

"That it is." Claudia stepped into the cold. "Bye for now."

Claudia paused, fingerpads light on the keyboard, trying to shake the feeling of being escorted to the door, of standing outside that trailer searching for her keys in her purse, only to realize she'd left her coat hanging inside the door with the keys in its pocket, and had to knock again with apologies and a quick dart of the hand to lift lapel from hook and be gone.

Do your work, she commanded herself. Get it right. It was hard to remember Dave's telling perfectly, but she had it down, at least.

Kwa-Ti takes many forms. Usually don't know it's him until he's gone. You can kill him, but he comes back. Like a craving, like I was saying.

My grampa used to tell it to me this way. Day's owner—you know, Moon's dad, the way your mom likes to tell it?—well, he did catch up to Kwa-Ti, who was a slave, you know, in that go-round, and he took back the light. Only in my family, it's in a box, not a shell, and Kwa-Ti got away by pretending he was asleep in the canoe. Rocked and drifted right out of there.

Day's owner, he killed Kwa-Ti, killed him dead. But before he got killed, Kwa-Ti asked not to be buried. He told them to season his body on the beach for four days. After that, he said to stick his head on a pole until it rotted.

That's what we used to do after a war party. All the women got on top of the houses, pounding the roofs with sticks when our warriors came home with heads in their canoes. Other tribes got real mad about it, their dead with the tongues sticking out for anyone to see. But that's how it was, eh.

She hoped people understood that hers was a memory of what happened, not its transcription. Still, Dave's version was remarkably similar to stories told in the 1920s by Young Doctor, the legendary carver, to Frances Densmore, the great documentarian of Native songs from the Atlantic to the Pacific, a real anthropological pioneer who traveled with a box camera, a cylinder phonograph and sometimes her sister. Called prim and opinionated by those who keep her in memory at all, Densmore saved thousands of songs from being extinguished by time, death and settlement policy, though she could be considered a plunderer by those who believe songs hold true power.

Claudia had wanted to ask Dave whether he could decode what she'd seen—that laughing mink, the whispering trees. But she would have to tell him about her despair, the betrayal and her unborn, who was his blood. The things she would have to admit stacked up around her, higher and higher. No way out but to eviscerate everything she built with strategy and self-denial.

Now, if she could just get it down—how Dave was correcting Maggie without telling her son she was wrong. Many coastal tribes shared this story, their versions naming Raven as bringer of light. The trickster's method for getting into the house changed, too. In one account, Raven becomes a pine needle swallowed by the daughter of day's keeper, born and raised within the house as its child, ever seeking to make off with the goods. Whatever Peter was taught was particular to the teller. Dave was highlighting the trapdoor of perspective, something all too familiar to anyone with a family.

Claudia had marshaled the evidence she could muster from Maria's point of view. While Claudia felt abandoned by their family—no one had claimed her when their mother was sick—Maria watched her sister vault into opportunities beyond her reach. Maybe it was too much for Maria to hear Claudia complain about her prospects, no end to her ingratitude. While she may not have built much of a career, Claudia was paid to learn and write, as long as she never stopped teaching. More than that, she had a calling. She cared about seeing the world anew through the beliefs of others. Claudia had thought Maria would follow in her footsteps. She meant for her sister to become a professional artist, and not a wife, but perhaps watching Claudia devalue the love she received was the final affront. She had no idea how Maria justified knifing her in the back, though Claudia had often, in her studies, plumbed that complex ecosystem of rationalizations that allow entire peoples to do horrendous things to others while convinced of their own goodness. But Claudia rarely asked her sister about her life or offered the curiosity, tolerance and patience that convinced people like Maggie to share their stories. Even in those interactions, she never truly showed up. The work it required dug too deep. Claudia once wished Andrew would treat her as well as he treated his clients. In her eagerness to take her rightful place at the table, she had repeated his mistakes and indeed those of too many men. Even so, Claudia was afraid to raise a child alone. She needed help.

Claudia would write a new ending, one in which her career was not engulfed by scandal, in which her intentions would be judged pure, an attempt at empathy through understanding others. She would model forgiveness of Andrew and Maria as a kind of cathartic transcendence. She would let Peter into their child's life. She would bring the baby to Maggie between academic quarters. She would, somehow, convince Thomas to accept his grandchild. She would tell her department chair the truth and rely on his kindness. Maybe they would see her as part of this place in a way that could benefit future research. If not, she would situate her work in a different community, perhaps urban immigrants, somewhere near where she taught, what she'd known. All she had to do was start sending emails.

Her cursor hovered in white space.

That harmony was a fantasy built for other people. This was real life. She had enough on her plate being one of the few of her kind on the rungs of academia. She would tell no one until she'd been to a doctor. Not someone local. She had to go back to Seattle. The question was when. Certain decisions would become more difficult, even impossible, as her pregnancy advanced. She'd been drinking at the most vulnerable time for a fetus. Smoking too. I didn't know, she thought. I didn't mean to. She closed her laptop and went to the fridge, yet again.

The sky faded from pink to gray, the waves dusky beneath dark clouds. To both sides of the beach, low headlands jutted, jet black, into the sea. At her feet was an old mussel, hinge intact, shells curved like wings. She held it up. Light spilled through wormholes woven in the barnacled crust.

The sea was wild in her ears. Behind her, someone crunched and squeaked through the dunes. It could only be him. She buried her find for later.

Peter sat, smelling showered, his thigh hot against hers. "The door to your place was wide open." He lit a cigarette. "The lights were on."

"I don't need you to know where I am."

"Why are you being such a hardass? It's wet out."

"I can look after myself, thank you."

"Randall and Roberta think you're an opportunist." He puffed out his cheeks. "But they're beginning to make me wonder."

"What exactly am I supposed to be getting out of this situation? I mean, really. I come here, I help out, and yeah, I take notes, and I reflect on them later in a book, which, while it may not affect your daily lives, could benefit future generations. It's a fair trade. I may not have been born into this community, but I've contributed. I earned my keep. Think about how things were when I got here." She waved her arms around. "And now?"

"We're making it happen."

"Yeah, you can say that now. But I helped you." She stood, doing her best not to place her hands over her stomach, a move that had become instinctive. "You've made me feel terrible. Just go."

"Roberta made me an offer. To share the song. They'll take care of Mom."

"Does she know?"

"We could have a life, Claudia."

She flinched and turned toward the bellow of the Pacific. What would he do with a baby? Hand it off, most likely. He barely wanted the best thing he had.

"Yeah, you're married. Whatever that means."

"You don't know anything about it. You're all about your pain, your problems. My sister is fucking my husband, Peter. My sister."

The cramp felt like a kick to her gut. "Oh my God." Not like this, out here, in the open. She started for the cabin, Peter scrambling to his feet.

"Claudia, why haven't you said something?"

She tried to shut the sliding glass, but he held the door. There was no way to win without hurting herself and maybe the baby, oh, the baby. Stress was bad in utero, she'd read that somewhere. Her baby felt what she felt. She lay down on the couch, rolled to her side and tucked her knees into the cushions, breathing slow, waiting for blood that did not come. He knelt beside her.

"I need this job, Peter."

His hand warmed her back. "People already know."

She spun to face him, furious. "How'd they find out?"

"Come on, my truck is parked here round the clock. I never confirmed."

She tried to hold back the tears, but soon her shoulders shook with hiccups and shudders that grew louder the longer she listened to herself. She hated being known for being small and afraid, so compromised.

"They've seen it before." He rubbed her arm. "Let go. You'll feel better."

"Don't tell me how to handle myself." She flung his hand away.

"Seriously?" He started pacing. "Know what your problem is? You don't want to hear that you have to change to be happy."

"Way to punish me for sharing. Thanks."

"You think you're the only one who's been forced to forgive?"

"Things didn't happen the way you think they did."

He stopped. "What?"

Claudia bit her lip against brandishing what she knew. Anything she said would be an intrusion. That story belonged to his mother. "I need time. Can't you see that?"

"The way you're going, you may not get there."

Who did he think he was dealing with? Anger flared bright in her chest. Claudia hadn't worked her whole life to be managed by another man. While he was washing out, she'd been on the grind. Easy to be hated for claiming the right to conduct herself like a man. Maybe power must be subverted to be gained in truth. But she had no intention of tethering herself to yet another framework of expectations, that of this family, this man who was talking to her like she was his child.

If she had to have a family, she would build one, her and her baby. Her pride.

She would choose a different path, an independence that recognized the background dissonance that plagued her around other people. So be it. Better off alone. A scholar, free to subject herself to the ironclad exertion of her discipline, as though being busy were a moral act and purity made accessible through the scourge of work. Single parenting would chain her to her home, it's true, but she could use that imprisonment to her benefit. Time to write. She could wear the baby and stand at her desk during the day. She could ignore deep exhaustion and carve pages from the dark hours. Burn herself out. Stay on the grind. She could make it work.

In return she would expect from herself a great flourishing made possible by being alone. Men had a way of working against her, telling her she was wrong. That it was unnatural to think so hard. That she needed to act different, or else.

She would do it her way. Damn the rest.

Chapter Twenty-Four

PETER PRACTICED HIS step hops outside the community hall. Scallop shells clacked and quaked around his ankles. He wiggled his cedar topknot to make sure the mask would stay put. His hand barely reached its crown. Soft trickles of sweat traced a line between his shoulder blades. He fought the urge to scratch beneath the wool blanket tied around his neck.

Otherwise shirtless, he was barefoot in jeans rolled to the knee. He flapped his elbows to let cold air beneath the blanket. Watching the other dances, he'd tried not to be obvious while scanning the crowd for Claudia. She had the good sense to seat herself in the back. Elders filled the front rows. Cedar boughs crowned the doors and windows. Drums dangled from hooks on the walls.

He spread his toes on the cool concrete and lifted his heels, listening. They would save the big giveaway for last, but everything was prepped in bright piles behind the giant curtain lent to his family for the potlatch. He was amazed at how his mother calculated just how much would be needed. He'd added coloring books, crayons, matchbox cars and a few action figures to keep things lively. He had been waiting behind the curtain, but the creak and shift of folding chairs, the echoes off the rafters and the occasional cry of a baby had become too much, and a swift draft beckoned him outside, where kids swirled over the jungle gym, shouting and jumping into damp mulch.

His breath doubled back on him inside the wild man mask. He hadn't been able to eat, though Roberta pulled together enough meat and seafood for the feast, calling in favors his mom didn't know about. He'd made the trips to P.A., their lists in his pocket, and filled the cart until it took a grunt to get rolling. Paid, too, but you can't just pick up one hundred pounds of elk.

The first thing they did after the dinner song was feed people. The spread filled the long lines of plastic tables that had to be broken down before the dancing began. There was elk meatloaf, breaded and fried halibut, baked beans, a shredded carrot salad, bowls of artichoke hearts, soft rolls, and best of all, baked salmon, copper oil soaking into mashed potatoes. He passed platters of grilled mussels and crab legs.

It took him an hour to make the rounds, wearing the cedar hat his mom made. The brim forced him to stand straight. All the while, folks filled up on coffee or stepped out front, texting or taking calls, swigging from bottles of water. He saw one kid eating a jar of blackberry jam, quietly, off by himself, looking around to see if anyone would stop him as he scooped fingers of purple jelly into his mouth, and Peter thought, go ahead, buddy, that's about as good as it gets.

It was hard to say how he felt as the old men clapped his back and the aunties patted his face with wrinkled hands. He thanked them one at a time for being there to remember things the right way. Looking back on their lives, he recalled stories no less riddled than his own, but here they were with their families, showing up to do the work. They would keep Makah culture alive.

The other people at Claudia's table milled around, filing off to the bathroom, talking to their friends, passing babies back and forth.

"Brought you this." He threaded a cedar rose through the buttonhole of her jacket. "We have a gift. For all you've done. Don't leave till the end."

"Of course not." A smile warmed her tired eyes. "You look wonderful."

He forgot himself. Her shoulder dipped away from his hand. The women around them glanced at each other. He stood back. There would never be a good time with her. "I have to go up front."

Peter made his way behind the curtain to double check his back pockets for the envelopes of cash they would press into the hands of those who stayed to watch him dance. He had been withdrawing the daily limit from the Mini-Mart's ATM for the last week, looking around to make sure pill-heads weren't casing him. After months of no money coming in, his bank account looked like it belonged to someone in his twenties, which lit in him that familiar panic that plagued his household as a child, anxiety he quieted by working, always working. If he wanted to be his own man, he had to keep moving.

He took the deal. His Indian name wasn't part of the trade. That was his to fold away with his very own wool blanket to protect him at night.

Inside, Dave told people—again—not to take pictures or recordings of the dancers. "And remember—don't post anything online. Once those pictures leave the village, they could end up on postcards or sold as art or whatever, so that's why we're particular. Thanks for being respectful of the families." Dave was doing a good job running the floor, as far as Peter could tell.

His mother waited in the doorway, and he did hug her, and he did not hold back, despite the mask. Her heart hopped against his ribs, a wild bird in its last winter. Once he'd done what she wanted, he could leave, and that freed him to love her the only way he knew how, which meant no questions asked.

"Proud of you." She patted his back with both hands. "My boy."

Back on the mic, Dave thanked everyone. "You are here to witness a great day for this family."

The drums began. It was just like they'd practiced, except his mind was blank. His body took over—the best thing it knew how to do—and now he was rounding the curtain, entering the floor by the drum circle, his stepping rhythmic, crouched down low, arms out, the mask heavy on his neck.

Randall and Beans and Dave drummed and sang in a circle with Roberta, his mother to one side, singing and keeping time with a feathered wing, showing him the steps—slow lift of the foot with a quick step down, and that's what he did. Through the mask, he saw his people watching, together guarding his claim to this place, and with it, their own. Slow lift with a quick step down, slow lift with a quick step down.

He nodded to all four directions, bearing the weight of the wild man's face. His feet turned like leaves caught in an eddy that circled the floor counterclockwise, the scallop shells rattling high and sharp.

Before, he went through the motions of learning this stuff, keeping his distance to placate his mom without put-

ting himself out there, but now, his feet moved with his heart
and his heart beat with the drums, and he felt his spirit rise,
knowing Makahs had danced this way since men dressed in
bear skins and stood barefoot on the beach, brandishing a
harpoon because they'd earned the right. They conquered
fear. So would he, moving in concert with a whole line of
men who kept going when it seemed impossible.

His shoulders were on fire. He kept his arms up. Slow
lift with a quick step down. Sweat rinsed his back and chest
and arms.

There were men all around him, not a one of them his
father. Peter wished his dad were here, wished he had been
around to teach him, wished he hadn't left it to Dave to sober up and face death on the level. Taking care of the hard
work—that was something Peter had in common with his
mom, and maybe they got it from her ancestors, who lived
from one day to the next, just like the chiefs. It was the dignity brought to daily life that mattered, not what they did.

Twin streams fell to either side of his nose, dropping onto
his chest. He was glad of the mask. The song shifted, sliding
into a tight, quick beat, and now he squatted with his back
to the crowd, propping his elbows to flare the blanket and
show the mother of pearl buttons on its back, twisting and
tipping his head over one arm so the mask seemed to float
above a large body. He coiled inside this illusion, holding
his breath until he spiraled up out of his crouch, hands flung
wide, knees rising and falling, rising and falling, rising and
falling, full stop.

Arms spread like wings, he pivoted for the families lined
up with kids in laps, their elders nodding in time with slow
claps. Cedar hair framed his eyes. All he could see was

brown. He reeled back and charged forward, thumping the floor with his steps. Again. Again.

The drums glided into another tempo. Time to leave the way he came in, shining for the eyes of his tribe, passing the drummers who looked ready to die, dancing for his mother who was singing and crying because he'd done it. They'd done it. And now it was done.

Acknowledgments

I write to improve the quality of ideas available to our society. In that endeavor, I have been lucky to find community with other thinkers, makers, readers and writers.

The Makah Museum, sustained by the Makah Cultural and Research Center, is a world class resource for tribal members and other peoples interested in the ancient, living culture of the Makah people. For their warmth, candor, wisdom and ready laughter, I am grateful to Makah tribal members Janine Ledford, Meredith Parker, Melissa Walsebot Peterson, Joseph and Mardell McGimpsey, Lila Parton and her children Duane Parton and Cheryl Sones, Keely Parker, Kirk Wachendorf and Edie Hottowe, among others.

For her advocacy and aesthetic, I thank Ria Julien of the Frances Goldin Literary Agency. For bringing my novel into the world, I thank Red Hen Press, a nonprofit independent press. Kate Gale, Mark Cull, Tobi Harper, Natasha McClellan, Monica Fernandez, Nicolas Niño and Rebeccah Sanhueza are tireless on behalf of books that better our collective thought.

From 2018 through 2020, I served as Prose Writer-in-Residence at Hugo House, a nonprofit writing center where I was given a space to work, a stage from which to perform, and students and mentees with whom I could share the lessons of this long journey. At Hugo House, writers are not only seen but recognized. For that, I thank Tree Swensen, Christine Texeira, Rob Arnold, Louise Kincaid, Nicole McCarthy, Katie Prince, Margot Kahn Case, John Peterman, Lily Frenette and the board of directors.

Libraries are the crown jewel of democracy. I thank Linda Johns, Lupine Miller, Andrea Gough and Stesha Brandon of the Seattle Public Library, where I teach writing, research and personal narrative in English and Spanish, and from whose stacks regularly emerge brilliant, borrowed books that sustain and inspire my own creative practice. For their writings about the Makah people, I thank contemporary historians Joshua Reid (Snohomish) and Charlotte Coté (Tseshaht/Nuu-chah-nulth), as well as Ruth Kirk, Richard Daugherty, Helma Swan (Makah), Linda Goodman, Erna Gunther, Alice Henson Ernst, Frances Densmore, Elizabeth Colson and the many Makah elders who gave their hours to that fraught work.

For their fellowships and aid of my development as a researcher and writer, I thank UC Berkeley's Knight Digital Media Center, the Jack Straw Writing Program, Harvard College, and the University of Washington Graduate School, where I was a Graduate Opportunities and Minority Achievement Scholar. Their support helped sustain me. So, too, the many weeks I've spent writing and learning in community at the Port Townsend Writers' Conference, where I now teach.

For their attention and counsel, without which I would be not only bereft but hopeless, I thank my earliest readers Sam Ligon, Elissa Washuta (Cowlitz), Patricia Henley, Robert Lopez, Kate Lebo, Steve Yarbrough, Anca Szilágyi, Jean Ferruzola, Shawn Wong, Jonathan Evison, Jarret Middleton, Alfa Demmellash, Alex Forrester and Kristen

Goessling. I thank Alfa for inspiring me to persist, Kristen for listening with wry kindness, Maggie Messitt for consolations and encouragements, and Patricia Gray for swimming before sunrise with a relentlessly positive attitude. Long may they guide me. For loaning their cabins so I could write in peace, I thank Neel Blair and Josie Clark (the finest neighbors one could hope to find), as well as Alex Loeb and Ethan Meginnes, and Todd and Mia Ellis.

To love a writer is no easy thing. I would like to conclude this litany of gratitude by thanking my family, which began as my abuela, grandparents, mom, dad and sister, and became my husband and our sons. I couldn't have expected so much joy.

Biographical Note

Kristen Millares Young is a prize-winning journalist and essayist whose work appears in the *Washington Post*, the *Guardian* and the *New York Times*, along with the anthologies *Pie & Whiskey*, a 2017 *New York Times* New & Notable Book, and *Latina Outsiders: Remaking Latina Identity*. The current Prose Writer-in-Residence at Hugo House, Kristen was the researcher for the *New York Times* team that produced "Snow Fall," which won a Pulitzer Prize. She graduated from Harvard College with an A.B. in history and literature, later earning her MFA from the University of Washington. From 2016 to 2019, Kristen served as board chair of *InvestigateWest*, a nonprofit news studio she cofounded in Seattle, where she lives with her family.